"You look different tonight, Catherine,"

David said as, without preamble, he swept her onto the dance floor.

"It's the new gown. I went shopping in the bazaar today."

"No, it isn't the gown; it's you." He danced her away from the others to the far end of the patio, under the shadows of the overhanging trees. Still holding her in his embrace, he asked, "What kind of perfume are you wearing?"

Catherine lifted the strand of beads that lay against her breasts. "It's sandalwood."

David took the strand from her fingers, drawing her closer as he did. He took a deep breath and, still holding her captive, said, "I've never particularly liked the aroma of sandalwood until now." He tightened his fingers on the beads, and he drew her even closer. "You *are* different tonight, Catherine," he murmured.

Dear Reader,

Welcome to summer, and welcome to another fine month of reading from Silhouette Intimate Moments. We have some exciting books in store for you, not just this month, but all summer long. Let me start with our June titles, then give you a peek at what's coming up in the future.

First, there's *That McKenna Woman*, the first book in Parris Afton Bonds' Mescalero Trilogy. Parris used her home state of New Mexico as the location of the Mescalero Cattle Company, then peopled the ranch with some of the most charismatic characters you'll ever find. Tom Malcolm and Marianna McKenna couldn't be less alike, but that doesn't stop them from discovering a love as big as the West. And the family created by their marriage provides the basis for the other two books in the series, books we know you'll look forward to reading.

Another special book for June is Kathleen Eagle's *More Than a Miracle*, a follow-up to *Candles in the Night* (Silhouette Special Edition #437). This is the story of a woman who, forced to give up her child, now embarks on a desperate mission to find her son. Her only help comes from the man they call McQuade, and even then, it may take more than a miracle to make her dream come true.

During the rest of the summer, look for books by old favorites like Lucy Hamilton (whose Dodd Memorial Hospital Trilogy ends in July with *Heartbeats*), Heather Graham Pozzessere and Emilie Richards. They're just a few of the writers whose work will be waiting for you—only in the pages of Silhouette Intimate Moments.

Sincerely,

Leslie J. Wainger
Senior Editor, Silhouette Books

Barbara Faith

Beyond Forever

Published by Silhouette Books New York
America's Publisher of Contemporary Romance

SILHOUETTE BOOKS
300 East 42nd St., New York, N.Y. 10017

Copyright © 1988 by Barbara Faith

All rights reserved. Except for use in any review, the reproduction or utilization of this work in whole or in part in any form by any electronic, mechanical or other means, now known or hereafter invented, including xerography, photocopying and recording, or in any information storage or retrieval system, is forbidden without the permission of Silhouette Books, 300 E. 42nd St., New York, N.Y. 10017

ISBN: 0-373-07244-9

First Silhouette Books printing June 1988

All the characters in this book are fictitious. Any resemblance to actual persons, living or dead, is purely coincidental.

® are Trademarks used under license and are registered in the United States Patent and Trademark Office and in other countries.

Printed in the U.S.A.

Books by Barbara Faith

Silhouette Intimate Moments

The Promise of Summer #16
Wind Whispers #47
Bedouin Bride #63
Awake to Splendor #101
Islands in Turquoise #124
Tomorrow Is Forever #140
Sing Me a Lovesong #146
Desert Song #173
Kiss of the Dragon #193
Asking for Trouble #208
Beyond Forever #244

Silhouette Special Edition

Return to Summer #335
Say Hello Again #436

BARBARA FAITH

is very happily married to an ex-matador, whom she met when she lived in Mexico. After a honeymoon spent climbing pyramids in the Yucatán, they settled down in California—but they're vagabonds at heart. They travel at every opportunity, yet Barbara always finds the time to write.

To Alfonso,
who shared with me
the wondrous experience of Egypt

Praise to you, O Nile, who issue from the earth and come to nourish Egypt; you who water the meadows, you that Ra has created to nourish all cattle, who gives drink to the desert places that are far from water.

You are verdant, you are verdant; O Nile, you are verdant.

—From the Pyramid Texts,
Nineteenth Dynasty, c.1359-1205 B.C.

A Note From the Author

The Temple of Philae was built by the last pharaohs during the thirtieth dynasty. After the construction of the first Aswan dam the temple was flooded for six months of every year. With the construction of the second dam it was condemned to vanish forever. Thus the complex of Philae was resited to the nearby small island of Agilka, where the ground was landscaped to provide the same surroundings it had when it was originally built.

Philae remains today, shimmering in the sunlight. As you approach from the boat that takes you across the Nile, you see the Temple of Isis standing just as it was so many centuries ago.

On your right when you arrive, there is a colonnade that opens up to six small rooms that were begun in fifty B.C. Above the exterior facade there are two bilingual inscriptions, one of which reproduces the text of the Rosetta Stone.

There is a second pylon, other rooms, towers and columns, the small, classically beautiful Temple of Hathor and the tall columns of the great kiosk of Trajan. Legend has it that this was a station chapel where ceremonies were performed so that Isis could leave her island and find it again.

If I have not mentioned in this book the fact that the treasures of Philae have been moved to higher ground, it is because I am a hopeless romantic and I choose to see the island exactly as it was when one could still hear the footsteps of the gods.

Prologue

So it was that in the first misty light of morning the young widow queen went to stand on the grassy bank of the River Nile. The servants waited at a distance, whispering among themselves at the look of sadness in the queen's dark eyes, the silent tears that fell down her lovely cheeks.

"Let him be alive," she prayed as she looked down the river for the first sight of the barge that would bring him back to her.

A week ago she had received word that the noble warrior who meant more to her than her very life had been wounded leading his troops against the Assyrians. For three days now she had kept her vigil.

When at last the barge came into view she stepped down to the bank of the great river, nervously fingering her sandalwood beads as she directed the servants onto the barge.

They bore him to her on a litter. His face, scarred by battle, was as pale as the morning light. She knelt beside him. She took his hand, and bringing it to her breast, she spoke his name. He opened his eyes. He caught the sweet-scented sandalwood beads she wore and brought them to his lips.

The servants carried him into her private chambers, and it was from there the queen gave the orders to prepare the tomb for her lover's voyage to the beyond.

"You will order the great artisan, Samiha, to build an alabaster boat so that this noble warrior may be safely carried on his voyage beyond the beyond. Take his chariot and put that in the tomb. Also his sword and his scimitar and a chest that is to be encrusted with jewels and will contain all of the things he will need in the other world."

For four days and four nights the young queen attended the noble warrior. During the times that he was conscious she remembered with him the early days of their love and the magic they had shared. She told him that a love like theirs would defy both time and death.

No one entered the young queen's chambers except for her favorite handmaiden, who waited and watched from one dark corner of the room.

On the morning of the fifth day the warrior opened his eyes. He looked upon the queen's face for one last time. "*Ana ohebok*," he whispered. "I love you."

She gathered her golden cloak about her as she knelt by his side. She kissed his dying lips; she took his dying breath.

And began to plan how she would follow him into the silent and mysterious beyond.

Chapter 1

The letter arrived two days before Christmas. Catherine carried it to the window that looked out over the desert, bleak now in the winter twilight. She held the envelope tightly, reluctant to open it, for inside would be the answer to all her hopes and dreams.

The dream was the only romanticism, the only weakness, Catherine Adair allowed herself. At thirty-seven she was a woman who'd long ago learned that life was a serious business. Except for her dream, her *passion* for a land she'd never seen, there wasn't a frivolous bone in Catherine's trim and compact body. Her bearing was erect, ladylike and controlled. She wore her straight brown hair in a blunt cut with bangs that came just to the edge of her brows. High cheekbones, a straight nose that never showed a hint of powder, and lips that were never touched with lipstick gave her face a look of severity.

She was conversant on any intellectual subject, honest to a fault, loyal to the few friends she had, and totally dedicated to her work as head of the archeology department of the small Arizona university where she'd taught for the past twelve years.

Clutching the letter, she went to the picture window that looked out over her cactus garden. She stood there for a moment, feeling the slight warmth of the sun on her face.

Three months had gone by since Catherine had applied to the Smithsonian Institution for a six-month grant to go to Egypt in search of the lost tomb of the young widow queen, Alifa. Now that the answer had come she was afraid to read it.

As she stood by the window, Catherine thought of all the reasons why she should get the grant. She was a brilliant student of Egyptology, and she could read and understand hieroglyphics. She'd written her dissertation on the lost tomb of the young queen. Dozens of her articles had been published in university publications and other scholarly magazines, and she'd made several important archeological discoveries in the past ten years.

Another factor in her favor was that she was Milton Adair's daughter. Professor Milton Adair had been, perhaps, the most famous Egyptologist to come out of the United States in the past fifty years. He'd instilled in Catherine the love she had for that ancient country. From the time she was old enough to understand, he'd talked to her about Egypt, telling her wonderful stories of the kings and their queens, of the pharaohs and the priests, and of the river that brought life to the land.

"We'll go together some day," he'd told her. "We'll see the great pyramids of Gizeh, the city of Thebes and the temples of the gods." With his stories he had given Catherine a dream.

The years had passed. There'd been school, then her mother's long illness. Her mother had died six years ago, and the following spring she and her father had planned the trip they'd talked about for so long.

But that wasn't meant to be. Two days before they were to leave, her father had a serious heart attack. Just before he lost consciousness he had whispered, "Go to Egypt for me, Catherine."

Perhaps at last that day had come. She wouldn't know until she opened the letter.

Her nerves overwhelmed her, and she thought of all the reasons why she might not be selected. She taught in a backwater university not one of the larger, more prestigious schools. The digs she'd done and the discoveries she'd made had all been in Arizona, New Mexico, the Yucatan and Guatemala, including several important discoveries and one rather spectacular one in the Yucatan several years ago. But she'd never been to Egypt. That would probably be the biggest single point against her.

A trembling sigh escaped Catherine's lips as she slid one plain rounded fingernail under the flap of the envelope and drew out the letter.

Dear Professor Adair,

We greatly appreciate the fine and scholarly work you have done in the field of archeology. We have read with interest your papers on the tombs of ancient Egypt, and we find your theories on the lost tomb of Queen Alifa most interesting.

The members of the board have spent a great deal of time over our decision. At last, though it pains me to tell you, we have awarded the grant to Mr. David Pallister, professor of archeology...

The letter slipped through Catherine's fingers, and she blindly stared out the window.

Several minutes passed before she picked it up to reread. She'd heard of Pallister of course, and she'd read his papers in the same university journals hers had appeared in. At thirty-one he was the fair-haired boy in the world of archeology—on his very first dig in the jungles of Belize, he'd made a discovery that had earned him world-wide praise.

He was a man to whom everything came easily. He'd sailed through Princeton on a scholarship and had graduated with honors when he was twenty. He'd gone on to get his master's and doctorate, and he'd received every grant he'd ever applied for, including this one. And if there was any truth to the rumors she'd heard linking his name with various women, it was a wonder that he found time to work.

As twilight seeped into the room she rested her head on her knees and began to weep.

Christmas and New Year's passed in a bleakness of despair, but as bad as the holidays were, Catherine was grateful for the break from her classes. Most of the other professors had left, and the few social functions she was invited to she refused, claiming a cold.

On the second day of January at six-thirty in the morning, she was awakened by the ringing of the telephone. She responded sleepily when the voice on the other end said her name.

"What?" She tried to rub the sleep out of her eyes. "Yes, this is Catherine Adair."

"Did I wake you?" Before she could answer, the masculine voice said, "Oh God, I forgot about the difference in time. Sorry."

"S'all right." Catherine sat up in bed.

"This is David Pallister, Miss Adair. I don't know if you know who I am, but—"

"I know who you are."

"I've just finished reading your last paper on the lost tomb of Queen Alifa. It's an interesting theory but..."

Catherine waited.

"I don't agree with you. Alifa is buried somewhere near her husband's tomb. That's where I plan to begin excavating."

"That's not where she is," Catherine said firmly. "King Amonset II died four years before she did. If she'd been entombed near him, her tomb would have been discovered years ago."

"Not necessarily. Alifa was Amonset's second wife. All trace of her disappeared when she was about twenty-two, but if my calculations are correct..."

Catherine tightened her hand on the phone as she listened. In her heart she knew he was wrong. But she remained silent. She listened, frowning until Pallister added, "But your theories interest me. That's why I'd like you to be a member of the team."

Catherine sat frozen, too shocked to speak.

"Miss Adair?"

"Yes, yes I'm here." Her mouth was desert dry.

"Professor Fletcher Garson is on the team, too—you've heard of him, I imagine. And we've got a young master's student from the University of Cairo. If you're interested..." Pallister let the words hang in the air.

"I'm interested," Catherine managed to say.

"Good." She heard him clear his throat. "Look, I know you applied for the grant. I'm sorry you didn't get it, but that's not why I'm asking you to be a part of the team. The discovery you made near Tikal two years ago was pretty amazing. I've read most of your papers on

Egypt, and while I haven't always agreed with you, I like the passion you have for the country. I imagine that's something you've gotten from your father. I've read all of his books, and I can't even begin to tell you how much I admire him. I really want you on the team, Miss Adair. Can I count on you?"

Catherine was shaking so badly by now she could barely hold the phone. "Yes," she said. "Yes, of course. Thank you for asking me."

"Okay. I imagine you've already arranged for a sabbatical, so that shouldn't be a problem. I want to be in Cairo the first week in February. I hope that's convenient."

"Yes." She was dizzy with happiness. "Yes, that's fine."

"We'll talk before that. I'll put a check in the mail tomorrow for your airfare and whatever other expenses you'll have. If you have any questions give me a call." He gave her his number in New Jersey, said he would talk to her soon and hung up.

Catherine sat right where she was for a long time. She was going to Egypt!

She got up finally, crossed the room and looked quickly through the stack of magazines on the second shelf of the bookcase until she found the issue with David Pallister on the cover. She carried the magazine back to the bed. There she sat cross-legged in her navy blue tailored pajamas, her expression thoughtful as she studied the photograph of the young man on the cover.

His blond hair was appealingly shaggy and fell rakishly over his clear blue eyes. His mouth was curved in a boyish smile, and there was a stubborn set to his chin. He leaned against a desk, dressed in a red crew-neck sweater and blue jeans that looked as though they'd been shellacked onto his body.

Catherine swallowed the lump of disappointment that had formed in her throat since the moment she'd read the letter from the Smithsonian. All that mattered was that she was going to be a part of the dig. She was going to go to Egypt, walk where the kings had walked and see all of the places that had existed in that ancient land for the past five thousand years.

She would stand on the banks of the Nile and dream of times long past.

Chapter 2

Cairo, ancient city of pharaohs and kings, of Ramses, Akhenaton and Tutankhamen, of Nefertiti and Cleopatra. Land of the ancient gods Ra and Amon, Osiris and Isis. It was now a smog-filled city of discordant noisiness, bleating horns, snarling buses and crumbling apartment complexes overrun by children and weeds and discarded trash. Too much humanity was crowded together in this hot and arid space, ruled in the hot summer months by a busyness of flies.

From the balcony of her twelfth-floor room in the hotel overlooking the River Nile, Catherine looked out over the domes and the minarets and down at the cars surging round and round the traffic circle below—six lanes of vehicles jockeying for position with their motors creating a steady raucous hum. Then, unbelievably, in the middle of the surging traffic, Catherine saw a rickety horse-drawn cart trying to make its way through the middle of the six lanes.

The incongruity of Egypt, she thought as she raised her eyes and saw in the distance, through the smog and the clouds, the faint outline of the pyramids of Gizeh. Her hands tightened around the balcony railing, and her heart beat fast with the knowledge that at last she was here in the land of the pharaohs.

The trip had been very long, from Phoenix to New York, to Madrid to Cairo. When she'd checked into the hotel, she had inquired whether Professor Pallister and Professor Garson had arrived and was told they had not. She asked about a trip to the pyramids and when she'd been informed that she could take an American Express tour the following morning, she immediately bought a ticket.

"Please to wear trousers," the man at the tour desk said. "It is the custom to ride the camels up to the pyramids. Only those who are old take horse-drawn carts. I am sure *madame* will prefer to ride the camels."

Madame wasn't so sure, but the next morning at nine o'clock, dressed in boots and a khaki jumpsuit, Catherine waited at the hotel entrance with a group of people for the tour bus to arrive.

The February morning was bright with promise, a perfect time of year to visit Egypt. In another two months, Catherine knew, the weather would be unbearably hot. What would it be like then, she wondered as she gazed out of the bus window at the crowded streets. They would be here until July, possibly longer according to David Pallister.

He'd told her that if they were close to a find the grant would be extended for at least another six months. He'd gone on to explain that he planned to begin excavations, using ground-penetrating radar and a magnetometer, near the Temple of Horus in Edfu. That was almost six hundred miles south of Cairo, far south where the temperature in the summer soared to more than one hundred and twenty degrees.

"We'll stake out the area within a quarter-mile radius of Amonset's tomb," Pallister had said. "That's where we'll begin."

That may be where they would begin, Catherine had thought, but it wasn't where they would find Alifa's tomb.

Her interest in the lost tomb of the young queen had begun years ago. Instead of the fairy tales that most children were told at bedtime, her father had told the young Catherine stories of ancient Egypt. She barely knew anything about Cinderella or Snow White, Jack and the Beanstalk or Hansel and Gretel. But as she grew older, she knew all there was to tell about Ramses, Tutankhamen, Cleopatra and Nefertiti. Catherine had grown up with stories of their lives and customs, and they peopled her dreams like old friends.

But of all the stories Catherine had loved to hear, her favorite was of the young and beautiful Queen Alifa.

"She was only fifteen, the daughter of a rich merchant from the Island of Philae, when she married King Amonset II," Catherine's father told her. "Alifa was a favorite of the people, as kind as she was beautiful. She treated her servants with gentleness and her husband as her lord. Amonset was already past middle age when he married Alifa, and he died when she was nineteen."

"What became of her?" How many times had Catherine asked that question? "She was so young, Dad. What happened to her?"

"No one knows for sure, Catherine. There were rumors that after the king's death she took a lover. There were other rumors that she'd returned to Philae. But no one really knows anything more about her except that she disappeared when she was twenty-two. Most scholars believe she's buried somewhere near her husband."

"What do you think?"

"I think she went away with the man she fell in love with," her father said thoughtfully. "Finding her tomb has always been a dream of mine, Catherine. Someday, when you're older, we'll go to Egypt together. We'll go to Philae, and maybe, if we're very smart and very lucky, we'll find Alifa there."

"And her lover," Catherine said. "If we only knew who he was."

"Yes," her father had said. "If we only knew."

The bus progressed along a wide boulevard where the shrubs in the center divider were trimmed in the shape of pyramids. As they neared the site the guide pointed out the tinted windows to the left, and Catherine turned and saw them, the giant pyramids of Gizeh—Cheops, Chephren and Mycerinus—and for a moment it seemed to her that time stood still. The sounds of the traffic and the excited hubbub of the voices around her diminished, for she was here at last.

As soon as the crowd of tourists stepped off the bus, they were led across the street to an enclosure where it seemed as though they were transported back three thousand years in time.

Dozens of camels, bedecked with tassels, ribbons and bells, were crowded into the enclosure with their drivers, robed men who called to the tourists, "*Sabah el kheir*, good morning, *madame*, good morning, sir."

One of them, a portly man dressed in a gray robe, ears sticking out under his white turban, motioned to Catherine. With a stick he whacked one of the camels across the knees and took Catherine's arm, saying, "Up! Up!"

She looked at the camel, an ugly beast who bared yellow teeth and let out a horrific sound that was somewhere between a yowl and a growl as Catherine cautiously approached.

"Up," the driver said impatiently. Catherine swung one leg over the wide saddle and clutched the saddle horn as the huge beast lurched to his feet. With the driver holding tight to the rein the camel rocked his way toward the giant pyramid. Halfway there both the driver and the camel broke into a run.

"No!" Catherine called. "No, wait, don't run!" She hung on to the saddle horn and tried to grip the animal's wide body with her legs as camel and driver headed toward the pyramid. When at last they came to a stop, the driver whacked the animal across the knees again. The beast yowled and spit, then with a great lurch knelt on the ground. Catherine freed her feet from the stirrups, swung one leg over the saddle and slid off. The driver held out his hand, pointing to his palm and yelling *"Baksheesh, baksheesh."*

Catherine paid him and quickly followed the people from the tourist bus toward the pyramid of Cheops. She barely listened to the guide as she followed the other tourists up to the entrance of the pyramid, so anxious to get inside that she paid no attention when he said, "If any of you have a problem with claustrophobia, I suggest you do not try to come in."

She was the last of her group, but before she had taken more than three steps inside, other tourists crowded behind her.

It was dark in the passageway under the pyramid, and just for a moment Catherine felt the first warning signals of the closed-in feeling that she hadn't felt since she was a child.

The only time it had ever happened she'd gone with her father to look at a Hopi Indian excavation. There had been a cave nearby that her father had wanted to see, and he'd taken Catherine in with him. She was ten, and the idea of accompanying her father had overjoyed her—until she'd started into the cave. Suddenly her mouth had gone dry, and the breath had clogged in her throat. But her eagerness to please her father had been so strong that she'd shrugged off her growing panic. She was frozen where she stood and gasping for air when her father had turned and asked her if she was ill.

But she hadn't been able to answer. Her father had picked her up and carried her out of the cave. When he saw her face, he'd soothed her and asked why she hadn't told him she was afraid.

That had been a long time ago. Catherine had gotten over her fear of deep, dark places. She'd worked in a lot of excavations, and while it was true that most of them had been open dirt digs, she'd never had a recurrence of the terror she'd felt that day with her father.

The passageway leading to the Queen's chamber, crowded with people in front and behind her, narrowed and slanted upward. The ground was rough beneath her feet. The light was dim. The smell of sweat and thirty centuries of sleep pervaded the dimness.

Perspiration broke out on Catherine's forehead, and her heart began to thud hard in her ears. Steady, she told herself. You've waited all your life for this. Don't be a fool. If all these other people can do it, so can you.

The passageway narrowed even more. They were walking on a cleated board now, pulling themselves up with a handrail. Her hands were slick with sweat, but still she told herself she was all right.

Suddenly the overhang of roof lowered. They were in a tunneled space no more than four and a half feet high, forced to walk in a bent-at-the-waist position. Someone in front of Catherine muttered, "Damn, this is awful!"

The sickness of panic rose in Catherine's throat, but she plunged ahead, forced forward by the crush of people behind her into the clot of people ahead of her. Until a fear so terrible that she couldn't control it froze her where she stood. She was paralyzed, unable to move either forward or backward, her heart beating so hard against her ribs she could scarcely breathe. She gasped, trying to force the fetid air into her tortured lungs.

"Move along," somebody behind her called out.

She shut her eyes tight against the encroaching terror, holding her arms close to her body, trying to tell herself this was a hideous dream and that she would awaken soon. But it wasn't a dream.

A hand closed on her shoulder. "What is it?" a man asked softly. "Are you ill?"

She was unable to speak because of the fear that gripped her body.

Behind her, behind him, the crowd tried to push forward, crushing her against this narrow, shallow tomb. The man shouted something to the group, took her arm and forced her around. He looked down into her pale face and put his arm around her.

"The woman is ill," he told the people behind them. "We've got to go back."

There were cries of protest in different languages. Everyone was uncomfortable and unwilling to make room for their untimely exit.

He hung on to Catherine and somehow, in spite of the crush of people and the muttered oaths, got her turned around. Still bent almost double, he squeezed her back through the passageway. When they came to where they could stand upright, he took one look at her face and headed toward the entrance. Half dragging her and trying to steady her stumbling steps, he got her outside.

"Steady." He eased her down on a rock and closing his fingers on the back of her neck forced her head between her knees. "Take some deep breaths," he ordered.

Catherine gulped at the fresh air. But her eyes were still tightly shut, her hands still clasped together.

He knelt beside her. "Easy," he said. "Take it easy. You're out now. You're all right. Come on, open your eyes."

She opened them. It took her a moment to focus. "Thank you," she managed to say. "I'm so sorry. I don't know what happened to me. I..." Her eyes widened in disbelief. She stared, incredulous, at the face she'd seen on the cover of an archeology magazine.

How many times had Catherine planned her first meeting with David Pallister? How many times had she told herself she would be the total professional, cool, collected, poised? For a moment she was half tempted to turn and run back into the pyramid.

Catherine swallowed hard. Then, straightening her shoulders and summoning every bit of her courage she said, "I'm Catherine Adair, Dr. Pallister."

David stared at her, his eyebrows drawn together in a frown.

"Nothing like this has ever happened to me before," Catherine said quickly. "I've been on other excavations, in the Yucatan, at Monte Albán and Uxmal, at Tikal..." Her voice trailed off. "It was the heat and the fatigue. I didn't sleep well last night. It was a long trip from Arizona..." Her voice trailed off.

David studied her face without answering. He'd formed a mental picture of her after he'd reread some of her articles, but she wasn't what he'd expected. He'd envisioned an intelligent, scholarly woman, a tough spinster who probably kept cats and hadn't had a date in twenty years. She would be strong, able to stand the heat of the Egyptian summer and do her share of the work without complaining. This pale and shaking woman certainly didn't fit his mental picture of Professor Catherine Adair. She was slender and small boned, her face paled by fear.

He took her proffered hand. "You have claustrophobia," he said accusingly.

"No, I don't!" she protested. "What just happened wouldn't have if I hadn't been so tired. I know how this looks..." She tried to laugh. "The idea of an archeologist with claustrophobia is ludicrous. But I assure you..."

David barely heard her. He knew that he'd made a mistake in asking her to be a part of the team. But dammit, he'd checked her out. She had a good reputation. She was a brilliant researcher, and she'd made some remarkable discoveries. The fact that she was the daughter of Milton Adair had helped in his decision to make her a member of the team. But the woman had claustrophobia! How had she managed all these years with a problem like that? And how in the hell was he going to handle it?

A faint blush of color flushed her cheeks. "I checked with the hotel when I arrived yesterday," she said. "About both you and Professor Garson. The desk clerk told me you hadn't arrived yet."

"I came in late last night. Fletcher will be in some time this afternoon." David got to his feet and still frowning asked, "Feeling better?"

"Yes. Thank you for helping me. I know how this must look, but I'm really not like this."

"Maybe." David looked away. "If you're feeling all right, we could make our way over to the other pyramids and the Sphinx. You haven't seen them yet, have you?"

When she said that she hadn't, he took her arm and led her to one of the tour buses that took them to the reclining Sphinx.

They stood before that damaged but indomitable face where pharaohs and kings and commoners, where Caesar and Alexander, Augustus and Napoleon had stood, here in this place where time began. They looked up at the marvel of stone sitting in somber and unassailable dignity.

"It's hard to believe I'm really here," Catherine said. "I've waited such a long time. I was going to come five years ago with my father."

"That's when he had the heart attack?"

"Yes."

"Couldn't you have come anyway, later I mean?"

She shook her head. "There were bills. My mother had been ill for a long time. Then when Dad died... I don't know, I kept thinking that next year..." She managed a smile. "But I'm here now, and all this is more, so much more than I ever dreamed it would be."

She followed him back around the Sphinx to the other two pyramids, out to the very edge of the Sahara. He was withdrawn but polite as he pointed things out to her. When it was time to leave, they boarded the same bus to take them back to their hotel.

"I'm meeting Fletcher for dinner tonight," David said. "There's a floating restaurant, the Nile Pharaoh. I'll make reservations for the three of us if that's agreeable with you."

"Yes, that's fine."

He looked at her. "Feeling all right now?"

"Yes, thank you."

"Shall we say seven-thirty in the lobby?"

Catherine nodded. "Seven-thirty is fine," she said.

When she was alone in her room, she closed the drapes, then undressed and took a shower. She stood under the hot water for a long time, washing away the dust, the smell of the camel and the mustiness of that deep, dark place under the pyramid.

"Fool!" she said aloud as the water cascaded over her head and down her body. How could she have behaved that way? Why, of all the people in Egypt, did it have to be David Pallister who'd rescued her? She'd seen his face when she told him who she was, had almost seen the words forming in his brain... I've got a woman with claustrophobia on my team!

Damn! Catherine pounded the wall with her fist. How could she have behaved like such an idiot?

When she came out of the shower and dried her hair, she put on a simple linen dress and a pair of brown shoes. Then, adorned with neither jewelry nor makeup, she went downstairs to meet David Pallister and Fletcher Garson.

"She did what?" Garson looked incredulously at David.

"She panicked. You should have seen her face! She was white as death, frozen where she stood. It was all I could do to get her out of there."

Fletcher took a long swallow of beer. "What did she say, once you got her out I mean?"

"She said it had never happened before, that it was the heat and the fact that she was tired."

"But if it has, if she really has claustrophobia..." Fletcher Garson tugged on his beard. "Can you imagine the kind of courage it must take her to go underground? She has a good reputation you know. I've read her papers, and I've talked to people who've worked with her. None of them has ever mentioned her having any kind of a problem. Paul Kinsky worked with her one summer in the Yucatan. He said it was hot as hell and that the work was backbreaking. But she worked as hard, if not harder, than any of the men on the dig. He also told me that she forged ahead of them into the jungle, wasn't afraid of snakes and that she never complained." He looked at David. "What's she like?" he asked. "I mean what does she look like?"

"She's plain. Straight hair, no makeup." David grinned. "She looks like somebody's maiden aunt. She..." He stopped and looked up as Catherine stepped off the elevator.

Both men stood up. "Good evening, Miss Adair. I'd like you to meet Fletcher Garson. Fletch, this is Catherine Adair."

Garson took her hand. "It's a pleasure to finally meet you. I knew your father, worked with him on digs in Ethiopia and Mauritania."

He didn't agree with David. She wasn't plain at all. She had a rather quiet beauty that she seemed totally unaware of. Her skin was fine, her features good, and her eyes were really quite lovely. Suddenly Fletcher Garson found himself wishing he were ten years younger.

"The boat leaves at eight," David said. "We'd better..." He glanced over Fletcher's shoulder, frowning at a man who advanced on him, camera in hand. An older woman, pad and pencil poised, followed behind.

"Mr. Pallister? May I have a few words with you, sir?" she asked just as a flashbulb went off in David's face.

"We're on our way to dinner," he said testily.

"Just a word or two for our readers, sir. You're a celebrity in the world of archeology, and I understand you're in Egypt to search for the missing tomb of the young Queen Alifa."

"That's right."

"Where do you hope to find her, sir?"

Another flashbulb went off.

"Near Edfu." David glared at the photographer. "But I'd rather not say too much about it now. I'll be glad to, later, after we find the tomb." He took Catherine's arm. "Please excuse us now. We're on our way to dinner, and if we don't leave immediately we'll miss our boat."

"The price of fame," Fletcher said wistfully as he followed David and Catherine out through the lobby.

"Those people drive me crazy," David shot back.

It was almost dark by the time they boarded the Nile boat. A thin slice of new moon shone overhead, and there was a slight chill in the air. The night smelled of jasmine and of the river, and the lights from the city reflected on the water as the boat moved away from the shore.

When Catherine put a brown sweater over her shoulders, David said, "Would you like to go in?"

She shook her head. "I'd rather stay here for a few minutes. This is all so beautiful."

"The Nile is even more beautiful farther on." Fletcher cupped one hand around his pipe and took a puff. "Between Luxor and Aswan is the most interesting part of the Nile, I think. You'll have to take a couple of days off this summer and take a cruise."

"Yes, I'd like that." Catherine glanced at David, then away.

He stood apart from her, looking out over the water. Tonight he'd worn dark trousers, a shirt and a tie and a suede sport jacket. The clothes made him look older, more serious. So much depended on him, Catherine thought. He was the one with the grant; he would decide whether she stayed or went. She tightened her hands on the railing. David had every right to replace her—the project was too important to have a member of the team he couldn't trust to do whatever needed to be done.

Catherine looked out over the water. She had to make him understand that what happened today would never happen again. And it wouldn't, she promised herself as she looked back on the lights of Cairo.

They went into the ship's dining room for dinner and after they had ordered Fletcher asked, "When do we leave for Luxor?"

"Day after tomorrow. I'm going to meet with Massaud tomorrow." David turned to Catherine. "Massaud Habib," he explained. "He's the Egyptian student who'll be going along with us. I've never met him, but he comes highly recommended. He's working on his master's degree, and he's familiar with the area where we'll be working. He'll be a great help."

David looked at Catherine over the rim of his wineglass. "It's going to be a difficult dig," he said. "We've got an awful lot of ground to cover, and we've only got six months to come up with something. Unless we do, we have to give it up, and I don't want that to happen." His voice hardened. "I won't let it happen. Every member of the team has to do his or her share of the work. You have a problem, Miss Adair, and frankly it worries me."

Catherine straightened in her seat. Using the same tone of voice she sometimes used when she addressed her students, she said, "I promise you that what happened today will never happen again, Dr. Pallister. If it does, I'll leave without your having to ask me to."

David tapped long slender fingers against the white tablecloth. "I'll hold you to that," he said.

The rest of the meal, except for the futile attempts Fletcher Garson made at conversation, was eaten in silence. When the ship docked back at the hotel, Garson said, "It's off to bed for me. I'm so tired I can barely keep my eyes open." He took Catherine's hand. "Why don't I show you the Egyptian Museum tomorrow while David looks up young Massaud? Is nine o'clock all right?"

Catherine nodded and with a grateful smile said, "Yes, thank you, Professor Garson."

"Fletch," he said. He shot a look at David. "We're all going to be working together, so we should be on a first-name basis. See you in the morning, Catherine."

When the elevator doors closed behind him, Catherine hesitated, then said, "I'd better go up, too."

"We'll meet for dinner tomorrow." David jabbed the elevator button. He let her precede him, but he didn't look at her until they reached their floor. He walked her to her door and took her hand to say a formal good-night.

Catherine looked up at him. "Good night, Dr. Pallister... David."

"Good night, Catherine." Her hand felt cool in his. Her skin was very smooth. He looked at her and wondered why he hadn't noticed before that her eyes were the clear brown color of Spanish sherry.

Chapter 3

At sixty-four Fletcher Garson was a splendid figure of a man. He was square and solidly built, with thick, wavy gray hair. His beard still bore tinges of red, which was accentuated by his deep rainy-day gray eyes. Catherine found him an excellent conversationalist and a wonderful guide.

The Egyptian Museum, with the treasures of King Tut and all of the other priceless objects, had overwhelmed Catherine. Fletcher had allowed her to take her time, remaining silent when she stopped to study something as beautiful as the quartzite head of Nefertiti or the famous Mycerinus Triad.

It was when they were having lunch that Fletcher said, "I don't think I've told you how much I admired your father. The last time I worked with him was in Mauritania in a village not too far from Néma. It was in the fall of 1967, and as I remember we both came down with malaria at the same time." He smiled at Catherine. "I had a miserable case. Your father recovered before I did, and he arranged transportation to fly me to Madrid for treatment. I still have flare-ups occasionally, but never anything as bad as that first time. What about him? Did he ever have flare-ups?"

"Not that I know of," Catherine said. "At least not while he was at home."

"Then he was a lot stronger than I am." Fletcher hesitated. "We all have our weaknesses, Catherine. I learned a long time ago not to be ashamed of mine. As you should not be ashamed of yours."

She looked into the kind gray eyes beneath the shaggy brows, and her throat tightened with suppressed tears—he reminded her so much of her father. She hadn't felt very close to anyone since his death, but there was something about this man, a warmth and understanding that seeped through her reserve and made her feel as though she could say almost anything to him and that he would understand, as her father had always understood.

She told him how she had felt in the pyramid yesterday. "I panicked," she said. "I was beyond rationally thinking that there was nothing to fear. Then the walls felt as though they were closing in on me, and I couldn't breathe. It was like a nightmare, a dream so real that when you awaken, your body is covered with sweat and your skin hurts from holding yourself so tightly."

A shiver ran down Catherine's spine as she tried to control herself. "I'm an archeologist, Fletcher. It's unforgivable for someone like me to have behaved that way."

Fletcher looked at her for a moment. He reached for his pipe and, when he'd filled and lighted it, said, "I think both you and David are blowing what happened all out of proportion. I've been through that passageway to the queen's chamber several times, and I've never felt good about it. A few years ago the chap ahead of me passed out cold. It's an eerie place, and if you're at all sensitive to that kind of thing, it can give you quite a turn. But I doubt that any excavation site will ever be as difficult as what you experienced yesterday."

"I hope you're right," Catherine said, somewhat reassured by his words. "Have you ever worked with David before?"

"Last year in Bolivia. He's very good at leading a dig, and he works harder than any man I've ever seen. He knows what he's doing, and he has a gut instinct, an amazing belief in himself that never seems to fail." Fletcher hesitated. "I've read your articles about the young queen's tomb, and I know that you don't agree with David about the location."

"But I don't suppose there's anything I can do about it," Catherine said.

"I'm afraid not. Once David makes up his mind about something, nothing will change him. He's had remarkable luck with everything he's done, Catherine. He's absolutely sure Queen Alifa's tomb is near her husband's, so I doubt anything you say can sway him." Fletcher smiled sympathetically. "What makes you so sure the queen's tomb isn't where he thinks it is? All the evidence points to her having been buried near Amonset."

"Not *all* the evidence." Catherine took a sip of her tea. "Alifa was born on the Island of Philae, Fletcher. Dad did a lot of research years ago, and it was his theory that after Amonset's death she returned there."

"That's pure speculation, Catherine."

"Speculation that Dad believed." She leaned across the table, her face intent because she wanted him to understand. "Dad used to tell me stories about her a lot,

Fletcher, and after a while Alifa seemed as real to me as you are. You know how children have imaginary companions? Well, Alifa was mine, and I was closer to her than to any of the little girls I used to play with. I knew everything about her—what she was like, how she felt about things, how she dressed, even what she liked to eat. I used to think about her just before I went to sleep at night."

"You were a child with a vivid imagination, Catherine," Fletcher said kindly. "Nothing very strange about that."

"But when I wasn't a child anymore?" Catherine shook her head. "When I was fifteen, the age Alifa had been when she married Amonset, I wept because I knew how awful it had been for her to marry a man so much older than she. Can you imagine what it must have been like for her, Fletcher? At fifteen my biggest worries were getting good grades and having a Saturday-night movie date. But Alifa had been torn from her home and forced to marry a man older than her father."

Catherine leaned back in her chair, and when she spoke again, her voice was reflective, thoughtful. "Maybe all girls that age are impressionable and romantic. God knows that I was. But it just seemed so real to me. I could imagine her standing before the priests the day she married Amonset. She was dressed in white linen, and her skin was perfumed. Her eyes were painted with kohl, and she wore a black wig that was so hot and heavy it made her head ache." Catherine's voice was low, intense with feeling. "I knew," she whispered, "somehow I *knew* the way she felt that day. And I knew she'd have given anything to return to Philae, that even as she stood beside her husband she dreamed of home."

Catherine took a deep, shaking breath. "I was obsessed with Alifa when I was fifteen years old, Fletcher. Maybe I still am."

Fletcher looked at Catherine for a long time before he said, "I don't want to sound like a male chauvinist, Catherine, but aren't most young women given to romantic flights of fancy? You're entitled to your dream, to the romanticism you felt when you were fifteen, but you're a woman now and based on all the facts—"

"Everything I've ever done, any dig I've undertaken, has been based on fact," she said defensively. "I'm a methodical researcher, Fletcher. I do my homework before I start a project, and believe me, I stopped having romantic flights of fancy a long time ago. To me it's perfectly logical that after her husband's death Alifa would have wanted to return to her home. She was only nineteen when he died, she had her whole life ahead of her."

Fletcher Garson stared at Catherine. The face that David had told him was plain was alive with passion. Her wide brown eyes were alight with an inner fire that told of the strength of her conviction. For a moment he almost believed her. Perhaps she was right, perhaps the young queen really had gone back to her island home. But even if he believed her, he knew in his heart that David never would.

The three men were seated in the lounge when Catherine appeared for dinner that evening wearing another dress that did nothing for her figure.

When the men stood, David said, "Catherine, I'd like you to meet Massaud Habib."

"Welcome to my country." The young man spoke in heavily accented English. He was short and stocky, with a pleasant face and skin the color of a copper penny. "I have read extensively of the mystery surrounding the missing tomb of the young queen," he said to Catherine when they sat down. "I have read your articles, and I understand you do not believe the queen is buried near her husband."

"No, I don't," Catherine said. "It's my opinion that she returned to Philae."

"I find that interesting, because in preparation for this dig I have recently discovered some forgotten transcripts written on papyrus about Queen Alifa in the archives of the Egyptian Museum. We have quite an elaborate oral tradition in my country—and it wasn't uncommon for the servants of royalty to be chosen for their gift of song. Often these songs were later written down by a scribe. The story that is told through the scribe's written words opens up a most interesting theory."

Catherine leaned forward in her chair, her eyes alive with interest. "What theory?" she asked. "What do you mean?"

"The papers tell of King Amonset's death, and it speaks of all the things that were later found in his tomb, which indicates the stories told through the songs were true, and that the servant who originally sang them was indeed near the king at the time of his death." Massaud looked at David and Fletcher. "The transcript also mentions a young noble named Ramah, who apparently was a favorite of the king's, so much that Amonset began construction of a tomb for Ramah before his own death."

"Ramah?" Fletcher nodded thoughtfully. "Yes, I've heard of him. He was killed in one of the wars, wasn't he?"

"Against the Assyrians," Massaud said.

"But what's that got to do with Alifa?" David asked impatiently.

"In the transcript there was a suggestion of a romance between the queen and a young noble."

"But that doesn't mean that Ramah was the noble referred to. Besides, from all the research I've done, it appears that Queen Alifa was completely faithful to her husband." David frowned. "I don't doubt there were as many illicit liaisons in the times of the ancients as there are today, but nothing I've ever read indicates that Alifa was an unfaithful wife."

"But King Amonset died before she did, Dave," Fletcher said thoughtfully. "Alifa was a young woman, at least thirty years younger than her husband. She would have been only eighteen or nineteen when he died. It isn't inconceivable that she would have had a lover after his death."

"Even if she did, Fletch, it wouldn't affect her place of burial. Those things were preordained."

"Is there any way we could see the papers?" Catherine asked Massaud, barely suppressing the excitement in her voice.

"Most certainly, Miss Adair. I copied the transcript into Egyptian—I will be happy to translate it into English for you."

Shooting an angry glance at Catherine, David said, "I'm sure the transcript makes interesting reading, but I don't see the connection between it and the location of Alifa's final resting place. Even if Ramah was the queen's lover, that doesn't alter the fact that she was entombed somewhere near her husband. I'll stake my career on it." The decision about where they would search for the tomb had been made months ago, years ago actually, while he was still in graduate school. The grant had been a heaven-sent opportunity to fulfill a lifelong dream, and now that he was here he didn't plan on letting Catherine Adair upset his plans.

He watched her as she turned to speak to Fletcher. She was a strange woman, introverted and withdrawn at times. At other times she was outspoken enough to set his teeth on edge. He knew her age to be thirty-seven, but she looked older. Probably, he speculated, because of the severity of style—or lack of style. Her bone structure was good, and her skin was as fine as porcelain, a perfect foil for the unusual color of her eyes.

David couldn't tell anything about her figure, not with the clothes she wore. The gray dress she had on tonight would have looked too old for his great aunt. He wondered why she dressed that way. Why she felt it was necessary to hide behind loose-fitting, nondescript clothes. He glanced down at her legs and felt a shock of surprise, because they were the best-looking, most spectacular legs he'd ever seen. Encased in pale gray silk stockings, they were smooth and curvy, and the ankles were so delicate he knew he could span them with his thumb and middle finger.

His gaze traveled up past the legs, trying to imagine what kind of a figure lay behind the folds of material. For a reason he couldn't explain he found himself unable to tear his gaze away. Her straight brown hair glistened like deep dark fur in the glow of candles, and her eyes were alive with excitement. Even as he told Fletcher and Massaud that they would leave on the afternoon flight for Luxor, his thoughts were on her. He raised his glass, and over the rim of it he watched the rise and fall of her breathing. He could see the almost hidden outline of her breasts and wondered how they would fit in his hands.

Abruptly a hot flame of desire shot through David's body. He put the glass down so hard the liquid spilled over the edge of it. He was angry, at himself for feeling this way and at Catherine who sat so cool and remote, so self-contained and professional across from him. Suddenly and irrationally David wanted to look behind that remote, cool exterior. He wanted to discover what thoughts lay behind those dark sherry eyes, what mysteries of femininity were hidden by the dull gray dress.

Somehow David knew that before their journey was over, he would discover the mystery of Catherine Adair.

The four of them flew to Luxor the next day. They would stay in this ancient capital of Thebes on the banks of the River Nile for two days before they boarded the ship that would take them farther south to Edfu, where they would begin their excavations.

"The workmen you instructed me to hire are waiting for us," Massaud told David. "I have worked with some of them before. Last year several of us from undergraduate school were sent to Abydos to work a dig with our professor. The men I have hired are reliable; you will have no trouble with them." The young man turned to Catherine and said, "The Temple of Luxor is very close to the hotel. If you like, we could walk down there, and I will show it to you this afternoon."

She looked at David. "If you don't need me for anything I'd like to go with Massaud."

"Sure, go ahead. I want to take in the Light and Sound Show at Karnak tonight though. The show in English is at eight-thirty. Let's all meet in the lobby at eight."

Catherine nodded her agreement, then quickly went up to her room in the hotel to change. She was back in twenty minutes, and she and Massaud crossed the street in front of the hotel so that they could walk along the Nile. There were hundreds of questions Catherine wanted to ask the young Egyptian, but the carriage drivers, who badgered them every step of the way, made conversation difficult. Finally Massaud turned and yelled something at the closest driver, who yelled back, then with an eloquent gesture snapped the whip over his horse's back and wheeled away from the curb.

"The temple was built in the latter part of the seventeenth dynasty and the earlier half of the nineteenth dynasty," Massaud told Catherine when they passed through the entrance, lined on both sides with lion-bodied sphinxes. "It was built on the site of an earlier temple of the Middle Kingdom about two thousand years B.C. and was dedicated to the powerful Theban god, Amon-Ra."

As the afternoon lengthened and the sun sank low on the west bank of the Nile, they wandered among the double rows of papyrus-shaped columns. In the last rays of the sun the strength and the grandeur of the ancient walls turned from ocher to golden. The tourists left, and the sounds of the day slowly faded away. Catherine looked about her. She'd never been to this place before, but there seemed a strange and dear familiarity about it.

When, into the quiet of her thoughts, Massaud said, "They will lock the gate soon, we must leave now," she hesitated, reluctant to leave. Only when he promised he would return with her in the morning did she let him lead her away.

"May the evening soothe and welcome you, for you are in the house of the father."

The voice rang out upon the cool night air, past the obelisks of Karnak, among the stupendous Hall of Columns, at the entrance of the great temple of Amon-Ra. Millions had trod here—pharaohs and kings and white-robed priests had moved in the incense-filled air. All was now quiet, except for this one voice.

"Hear the whispered response of the ever-present gods who speak to you of the past."

Out of the blackness of the night a light shone upon the papyrus-flower columns. "Decayed and desolate now," the voice went on, "leaving only this record of the greatness of the time and these structures, so vast, even in their ruins, that they must have been designed not by men but by the grand scale of the gods."

As the light that had shone on the columns dimmed, the crowd moved forward to their seats. But Catherine wasn't aware of the crowd or of David's hand on her arm.

"I'm afraid we've lost Fletch and Massaud," he said as he led her to a seat facing the span of Karnak. "We'll catch up with them later." He glanced at her. "Impressive, isn't it?"

Impressive wasn't the word. It was magic, it was being transported back thousands of years to a civilization that was unlike anything the world had ever known or would ever know again.

A breeze through the trees whispered like the sighing voices of the ever-present gods of the past. A thin slice of new moon reflected on the sacred lake. The papyrus quivered, rustling its leaves.

A voice said, "I open my mouth to speak in the midst of silence. Listen now, for our journey to the start of the night will take us to the stars. We will travel through thirty centuries of sleep. . . ."

"I remember the first time I saw this..." David started to say, then stopped and stared at Catherine. She sat forward in her chair. Her face in the moonlight was transfixed, motionless and strangely, exotically beautiful. Was this the woman he had thought of as plain? Plain! Good lord, she was either one of the most beautiful women he'd ever seen, or his eyes were playing tricks on him.

David didn't speak again, he only watched Catherine, the mobility of her mouth, the strange, haunting sadness of her dark eyes, the slender white fingers that brushed tears from her cheeks. He wanted to touch her, but because he was afraid of breaking the magic that held Catherine in this spell, he neither moved nor spoke.

At last the voice that had taken them on this voyage into the past faded away into the night, and the lights came on.

"Catherine?" David touched her hand. "It's over, Catherine."

She looked at him, still bewitched by the spell of Karnak. "I've never..." She seemed to be struggling her way back to reality. "I've never experienced anything like that before. It was as though I could see the men and women who have walked here before us."

Catherine looked out over the lake where blossoms of night flowers drifted, and it seemed to her that even from here she could smell their fragrance. "The sacred lake of Karnak," she said softly. "Upon which you have come to dream and to know the splendor that was Thebes."

The people sitting near them had left their seats to drift back through the columns. They were alone in the stillness of the night. David looked at her tear-streaked face—a sensitive face made beautiful by what she'd experienced, and knew that he had to touch her. Very gently he brushed his fingers along her cheek to turn her slightly toward him. Her dark eyes widened, but before she could speak he kissed her.

It was a brief kiss, light and softly caressing, but as his lips touched hers David felt something stir within him. He let her go, and in a voice that didn't sound like his own, he said, "For Karnak, Catherine. Because you understand."

But David didn't understand. He only knew that he was drawn to this quiet, solemn woman and that he wanted to fold her in his arms and hold her close, here in this ancient and magical place. Instead he took her cool hand in his and said, "Come, it's time to leave."

Still under Karnak's spell, with the memory of David's lips on hers, Catherine let him lead her through the now silent columns.

Chapter 4

The Nile, called by the ancients a sacred avenue in the shade of the sycamores, sparkled in the morning sun as the four archeologists boarded the boat that would take them farther south to Edfu.

It had all been almost too much to absorb, Catherine thought as she watched the receding shore of Luxor from the upper deck of the ship. Only a week ago she had been in Arizona, excited about the impending trip to Egypt. But not even in her wildest dreams had she anticipated how magnificent everything would be. She needed time to think about all she'd seen and experienced in these past few days—the pyramids and the Sphinx, the glory of Karnak and the immensity of the Valley of the Kings where she'd seen the tombs of Seti I, of Ramses and Tutankhamen.

And yes, she needed time to think of the way she'd felt when David kissed her.

Very few men had kissed Catherine since the long-ago summer when she completed her first year of graduate school. She'd worked to the point of exhaustion that year, and when she told her father she planned to take extra courses during the summer he'd turned to her in amazement. "No, you're not! You're going to take a vacation." He'd bought her a round-trip ticket to Jamaica and arranged a three-week stay for her at one of the plush hotels on the north shore.

It was the first time Catherine had been on her own without the protection of her parents or her school. She spent the first few days secluded under a palm tree on a chaise with her nose in an archeology book. On the fourth day of her stay she was pulled to attention by a masculine voice that asked, "Don't you ever stop reading?"

She'd looked up into a pair of warm brown eyes in a laughing, freckled face.

Ron Palmer, from Fort Myers, Florida, looked as harmless and as friendly as the boy next door. He coaxed Catherine out from under the palm tree into a whirl of activity she'd always been too busy to enjoy. They swam in the blue Caribbean, sailed and snorkeled and splashed in Dunn's River Falls. And every night when the trade winds stilled, they danced to the slow and lazy rhythms of a calypso band. At the beginning of Catherine's second week at the hotel they became lovers.

It was for Catherine a time of incredible magic. She had dated very little in high school and college, and certainly she'd never had a whirl like the kind she enjoyed that summer in Jamaica. She'd been reluctant about letting Ron make love to her, and even now, standing here on the deck of the Nile steamer, she wasn't sure whether she'd been coaxed or forced.

Ron had come to Jamaica with a friend. She didn't like Guy Lockwood, but she'd pretended to for Ron's sake. When one afternoon Guy asked her to go for a sail and Ron agreed, she'd reluctantly gone with him.

The skiff was little more than a flat board with a sail. There was room for only two people, if the two people sat close together. A few feet from shore the wind caught the sail, and they were off. Caribbean clouds drifted fat and full overhead, the wind was up and the sea had just enough of a chop to make it exciting.

Instead of staying near the hotel, as most of the skiffs did, Guy headed down the beach and out of sight of the buildings. When a wave threatened to topple them, he told Catherine to move closer, and before she could protest he pulled her up against him. For a minute she didn't say anything, then, not wanting to make an issue of it, she moved a fraction of an inch away.

"Hey," Guy said with a laugh. "Where're you going?" He pulled her back, put his arms around her and slid both hands up to cup her breasts.

Catherine tried to jerk away from him. "Stop it," she ordered. "What do you think you're doing?"

"The same thing Ron's been doing for the last week." Guy turned her around to face him, fastened a hand in her hair, glued his mouth to hers and, with his other hand, pulled down the front of her bathing suit.

"It's okay," he said when he came up for air. "Ron doesn't mind if we share the wealth. He said you were hot enough for both of us." Guy tightened his grip on her arms. "I'm going to head for that cove. You and I are going to have us some fun, and later you can tell old Ron whether or not I'm better than he is."

Guy reached for the tiller, and when he did, Catherine hit him as hard as she could. He sprawled back on the board, and she jumped off the side of the skiff and swam to shore. She managed to get back to the hotel without anybody seeing her, and the next morning she left the island.

In the weeks and months that followed, Catherine tried to tell herself that what had happened in Jamaica hadn't been her fault. Ron Palmer *had* looked like the typical boy next door. She'd trusted him with her love and with herself, and he'd made a fool of her. But the memory of that day on the boat with Guy Lockwood had chilled a very important part of Catherine. It was a part of herself that, since then, she'd chosen to hide behind the dark and unattractive clothes she wore.

She hadn't felt anything for a long time, not until Karnak—and David.

Catherine stayed out on deck most of the afternoon, watching the Nile flow past adobe villages, peasants in flowing *gelabayas*, ancient waterwheels, camels, donkeys, water buffalo and the tall-masted feluccas sailed by dark-skinned Nubians. It was a world that was foreign to her, yet one she felt oddly at home in.

At noon the following day the ship docked at Edfu. As it edged toward shore Catherine saw that the few people who waited on the pier were overshadowed by a dark-skinned man of medium height who weighed well over two hundred pounds. Bald except for a fringe of dark hair that circled his head, he was dressed in a wine-colored *gelabaya* and leather sandals.

"*Sabah en-nur*, greetings," he called as they came down the gangplank. He rushed forward to grab Fletcher Garson's hand.

"*Ahlan wa sahlan,*" Fletcher responded. "It is good to see you again, Abdel Moustafa. May I present Professor Catherine Adair and Professor David Pallister from the United States. I believe you've already met Massaud Habib."

"Indeed I have. It is good to see you, young Massaud." The fat man looked at Catherine. When she extended her hand, he bowed low and kissed it, then greeted David. "I know of your fine reputation," he said. "It will be an honor to have you in my house."

"It is most gracious of you to offer your hospitality," David said. "*Shoukran*, thank you."

Catherine looked questioningly at Fletcher, who said, "Abdel Moustafa has kindly offered us his hospitality until we've established our base camp." He looked around at their luggage. "I guess we have everything. Shall we go?"

Abdel Moustafa's chauffeur-driven Mercedes sedan turned back in the direction they had come on the Nile. He sat in the back seat beside Catherine, his body spread about him in folding waves of flesh, waving thick, ring-covered fingers while he talked.

"My house is yours for as long as you like," he told David, who sat next to Fletcher and Massaud.

"That's kind of you," David said. "But the camp will be ready in three days."

"A camp of tents! Would you not be better to stay here? I will loan you a car so that you can drive back and forth to the site of your work. Why be uncomfortable when you can so easily enjoy the luxury of my home?"

"Archeologists aren't supposed to be comfortable," Fletcher said, grinning. "We like living in tents and digging in the ground in hundred-degree heat, eating off plastic plates and shaking sand out of our clothes before we put them on." He looked out of the window as they passed a man leading two camels. "It's good to be back," he said. "It's like coming home."

They passed through a village, and Abdel pointed out the marketplace to Catherine. "You can buy anything you want there," he told her. "Clothes, jewelry..." He laughed and winked at her. "Love potions. It's an interesting place, and you must visit it while you're here." He shifted his mammoth bulk as the car slowed and said, "We are arriving at my most humble home."

The most humble home was a two-story, multiroomed house that looked part English palace and part Italian villa. Manicured terraced gardens sloped down to the Nile. A waterfall at the highest part poured a cascade of water to form the swimming pool.

"Swim if you like, or rest if you prefer," Abdel said. "The servants will show you to your rooms now, but we will meet at seven for an aperitif. Dinner will be served at eight. If there is anything you desire, please do not hesitate to summon a servant."

Catherine's suite of rooms overlooked the waterfall, the pool and the Nile beyond. She was stunned by the beauty and the luxury of the place and found herself smiling both with pleasure and surprise at yet another side of Egypt.

Dinner that evening proved to be another surprise. After a salad of artichoke hearts and endive they were served a marvelous chateaubriand and a variety of perfectly cooked vegetables. Chocolate crepes and American coffee were served for dessert. It was while they were having an after-dinner cognac that their host said, "I am giving a dinner party in your honor tomorrow night."

A frown puckered David's brow. "That's not at all necessary, Mr. Moustafa."

"But it will be my pleasure to introduce you to my friends," Abdel protested. "I assure you that it will be a small affair, no more than twenty." He patted Catherine's hand. "You will enjoy it, my dear. All lovely ladies enjoy parties."

Catherine forced a smile. Not this lady, she almost said. She didn't like meeting strangers and making small talk, and she really didn't have anything to wear.

That night when Catherine got into bed, she looked up and frowned at the mirrors above her head. In her tailored pajamas she looked totally out of place in this four-poster bed with the pale mauve hangings and pink satin sheets. Everything was so opulent, so unlike the sterile neatness of her bedroom back home. This wasn't a bed one slept in, this was a bed one gamboled in. She had a sudden clear picture of other guests who'd occupied this suite of rooms and made a face at herself in the mirrors.

Finally, with a sigh of exasperation, Catherine threw back the satin sheet and crossed the room to the balcony. The air was sweet tonight, faintly scented with jasmine, as calm and still as the river flowing so timelessly past. As she leaned against the rail Catherine's frown slowly faded, and a sense of peace softened her face. A faint shadow of moon shone on the palm trees that grew near the bank where reeds and flowers sloped gently to the water. She breathed in the soft night air and thought of the centuries of people who'd gone before her, of the silent passage of boats on the great river, of the men and women who'd taken their lives and their strength from the waters of the Nile.

Catherine stayed out on the balcony for a long time, and when at last she went back into the room, she left the doors open so that she could smell the jasmine and hear the gentle flow of the water. She paused by the bed. A smile softened her face as she unbuttoned her pajamas. She folded them over a chair, then got into bed and switched off the bedside light.

The satin sheets were cool against her naked body, and with a contented sigh she closed her eyes and let herself drift into a sleep, but not a dreamless sleep.

Sleep...

The air was filled with the scent of jasmine when she slipped from her chamber down the silent path in the shadow of the trees toward the water, her heart beating like a frightened bird against her ribs.

"Meet me tonight," he had pleaded. "If I do not touch you, if I do not hold you in my arms, I think I will die. Come, my sweet love, come to me tonight."

She wore an indigo-blue cape over her short, white gown and gold sandals on her feet. I will tell him we cannot meet again, she thought as she nervously fingered her sandalwood beads. It is not proper that I... She heard the whisper of his voice and paused, wondering if she should turn back.

He stepped from a spread of palms in front of her. "My love," he whispered. "You have come."

Before she could speak, he pulled her into a bower of overhanging trees. She protested, even as he folded her in his arms. His lips were cool, but the arms that held her were as warm as the body pressed so close to hers.

The cape slipped from her shoulders, and she swayed against him. How long, dear Isis, how long had she dreamed of this moment? How many times had they looked at each other across the temple courtyard? How many times had he whispered, "My queen, most royal, more beautiful than any woman in Egypt."

The kiss deepened. She could no longer think for the waves of heat that warmed her trembling body. He knelt, gently urging her down beside him, and like a slave with no will of her own she followed him. She felt his hands upon her breasts and moaned softly against his lips. She offered no word of protest when he laid her down upon the flower-filled bower. She was a prisoner now, of the body that covered her and of the treacherous heat that throbbed through her veins. Once again his mouth claimed her, and his arms went around her, urging her closer, closer. With a cry of surrender she yielded to him.

It was more, it was so much more than she had ever dreamed it could be. Dreamed...

Dreamed...

Catherine awoke with the first rays of the sun and looked around the room in puzzlement. The morning air was cool, and she pulled the sheet up to cover her body, wondering what flight of fancy had made her take off her pajamas the night before. She sat up in bed, feeling strangely disoriented.

Quickly she got up and, going to her suitcase, pulled out her black maillot and a beach robe. When she'd dressed, she went out on the balcony. No one was out yet; everything was quiet. Silently Catherine went out of her suite of rooms and down the stairs.

The grass was damp and cool against her bare feet. She dropped her robe when she reached the pool and looked out to where the mists rose over the Nile. Her face was thoughtful, puzzled, because it seemed to her that through the mists she could hear the sound of voices, not one or two, but the murmur of centuries, soft upon the morning air. She put her hands to her temples, then shook her head as though to clear it and dove into the pool.

Pale arms cut the water cleanly. She swam back and forth three times, then let herself drift faceup, alone and remote, removed for this brief moment from all thought and care.

At last Catherine came out of the pool and stood, eyes closed, facing the sun, feeling the warmth of it on her body and seeping into her bones, unself-conscious because she was alone. There was no one to share this quiet morning with, no one to see as she raised her arms to the sun god, Ra. No one.

Only David. Like Catherine he had come out on his balcony. He'd gazed around him at the terraced gardens and the Nile beyond, where two feluccas, tall sails furled in a quickening breeze, crossed the river to the opposite bank. He had just turned to go back into his room when he saw her.

She stood with her arms raised to the sun, her slender body poised and graceful. Her breasts were firm and high, her waist narrow, and her legs were even more lovely than that first brief glimpse had indicated. Here, with her body outlined against the sun, unaware that anyone was watching, she was more alluring, more exciting than any woman he'd ever known before.

The breath caught in David's throat with the thought that he and Catherine would be together every day for the next six months, even longer if the dig went as well as he hoped it would. He'd expected it to be a period in his life completely devoted to his work. It would be, of course, but now he knew he would make time for the pursuit and the seduction of Miss Catherine Adair. He would discover what lay behind those unfathomable, sherry-colored eyes, what mysteries of feminine warmth lay hidden behind that cool mask she wore. One glance at the woman who stood with her arms raised to the sun would tell even the most casual of observers that here was a woman of passion.

He would be the one to unlock that passion, to awaken that smooth sleek body to joys she hadn't even imagined.

He whispered her name and felt his body tighten with need.

Chapter 5

Catherine couldn't say why she began to look forward to Abdel Moustafa's party, she only knew that as the day passed she felt a growing sense of excitement.

That afternoon her host asked if there was anything she needed, and when she told him that she would enjoy going to the bazaar, he immediately had his car brought around. The car arrived with a servant who would accompany Catherine, a young woman who was almost as corpulent as her master.

"This is Safa," Abdel said. "She will go with you."

Catherine opened her mouth to protest, but before she could speak Abdel said, "Please, I insist. It would not be proper for you to go alone. Safa has some English. She also knows how to bargain with the shopkeepers."

The young woman smiled appealingly, bobbing her head, saying and motioning for Catherine to enter the car.

Because it was Saturday, the huge souk was crowded with people. As she made her way among the shops, Catherine was assailed by a babble of voices—sellers hawking their goods, men with pushcarts who shouted warnings as they barreled their way through the narrow alleys, housewives bargaining for a chicken or lamenting over the price of onions. The stalls were filled to overflowing with apricots and dates, pomegranates, oranges and bright red strawberries. The scent of rosewater, flowers and incense hung heavy in the air, mingling with the smell of garlic and onions.

This was a new world to Catherine. Smiling, bemused, with Safa trailing close behind, she made her way from stall to stall. She stopped to finger the fine material of the caftans, to slip golden bracelets on her arms and rings on her fingers. As she lingered over soft, green velvet slippers, she thought of the sensible brown shoes she almost always wore, and before she realized what she was doing, she asked "*Bekam*, how much?" of the robed man behind the counter.

He told her the price. Safa stepped forward, one hand clutching her breast as though in pain. She shook a fat finger at the man and said something Catherine didn't understand. The man whined a reply. Safa snapped back at him and held up ten fingers. With a sigh the man put the velvet slippers in a bag. Catherine paid him, and a triumphant Safa took the package.

Glad now that Abdel had insisted on the servant accompanying her, Catherine returned to the shop where she had seen the caftans. The shopkeeper, excited because Catherine had returned, quickly took a dozen or more of the garments and spread them on the counter. They were all beautiful, soft to the touch, bright and shimmering in rainbows of exotic colors that a week ago Catherine wouldn't have dreamed of wearing.

She eagerly touched the delicate fabrics and at last selected a silk chiffon in variegated shades of green and gold. The robed man pointed to a screen, and Catherine went behind it. She undressed, then slipped the caftan over her head and looked at herself in the mirror hung on the back of the screen. The silken material lay in a graceful flow around her body. It dipped low in front, just to the rise of her breasts, more revealing than anything she'd ever worn. But oh, the silk was so soft, the colors so vivid. She hesitated for only a fraction of a second before she decided to take it.

Handing it over the top of the screen Catherine said, "Safa, will you be kind enough to ask the gentleman how much this is?" and smiled as the Egyptian woman began to bargain.

At the shop next door Catherine bought gold loop earrings and a gold, green-eyed snake bracelet for her upper arm. She was about to leave the shop when the seller picked up several strands of beads and held them out to her. They were different than anything she'd ever seen, not made of glass or imitation jewels, nor of gold or silver, but of what looked to Catherine like small stones or pods of some unknown plant. She shook her head and with a smile tried to step around the man. But before she could, the seller held a strand to her nose. Catherine sniffed, then took the beads from him and, closing her eyes, breathed in the scent of sandalwood.

He put three strands around her neck and said something to Safa, who turned to her and said, "These are a gift, Miss Adair. Most unusual."

Catherine thanked the man, and with the aroma of sandalwood wafting about her, returned with Safa to the car and went back to the villa.

"Dr. Pallister and Professor Garson have gone to look over the excavation site," her host told her when she arrived. He insisted that Catherine sit down to enjoy a cool drink and a light lunch, and when she'd finished, he suggested that she rest in her room until the party.

"Safa will come later to help you dress," Abdel said, and when Catherine protested that she really didn't need anyone to help her, he politely but firmly replied, "But it is our custom, and you are my guest."

Her rooms were hot. She spread her new purchases out on the chaise near the French doors, then went out to stand on the balcony. The sun was high, and the oppressive heat shimmered in the air. She could feel beads of sweat break out on her forehead and upper lip. Closing her eyes, she lifted her face to the sun and stood, still as a statue, until she was light-headed and dizzy. Then she went back into the room, undressed and, wearing only the sandalwood beads, lay down on the bed and gazed at the mirrors overhead. Her eyes felt heavy, and soon, like the mirrors in a fun house, the ones above her head seemed to slide together, uneven and distorted so that her face became not her face but a kaleidoscope of faces that slid out of focus, reformed and slid away again.

Away...

A lark sang in the bower of trees that shaded them, a song so hauntingly sweet that tears came unbidden to her eyes. He caught the silver tears with his tongue and gave them back to her, salty against her lips. His arms, as strong as temple stone, tightened around her.

"Do not weep, sweet love," he murmured. "We are here to celebrate our love." He kissed her eyelids closed

and began to trail kisses as soft as the feathers of the bird who sang above them over her face. Then gently he caressed her breasts, tracing the roundness and the tender buds with his fingertips until she moaned with pleasure.

When she whispered his name, he caught the strands of sandalwood beads between his teeth and rubbed them slowly across the rise of her breasts to perfume her with their fragrance. Finally he raised himself over her. "Most lovely of women," he whispered. "My queen, my love." He kissed her lips and eased his body over hers. "Now," he whispered. "Now my heart..."

"Miss Adair? Miss Adair, please?"

Slowly, reluctantly, Catherine opened her eyes. She lay for a moment uncertain where she was as fragments of the dream drifted in the fading light. Voices, like the half-remembered words of a song, hung in gossamer threads in the room, an echo of a whisper, "Now, my heart." Then the dream and the memory of a beloved face slowly faded into the gathering shadows of the room, and Catherine looked up to see herself in the mirrors above the bed, naked except for the sandalwood beads.

There was a knock at the door, and finally, as though from a distance, Catherine heard Safa call her name.

Catherine sat up and pulled a robe on as she hurried to the door. When she opened it, Safa smiled and in careful English said, "I am come to help you."

Still in a fog of sleep, Catherine murmured, "That's kind of you, but really I don't need any help."

But Safa was already in the room. Before Catherine could stop her, she hurried to the bathroom and began to run water in the large sunken tub. By the time Catherine entered the bathroom, the tub was filled with scented, bubbling foam, and Safa was waiting with her arms outstretched to take Catherine's robe.

Catherine shook her head and began to step aside, but Safa took the robe from her shoulders and clasping Catherine's hand helped her down into the tub.

With a sigh Catherine lowered herself into the scented water. She leaned back and closed her eyes in contented luxury as the hot water covered her. But when she felt a soapy sponge on the back of her neck she said, "No, I'll bathe myself."

Safa placed her hands on her full hips and looked uncertain. "It is my job to assist you."

"You can put out the clothes I'll wear to the party tonight. There's a gray dress in the closet. I'll wear that with gray shoes."

"Gray?" Safa shook her head. "I do not understand."

Catherine picked up a fluted jar of crystal bath salts. "This color," she said.

Safa frowned. "A gown that color?" She shook her head and, muttering to herself, left the room.

When the door closed, Catherine leaned back, letting the heat of the water seep into her skin, drifting in the hazily remembered dream of two lovers in a quiet garden with only the song of a lark to break the stillness of the evening.

At last Catherine stepped out of the tub. She wrapped herself in a large towel and went into the other room to dress. Safa hurried to her and, motioning Catherine to a chair in front of the dressing table, said, "I do your hair, yes?"

"No, thank you," Catherine said, shaking her head. But Safa, humming softly to herself, paid no attention as she picked up Catherine's hairbrush. She brushed Catherine's dark brown hair and with a few turns of her wrist coaxed enough curl into the ends so that dark wings curved softly, close to Catherine's face. Then Safa took a comb and teased the straight bangs into wisps of softness.

"Where is the paint for your face?" she asked when the hair was finished.

"I don't paint my face," Catherine said.

"But your eyes are beautiful, Miss Adair. Surely you do something with them."

Catherine shook her head. "I'm a plain woman. I prefer to go without makeup."

"Just a bit of kohl, yes?"

Quickly then, before Catherine could object, Safa pulled a small jar out of the pocket of her robe. "Just let us see," she coaxed. "If you do not like it, I will wipe it off. Only a touch. Close your eyes. Yes, that's it."

When Catherine opened her eyes, she saw that the lids were darkened and smoothed at the corner to make her eyes look bigger, longer and strangely exotic. She glanced around for a tissue to wipe it off, but instead found herself saying, "Thank you, Safa."

Catherine rose and went to the closet. Opening the door, she asked, "Where is my gray dress?"

"There was a spot on the skirt, Miss Adair," Safa answered with a look of total innocence. "I gave it to one of the servants to clean. You will have it tomorrow."

"But I have to wear it tonight."

Safa shook her head. "The caftan you bought today will be perfect for the party. Here, I have put it out for you."

Catherine hesitated. The only other garment she had, other than jeans and a jumpsuit, was a casual denim suit, hardly suitable for a dinner party. She had no choice; she had to wear the caftan. "All right," she said to Safa. "The caftan will have to do."

With a smile of satisfaction Safa slipped it over Catherine's head, then watched while Catherine fastened on the gold earrings and gold snake bracelet.

Just before she left the room, Catherine remembered the sandalwood beads and put them on.

The silk chiffon caressed her skin and drifted about her ankles as she descended the stairs. The velvet slippers made no sound, and yet several people turned to watch her. But it was Fletcher Garson who came forward to take her hand when she reached the last step.

"My word," he said with a pleased smile, "you look absolutely lovely."

"Thank you." Catherine felt her cheeks warm with color. "I went shopping today."

"You must do that more often. The gown quite becomes you. Would you like a glass of champagne?"

"Yes, please."

Fletcher lifted two glasses from a passing waiter's tray. He handed one to Catherine, but before she could take a sip, Abdel Moustafa said, "Good evening, dear Professor Adair. Please come and let me introduce you to my guests."

Catherine raised her eyebrows to Fletcher and with a helpless shrug allowed Abdel to take her arm and lead her to his other guests. She smiled and nodded, shook hands and even managed to say, "*Massaa el kheir*, good evening," once or twice.

She was chatting with a French diplomat and his wife when she saw David watching her from across the room. He raised a martini glass in a mock salute, and Catherine paused while the conversation went on around her.

Stilled by the intensity of David's gaze, locked in the magnetism of his blue eyes, she rubbed the crystal champagne glass across her lips. Suddenly the room had become too warm, and the glass was cool against the heat of her skin. Slowly, without conscious thought, she lowered it down her throat, down to the full rise of her breasts.

And all the while David's gaze held her, until it seemed that time stood still, that they were the only two people in the room. Catherine was caught, mesmerized, scarcely daring to breathe when he raised the martini glass to his mouth. Deliberately he looked at the rise and fall of her breasts, then he lifted the olive to his lips and carefully, slowly, bit it.

Frozen, Catherine watched David move toward her, knowing that in another moment he would reach her.

Suddenly, like the shattering of a dream, a gong sounded and Abdel called everyone to dinner.

David took her arm, and Catherine flinched, for his touch, like a shock of electricity, was alive and hot. Without speaking he led her into the dining room. He held a chair for her, and when she sat down, he slid her chair forward, his hands lingering for a moment on her shoulders.

The buzz of conversation, in Egyptian and English with a smattering of French, flowed all around Catherine. She spoke to the French diplomat on her right and to the people sitting across from her, and she had little idea of what she was even talking about. She didn't speak to David, but she was breathlessly aware of him next to her. When their host stood to offer a toast, she raised her glass with the others, and when several of the guests near them touched glasses, David turned toward her.

Once again it seemed to Catherine that time stood still. She felt as though she could drown in the deep blue of David's eyes as their glasses touched.

When dinner was over Abdel led his guests outside to the terraced gardens. There, at the end of the wide patio, an orchestra played, and the guests began to dance. The French diplomat led Catherine out on the patio. They danced for only a few minutes before Fletcher cut in.

"It's quite a party," he said as he looked around him. "Having a good time?"

"Yes, Fletcher." Trying desperately to make conversation, she said, "It's a lovely night, isn't it?"

"A relief after the heat today. Seems unusually warm for February, and if it's any indication, we're in for a hot summer. You don't mind the heat?"

"I grew up in Arizona. Heat doesn't—" But before she could finish the sentence, someone cut in. Then someone else. And finally, finally she found herself in David's arms.

"You're different tonight," he said without preamble.

"It's the new gown. I went shopping in the bazaar today."

"No, it isn't the gown, it's you." He danced her away from the others to the far end of the patio under the shadow of the overhanging trees. Still holding her in his embrace, he said, "What kind of perfume are you wearing?"

"I'm not wearing perfume." Catherine lifted the beads. "It's sandalwood."

David lifted the strand from her fingers, drawing her closer as he did. He took a deep breath, and still holding her captive, said, "I've never particularly liked the aroma of sandalwood until now." He tightened his fingers on the beads, and he drew her even closer. "You *are* different tonight," he murmured.

Catherine felt his breath on her skin and knew she should pull away.

He lifted the beads to his mouth and rubbed them against his lips, whispering her name.

The beads slipped from David's fingers, and his mouth found hers in a kiss that shattered the calm of the night and made her tremble with longing. Above them in the tree Catherine heard the song of a lark, and suddenly feelings she hadn't even known existed turned her body to a liquid fire that threatened to envelop her in its flame.

Catherine swayed against David, helpless against the arms that bound her to him and the passion that fevered her body.

The lark song stilled. She stepped away from David and touched trembling fingers to her lips. Then with a smothered cry she turned and ran toward the house.

Chapter 6

Two years had passed since Catherine's last dig. It had been at Tikal, and the discoveries she and her crew had made there had been good ones. Now, sitting next to David in the Jeep that would take the four of them to the excavation site at Edfu, Catherine remembered the hardships she'd faced in the steaming Guatemalan jungle. One of the local boys on his way into Guatemala City for supplies had been stopped and arrested by the federal police. Her student assistant had almost died from a bout of dysentery, and she'd been struck by a bushmaster snake, whose bite, though treated immediately, had left her ill for a week.

Catherine looked ahead of her at the bleak ocher land and wondered what perils lay ahead. Then, eyes hidden by dark glasses, she looked down at David's hands on the steering wheel. They were strong hands, tanned dark by the sun, the fingers long and slender, the nails trimmed. He had the hands of an artist, she thought, of a man who could bring antiquities up from the earth, recognizing their beauty and priceless worth.

Again, as she had through most of the sleepless night, Catherine wondered what had possessed her last night, what hidden demon had made her behave the way she had. She'd flirted outrageously with David, and later, when he kissed her, her body had melted against his, and a trickle of flame had coursed through her body, softening her, making her long for things she'd never dared dream about. She had wanted David with an urgency so powerful it had almost overwhelmed her.

Catherine's face burned with shame as she looked out over the desert. How ludicrous, how silly she must have seemed to him, an older woman hungry for romance, openly lusting after a younger man. And a man as supposedly experienced as David Pallister as well!

"The place where we'll begin excavating isn't too far from the Temple of Horus," David said, breaking in on her thoughts. "We'll pass right by the temple, but we won't stop now. We can see it some afternoon when we've finished work."

He glanced at Catherine as he spoke, then away, his forehead creased into a frown. It hardly seemed creditable that the poised woman who sat beside him now, dressed in the khaki jumpsuit she'd worn the day he'd first seen her at the pyramid in Cairo, was the same woman he'd kissed last night.

She'd been having breakfast alone this morning when he went out onto the terrace. She'd looked up, her eyes bright and clear in the morning sun, and the hand that held her cup had trembled when she'd bidden him good-morning.

"Good morning." He'd poured himself a cup of coffee while he searched for words to put her at ease. When he sat down, he saw the flush on her cheeks, and a wave of tenderness flooded his body because she was shy, embarrassed by what had passed between them last night. He reached for her hand. "Did you sleep well?" he asked.

"Yes. No." She pulled her hand away. She took a deep breath and coolly said, "I'm afraid I behaved badly last night, David. What passed between us was a mistake, and I'm sorry." Her back was ramrod straight; her eyes were level. "I hope I haven't given you the wrong impression, because I want you to know that nothing like that will ever happen again."

David had leaned forward, angry and bewildered, but before he could answer, Fletcher and Abdel had appeared. Now, through the mirage of heat and dust from the desert road, David's anger faded, and it seemed to him that he could still see Catherine as she'd looked at him across the room last night. The Egyptian gown had shimmered under the reflection of the chandelier. The dark wings of her hair curved softly around her face, and her sherry-brown eyes, outlined by Egyptian kohl, had given her a look of smoldering sensuality. Mesmerized, he'd raised his glass as she touched her own glass to her lips. The breath had caught in his throat when, instead of drinking, she had rubbed the glass against her full bottom lip, then had slowly lowered it down the lovely line of her throat to the cleft between her breasts.

God help him, he'd felt desire surge in his loins like a hot brand of fire. He'd wanted to rush to her side, to sweep her away to some dark, quiet place where he could slip the cool green gown from her body. He'd wanted to kiss those lips that caressed the edge of crystal and lose himself in the rise of her breasts dampened by the champagne glass.

The Jeep jarred over a rock, and Fletcher said, "Take it easy, Dave. You almost lost Massaud and me that time."

"Sorry. My mind was on...the excavation." He looked at Catherine again and felt an edge of anger. Last night she'd looked like a seductress skilled in every art of love known to man since the beginning of time. But this afternoon she looked as prim and proper—and yes, dammit—as forbidding as a maiden aunt. What in the hell kind of woman was she?

David pushed the windswept hair back from his face and swore under his breath. The idea of spending the next six months with Catherine Adair dismayed him. He'd never before let anything or anyone interfere with a project. His romances—and despite what the press said, there hadn't been a lot of them—had always been conducted on his own time. He never mixed business with pleasure, and he didn't intend to now. But he had to admit that Catherine intrigued him.

When at last David turned off the narrow gravel road onto what was little more than a wide, rutted path leading to the excavation site, he said, "Hang on. We've got nearly twenty minutes of this."

The dun-colored land was barren, with only an occasional patch of palm trees swaying in the morning breeze. They passed a robed man riding a mule, and it seemed to Catherine as though time had turned back a thousand or more years. Her gaze drifted out over the desert, and she watched the landscape go by, grateful for not having to look at David.

At last he slowed the Jeep and pointed to a small, but beautifully constructed temple. "That's King Amonset's tomb," he said. "We'll see it later."

"I visited the temple last year." Massaud paused. "It is not large, but as you say, Mr. David, it is exceedingly beautiful. It is a shameful thing that over the centuries it has been pillaged."

Fletcher took the unlit pipe out of his mouth. "Tomb robbing has been a profitable business for a couple of thousand years. The sand rats know all the tricks, how to dig and work their way along passages as cunningly as the most expert excavators."

"The thieves certainly knew how to break in there." David pointed to the temple. "You see the columns there on your right? When the tomb was discovered in 1933, that part of the structure had almost been destroyed. But when the archeologists entered the tomb they found everything apparently undisturbed; the bronze bowls, glass bottles, ivory-inlaid chests and, of course, the sarcophagus. At first it seemed as though everything were intact. Then they discovered a hole in the wall just beyond the head of the sarcophagus and two or three fallen beads. So they knew a string of beads had been snatched away and that whatever jewels there'd been had been stolen as well. The thefts had been committed by men who knew exactly what and where the booty was, probably not too long after Amonset's death."

"There's a guard on the tomb now," Fletcher said. He looked at David. "I imagine we'll post guards on the excavation site, won't we?"

David nodded. He put the Jeep in gear, and when they reached a rise of land less than a quarter mile from the tomb, he pointed to the right. "There it is," he said. "You can see it from here."

Near a crumbling stone wall, terraced against the sand dunes, was the place where they would begin their excavations. Scaffolding had been built, and as they drew closer, Catherine could see parts of what had once been some sort of structure. Several hundred yards from the excavation site was a row of tents.

"This part of the dig was started last fall," David said. "A lot of it has already been uncovered." He looked at Catherine with what could only be described as a triumphant I-told-you-so expression on his face. "There's a tomb under there, and I'll bet my reputation it's Alifa's."

He was so damned sure of himself, so confident that he was right that Catherine had to bite her tongue. Just for a fraction of a second she wondered if she'd been wrong all along. But none of that showed on her face when she spoke. "Then the sooner we get started, the better."

At the sound of the Jeep four men emerged from near the dig. Three of them wore robes as somber as the landscape. The fourth, younger than the others, wore faded jeans and a sweat-stained undershirt.

"*Ahlan wa sahlan,*" the oldest of them said in greeting. He was tall and thin. His skin was the color of old parchment, and when he spoke, Catherine saw that three of his front teeth were missing.

"*Sabah el kheir,*" Massaud said as he jumped down from the Jeep. "Good morning, Nawab. You have already met Professor Garson and Professor Pallister." He took Catherine's hand to help her down. "This is Dr. Catherine Adair. Catherine this is Nawab Hassan. The young man next to him is his son, Azan. The short fellow is Sahibzada, and the disreputable-looking one in jeans is Gamal."

"*Saeeda*, hello," Catherine said.

Three of the men nodded politely, but Gamal merely looked at her, disconcerting her with the appraising expression in his dark eyes.

While Nawab Hassan spoke to David and Massaud, Fletcher picked up Catherine's canvas bag. "Come on," he said. "Let's get you settled." He indicated one of the tents as they approached. "This one's yours. Not very comfortable, I'm afraid, but then I suppose you're used to this."

"I've been on enough digs to expect it." Catherine lifted the flap and went in. There was a cot with a thin mattress—an improvement over her last site—a table, a stool and a small chest of drawers.

"The mess tent's at one end, the facilities at the other. David has the tent next to yours; Massaud and I are next to him." Fletcher placed her bag on the chest. "Like to rest, or would you prefer to have a look around?"

"I'd like to look around." Catherine hesitated. "Fletcher, why did David decide to dig here?"

"It seemed the logical place. The site had obviously been worked on, then abandoned years ago. It's just about the distance from King Amonset II's tomb that most of the tombs of other wives of pharaohs have been. As a matter of fact Amonset's first wife is buried close by." Fletcher lifted one shaggy brow. "You're still not convinced we'll find Alifa here, are you?"

"No, I'm not, Fletcher. But that won't prevent me from doing my share of the work."

"I'm sure it won't." He raised the tent flap. "Well come along, I'll show you where we'll start tomorrow." He took her hand as they scrambled down the rocky slope. "Watch your step," he cautioned. "The men haven't finished shoring up the sides and there're apt to be slides."

The shallow entrance beckoned, a dark hole in the earth that led downward. The work here had progressed Catherine saw as she looked around her, but at this stage of an excavation it was necessary to go slowly. Stones and boulders had to be moved. Dirt had to be cleared and carried away, and every basket of it had to be carefully sifted for potsherds. Four stone steps had already been uncovered, and rubble had been removed to clear a path for further excavation.

"Nawab and the others have been chipping away at the stone," Fletcher told Catherine. "A few days ago they discovered what might be part of a passageway. Like to have a look?"

"Yes, please."

"Watch your head." He took a flashlight out of his jacket pocket and beamed the light on the wall of rocks in front of them. "We'll rig up the generator so we'll have more light to work by and start in here tomorrow. The trucks with some of the heavier equipment should've been here by now. We need another winch, and we'll have to build more scaffolding." Fletcher turned to look at her. "It's a tomb all right. There's no mistaking it."

Fletcher was right, there wasn't any mistaking it. *Someone* had been buried here. But Catherine knew—although she didn't know how she knew—that it wasn't Alifa. The young queen couldn't be here, not in this arid desert so far away from the blue waters of the Nile, away from the place where she was born.

Fletcher touched her arm. "Are you all right?" he asked. "Not having trouble, are you?"

Catherine shook her head and smiled at him. "No, Fletcher, I'm fine."

That night at dinner she asked Massaud if he'd started on the translation of the papers he'd told her about.

He nodded. "Yes, I have already begun. They are most interesting. I'll give you the first pages after dinner if you like." He turned to the others. "The handmaiden who sang to the scribe must have been a favorite of the queen, since she accompanied her from Philae when Alifa was chosen to be King Amonset's wife. The stories tell that the young queen dreamed of one day returning to Philae. It is most interesting."

"That's what it is—a story," David said with a frown. "I don't doubt that the servant girl was devoted to the queen, Massaud, or that the two women loved their home. But Alifa's life was here with her husband. This was where she belonged, this was where she stayed." He looked at Catherine across the table. "Anything else is pure conjecture. Alifa is buried here, and I intend to prove it." He shoved the bench away from the table. "I'm going to have a look around before dark," he said angrily, and strode out of the tent.

"I did not mean to upset him," Massaud said.

"It's not you he's upset with." Catherine looked at David's retreating back, then she, too, pushed away from the table. With a murmured "Excuse me," she hurried after David. If they were going to work together for the next six months, there couldn't be this kind of dissension between them.

David had walked beyond the site to the crumbled wall where he stood staring out over the desert. He turned when he saw Catherine, thumbs hooked into the pockets of his jeans, his face set and angry. "If you've come to argue about Alifa, I'm not in the mood," he snapped.

"I haven't come to argue, I've come to say I'm sorry. I know I get carried away when we start to talk about her, but she's been a big part of my life ever since I can remember."

"What do you mean, she's been a part of your life?"

"My father started telling me about Alifa when I was a little girl, David." The hint of a smile softened Catherine's mouth. "He made up all kinds of stories about her, and after a while she became as real to me as the friends I played with. Maybe she's the reason I became an archeologist." Catherine looked at David and, taking a deep breath, she said, "This is your dig. I don't agree with you that we'll find Alifa here, but I promise you that I'll work harder for you than I've ever worked before. There's a part of me that almost hopes we *do* find her here, because I want so desperately to know where she is." Catherine shook her head. "But I don't think we will, David. I honestly believe she went back to Philae."

The frown that had formed as David listened to Catherine faded. "I don't understand this conviction of yours, this absolute certainty you have that she's buried in Philae. Childhood dreams are one thing, Catherine, but we're archeologists, scientists who base our actions on the facts and the research available to us. We all have instincts, gut feelings, and God knows they've played a big part on a lot of my digs." His voice softened as he looked at her. "I can understand the way you feel. You were an impressionable child, and you romanticized Alifa until she became real to you. You *wanted* her to go back to Philae, so you convinced yourself that she did."

David paused while he tried to form the words to make her understand. "It isn't that I don't respect your ability, Catherine. I know your reputation. I know how competent, how thorough you are in your research, and I know the success you've had on other digs. I don't want to be unreasonable, but I'm convinced we'll find Alifa's sarcophagus here. If we don't . . ." He hesitated. "If we don't, maybe we'll check out your theory about Philae."

The breath caught in Catherine's throat, and she felt the sting of tears behind her eyes. It was a moment before she could speak. "Thank you, David."

He looked out toward the excavation site, shadowed now in the fading light. There was a hush over the desert, a calm in the air as though the land, waiting for night to fall, had stilled. David looked at the woman standing beside him, at the fine clean lines of her face and the dark hair that curved against her cheek. He remembered how she'd felt in his arms last night.

Before David could stop himself, he put his hands on Catherine's shoulders and turned her toward him. Her dark eyes went wide with surprise, and he felt her body tense. "We're going to be together for the next six months," he said. "It would be nice if we..." He smiled softly. "If we could get along."

"Please let me go, David," Catherine said, trying to free herself from his grasp.

"Dammit, woman, I don't understand you. Last night your come-hither signal rang out loud and clear. I kissed you and you responded, and something very special passed between us. But today you've acted as though we're strangers."

Her dark eyes filled with confusion, Catherine searched for the words to explain to David what had happened last night. But how could she explain what she didn't understand herself?

Still a prisoner of the hands that held her, Catherine said, "David, I don't know what happened to me last night. I'm usually not like that." Her lips quivered as she struggled for the words. "I've dreamed all my life about coming to Egypt. Now the dream has become a reality, and I'm feeling things I've never felt before, things I don't understand." She raised her eyes to his. "It's as though I'm dreaming. As though I—"

"Is this a dream, Catherine?" Before she could pull away, David covered her mouth with his. She froze, her lips closed tight against his, her body stiff and unyielding. When he let her go, his eyes burned with anger. "Last night you were warm and passionate, and you wanted me just as much as I wanted you. Why don't you just admit that, Catherine?" he demanded hoarsely.

"No!" Catherine stepped away from him. "That's not true, David. I didn't. I..." Suddenly a shiver ran through her. "I'm sorry," she whispered.

"Don't be such a tease, Catherine," he said scathingly. "I wish to hell I hadn't asked you to be on the team. But I did, and there isn't anything I can do about it now. But I won't play your game again. The next time you look at me the way you did last night, the next time your body turns soft against mine, I won't let you go."

David turned and walked away from her, back over the dunes, turned golden in the last rays of the sun. He didn't see the tears that streaked her cheeks or the look of confusion in her dark eyes.

By the light of a kerosene lamp Catherine began to read the papers that Massaud had handed her when she'd returned to the camp. "This is as much as I have," he said when he gave them to her. "Transcribing them into English is a slow process. But it is a fascinating story, one I think you will enjoy."

And Massaud was right.

> The daughter of Yahwa el Salir was a beautiful child, and it was plain to all who saw her that she would grow to be a lovely woman. Her nature was sweet, her voice as soft as a dove's. She was a dutiful and obedient girl, but one given to daydreaming. She wrote poetry, and she sang in a lyrical voice,

so beautiful that even the birds stilled their song to listen.

She loved Philae, and for the young Alifa there was no other place on earth half so beautiful.

This was as far as Massaud had gone with the translation.

Catherine closed her eyes, picturing the child that Alifa had been, seeming to hear in the quiet of the desert night a little girl's voice raised in song.

She read the words again and again. At last she turned out the kerosene lamp and undressed. She lay down on the cot and pulled the sheet up to warm herself against the night chill of the desert. She thought about Alifa, who'd lived on an island surrounded by the blue waters of the Nile and smiled at the thought of a voice so beautiful that even the birds had stopped their singing to listen.

Then her thoughts turned to David, and her smile faded. What had happened between them was her fault. How could she explain to him what she didn't understand herself? She'd always been in control of her emotions—but when David kissed her.... Catherine's eyes drifted closed on the thought of his name.

Chapter 7

By the first week of April the midday temperature at the excavation site rose to more than one hundred degrees. A dozen more men had been hired, and with the aid of a winch, rocks had been levered away from the entrance. A wooden platform had been rigged, and an arrangement of pulleys constructed.

Work started at daybreak every morning after a piece of the traditional flat bread and coffee prepared by Sahibzada. Eyes red rimmed, dark bags beneath them that seemed almost to rest on his sallow cheeks, Sahibzada would mumble, "*Sabah en-nur,*" then go to join Nawab and the other men, who'd already begun their day's work. They were good men, all but Gamal, who seemed out of place among them. He was resentful of orders, smoked endless cigarettes and looked at Catherine with knowing, insolent eyes.

"I don't like that fellow," Fletcher told David one morning when they stopped to rest. "Have you seen the way he watches Catherine?"

"She can take care of herself," David snapped.

Fletcher's eyebrows raised. "Nevertheless, Dave, I think we'd better keep an eye on him. He hangs around Catherine as though he's waiting for an opportunity to catch her alone. I don't like it."

David shrugged and turned away as though unconcerned, but that afternoon when they resumed work, he watched Gamal. Wearing tight jeans, his bare, brown chest gleaming with sweat, the young Egyptian slouched close to Catherine. If she noticed or was bothered by his presence, she gave no indication of it. Only once, when his hand touched hers as she reached for a potsherd, did she draw away. She looked angry and said something that David couldn't hear.

It was after dinner that night when the trouble started. David, Fletcher and Nawab were sitting outside the tents cleaning a few pieces of broken pottery they'd found that day when Massaud approached.

"Those are good pieces," Massaud said when he squatted down beside the other three men.

Fletcher nodded. "We're piecing together centuries of history here, Massaud. Every time we dig something up from the past we give more meaning to the present."

"That is true, Professor. In Egypt the past and the present are as one. That is why we Egyptians are so excited when we see people such as yourselves with the same love we have of ancient times. It pleased me to see Miss Catherine as interested as I am in the transcript I have been working on. I have translated additional pages. When she returns, will you give them to her?"

"Returns from where?" David asked.

"From out beyond the rise of the dunes. She walked there a little while ago."

Fletcher looked at David across the pot he was polishing. To Nawab he said, "Where's Gamal?"

"Who knows with that one."

A frown marred Fletcher's forehead. He took his pipe out of his mouth. "I think I'll have a look," he said.

"No, I'll do it." David got quickly to his feet and started walking in the direction of the dunes. He'd meant it when he'd said Catherine could take care of herself. She probably could. Nevertheless... The thought hung in the air as David hurried up the dune. Just as he neared the top, he heard Catherine scream.

He ran the last ten yards to the top of the dune.

Catherine was on her knees in the sand, struggling with Gamal, who had imprisoned both of her wrists with one hand. He grasped the top of her khaki shirt with his other and ripped it open. She screamed again, and the cry tore through David, blinding him to all sense of reality as he sprinted forward. He lunged at Gamal, hit him in the back with his shoulder, then spun the Egyptian around. One fist connected with Gamal's chin, bone against bone. Gamal cried out, pain and surprise distorting his face as he skidded down in the sand. He shook his head to clear it, then bounded up, screaming in rage as he charged. David blocked the blow with his forearm, and the edge of his hand shot out to catch Gamal across his neck. Gamal dropped to the sand, gagging for breath.

David leaned over him, feet apart, fists clenched. When Gamal groaned, David yanked him to his feet. "Get out of here," he growled. "Be gone by the time I get back to camp, or I'll turn you over to the police." He shoved Gamal down the slope of the sand dunes. "Never show your face around here again," he threatened.

David turned back to Catherine. She stood silent, staring at him, her face pale under the tan. Before she could speak, David strode toward her. Still shaking with anger, he said, "Are you all right? Did he hurt you?"

"No." She breathed shakily. "No, he didn't hurt me."

David grasped her arms. "That was a damn fool thing you did, coming up here alone. Haven't you seen how he's been looking at you? What in the hell's the matter with you? Haven't you—"

"Don't," Catherine whispered. She lifted her hands, palms open. "Please, don't."

David looked at her. He took a deep, slow breath and released her. She pulled the front of her torn shirt together. "I came up to see the sunset from here," she said. "I didn't think..." She looked at his hands, and her dark eyes widened. "You're bleeding," she said. "Oh, David, you've hurt your hands." She soothed the skinned knuckles with her thumbs, then took the white scarf she had knotted around her throat, tore it in half and carefully wrapped his bleeding fingers.

The gesture was nothing and it was everything. A feeling unlike anything he'd ever experienced shook David. This was another side of Catherine, a side of her he hadn't even suspected existed. He pulled one hand away and touched the side of her face.

She looked at him and in the last rays of sunset her sherry-brown eyes were touched with gold. Her face softened, her lips trembled.

"Catherine, I—"

"Yo!" Fletcher called as he came up over the rise of the dune. "Are you two all right? Gamal came back to camp all bloodied up. Grabbed his things and took off." He saw Catherine's torn shirt, David's bandaged hands. "What the hell happened up here?"

David stepped away from Catherine. "He had Catherine down on the sand," he said.

"I'll be damned!" Fletcher swore under his breath. He looked at Catherine. "Are you all right?"

"Yes, I'm all right, but David's hurt his hands."

"Good." Fletcher grinned. "Sorry you hurt them, Dave, but it was for a damn good cause." He put his arms around Catherine's shoulders. "Come on," he said, "let's get back to camp."

Catherine looked at David for a moment, then the three of them went down the dune to the tents.

It was easier between Catherine and David after that. They didn't speak about what had happened there on the dune, but they were friendlier, more at ease with each other.

Each day David became more aware of Catherine, and it seemed to him that she was changing—there was a softness to her face that hadn't been there before, and her voice had taken on an almost lyrical quality. She intrigued him as no other woman ever had.

He pushed ahead with the dig, using ultrasonics as they probed deeper into the earth. The four of them, along with the Egyptians, worked from sunup to sunset with scarcely a break in spite of the heat. Once or twice there were slight earth tremors. "It is nothing," Nawab said each time. "Only the gods grumbling a little."

In the evening after they had eaten, they lingered over coffee, talking of the day's progress.

"We're close," David said one night. "I can feel it. Another two weeks should do it if we're lucky." He looked at Catherine. "I know you had your heart set on finding Alifa on Philae. I hope you're not going to be disappointed when we discover her here."

"The important thing is that we find her. It will be wonderful if you do, David, for you, for your career."

"For all of our careers. We're a team, remember." His gaze met hers across the table. "When we find her, maybe we'll take a break before we begin the final excavation and the cataloging. We could go back to Cairo for a few days or take a cruise on the Nile. You'd like that, wouldn't you?" His gaze swept Fletcher and Massaud, including them, but it was to Catherine he spoke.

They needed a break, David thought that night when he went into his own tent. The hard work and the heat was getting to all of them. He'd seen the patches of fatigue under Catherine's eyes, and although she never complained, it was plain to see that the heat was bothering her.

He worried about Fletcher, too. At his age, this could easily be Fletch's last time on the working end of a dig. Only two days ago, suspecting that he might be having a flare-up of malaria, David had asked if he were feeling all right.

Fletcher had assured him he was perfectly fine. But his color was bad, and David was worried about him, so worried that he finally insisted his friend take a day off.

"We need supplies," he told the others at breakfast one morning. "Fletcher, I want you and Massaud to take the truck into Edfu and get what we need. Spend the night with Abdel, have a swim in the pool, cool off and relax. It'll do you both good."

"There's too much to be done here," Fletcher objected. "I'm not going to leave and let you and Catherine do all the work."

"We'll take the day off, too. I've been promising Catherine I'd show her King Amonset's tomb. We'll do it tomorrow." David looked at her. "All right with you,

Catherine? Of course, if you'd rather go into Edfu, that's all right, too."

She shook her head. "No," she said with a smile, "I've been wanting to see the tomb."

"Then it's settled." David stood up. "Fletch and Massaud will go to Edfu; Catherine and I will head for the tomb." When the older man started to object, David said, "No arguments, Fletch. You're going to Edfu." He turned to Massaud. "You be sure he takes it easy."

"I will, David."

David looked at Catherine. They hadn't been alone since that evening at sunset after his fight with Gamal. He remembered the way she'd looked when she held his hands in hers; he didn't think he could wait for morning to come.

Fletcher and Massaud left at daybreak, with Massaud at the wheel of the truck. An hour later David and Catherine set out in the Jeep for King Amonset's tomb.

"I asked Sahibzada to pack us a lunch," David said. "I didn't know how long we'd want to look around, so I thought we'd better be prepared." He glanced at her. She looked as fresh and cool as the morning with her dark hair pulled back off her face with a wide, blue band. She wore a white shirt and khaki shorts that showed off her tanned, shapely legs.

"Not too much is known about the temple," he said to keep his mind off her figure. "At the end of the pre-dynastic period, about thirty-one hundred B.C., Egypt was divided into two kingdoms, Upper and Lower Egypt. Upper Egypt extended from El Faiyûm in the north to Aswan in the south, while Lower Egypt consisted of Memphis and the delta. When Amonset came to power after the death of his father, Amonset I, he was almost forty years old. He began construction of his temple the first year of his reign, and he took a wife, Batsira of Memphis, to unite Upper and Lower Egypt."

The Jeep rattled over the rutted road as David continued. "She died without giving Amonset children when he was fifty-two."

"So he looked around for another wife," Catherine said, bracing herself against the jar of the Jeep. "And he found Alifa."

"He'd heard stories of her beauty from men who'd been to Philae, so he sent an emissary there to ask Alifa's father for her hand in marriage."

"Of course she had no say in the matter."

"None." David looked at her. "That's the way it was in those days, Catherine. A woman did whatever she was told to do." The Jeep slowed. "There it is," he told her, and she turned to see the temple, which had been built of sandstone more than two thousand years ago.

This was where Alifa had watched them entomb her husband, Catherine thought as she stepped out of the Jeep and looked up at the temple. She stood where they were standing, with the lords and nobles surrounding her, Queen of Egypt now that the king was dead. His subjects were weeping, calling out to him, "Come, Amonset, return to us, oh mighty sovereign, gone now to live among the gods. Return, return..."

"Catherine?" David looked at her with a puzzled smile. "What is it? You look as though you're a million miles away."

Not a million miles, she thought to herself—just two thousand years.

He left the lunch in the Jeep and slung one of the canteens over his shoulder. "Let's get started," he said. "We can eat later." He looked around for the guard who was supposed to be on duty. "*Saeeda*, hello?" he called out. "Is anyone here?" He listened for a moment, then with a shrug said, "Come on."

There were four columns on either side of the courtyard. Inside there was a gateway, which in the time of Amonset II had been closed by a cedar door inlaid with bronze and gold. As they entered, Catherine saw an elaborate series of reliefs, which showed the king with the four standards of Upper Egypt, the jackal, the ibis, the hawk and the totem. Beside the king was falcon-headed Horus, holding a scepter in his hand and Maat, the goddess of truth.

It was cooler here inside the walls as David and Catherine entered the antechamber that led down to the tomb. "This isn't like the dig we've been working on," he said. "This goes back some distance under the ground." He hesitated. "If you'd rather not attempt it, I'll understand."

Dark eyes snapping with anger, Catherine said, "What happened to me in the pyramid in Cairo had never happened before, and as I told you, it won't happen again." She started toward the stone steps that had been cut out of rock.

David looked at her retreating back. He wasn't surprised by Catherine's anger, because in the last few weeks he'd come to know what a strong woman she was. But the strong had fears too, he thought as he followed her. What Catherine had felt in the pyramid had been very real. She'd denied that she had claustrophobia, but if she did have it, and she'd been able to handle it all these years as an archeologist, then she really was one hell of a woman.

He beamed his flashlight forward, on Catherine rather than on the crumbling walls, following the line from her shoulders to her waist with the webbed belt that held a flashlight and extra batteries. Then to her hips and around her trim bottom, down to the splendid legs. Wondering, because he couldn't help but wonder, what it would be like to have those magnificent legs wrapped around his body.

Catherine turned. Crossly she said, "We have to climb over some rocks here. Can you turn your flashlight this way so I can see?"

"Sure." David hurried to her, but instead of doing as she asked he said, "Better let me go first. It's hard to see in there." He squeezed past her, then flashed his light back so she could enter.

They were in a dark passageway. He wanted to ask again if she was all right but knew that he shouldn't. He looked for a railing and found one on his right. "Hang onto this," he told Catherine. "We're going down now. It's not too far, but it's hard going."

With every breath she drew, Catherine told herself she was all right. The smell of lost centuries choked her nostrils. The passageway narrowed, and the rock ceiling above them slanted down as drastically as it had in the pyramid.

"We're here." David reached back to grasp her hand and lead her into a small room. He beamed his light over the walls, then to the rocky floor. "That's where the sarcophagus was," he said. "Let's have a look at the walls."

Catherine followed the beam of their flashlights. The colors, because of the dryness of the climate, were still vivid, and it was possible to see life as it had been almost two thousand years ago. The paintings depicted servants bringing offerings for the dead king to take to the next world. A deity wearing the priestly leopard mantle was followed by a line of gods carrying scepter and ankh. A gold falcon with obsidian eyes, along with other animals and birds, waited at one side of the king as he stood, both arms outstretched to two women. One wore a black wig that fell past her shoulders, a gown of gold, a jeweled collar. The other, the younger woman, was dressed more simply in white cotton. She was unadorned with jewels, except for a gold snake bracelet wound around her upper arm.

"Batsira and Alifa," David said. "Batsira's tomb isn't too far from here; that's why I'm so sure we'll find Alifa's close by."

Catherine stared up at the three figures, then concentrated on Alifa. She had a high, noble forehead and brows that curved to frame almond-shaped eyes. Her nose was slim and straight, and there was a delicate indentation that led to the sweetly curved lips. Her neck was slender, her breasts high. Catherine didn't know how true to the young queen the painted figure was, but presented here she was quite beautiful.

David took Catherine's arm, then paused as a slight tremor shook the earth beneath his feet.

Startled, Catherine looked at him. "What—"

The earth moved, more violently this time. There was a roar from the very bowels of the earth and a jolt so strong that they staggered and almost fell.

Catherine cried out as David clasped her to him. "My God!" she cried.

"Earthquake!" The floor rocked like a roller coaster beneath their feet; the terrible roar grew louder.

"David!" She buried her face against his chest, and there was a part of her, even in her terror, that was grateful that if this was the end, that she was here with David.

The earth steadied. But still David held her. "It's all right," he said at last. "It's over, Catherine, but we'd better get out of here." He rested his hand against her hair. "Are you all right?"

Catherine summoned a smile. "I've never experienced anything like that before. I'll be a lot happier when we're back outside."

"So will I." David let her go, but still holding her hand, he moved ahead of her toward the entrance. "We can come back another day," he said, "but now we'd better—" He stopped, and she heard the harsh intake of his breath.

"What is it?" Catherine moved up beside him. "Why did you stop?" She followed the beam of his flashlight and froze.

The entranceway was blocked by fallen boulders. They were trapped.

Chapter 8

Catherine stared unbelievingly at the blocked entranceway. "We can't get out!" she said. "Oh God, David, what are we going to do?"

"Maybe it's not as bad as it looks." David hurried to the entrance and beamed the light around the fallen rocks.

"Hold this." He handed his flashlight to Catherine. "Let me see what I can do. It's not completely blocked, you can see the light coming in. If I can move some of the rocks blocking the exit, we'll be able to squeeze through."

For the next thirty minutes David exerted every bit of strength he had in his lean, hard body, but he only succeeded in dislodging a few rocks near the top of the opening. The others, the ones they would need to move if they hoped to get out, were too big to budge.

"I'm afraid we're going to have to wait for help to come," he said as he wiped the dust from his hands onto his jeans.

"Wait? We can't just wait." There was an edge of panic in Catherine's voice. "We've got to get out of here! There isn't any air. We'll suffocate. We'll—"

"Take it easy, Catherine. There's plenty of air coming in from the top of the entrance. When we don't return to camp, Nawab and the others will come looking for us. All we've got to do is sit it out and try to be patient."

"For how long? We've only just gotten here. Nawab won't begin to worry until late this afternoon or tonight when it's dark. We can't stay here all that time." Catherine shoved the flashlights into his hand and began digging frantically at the rocks.

David put his hands on her shoulders and pulled her away. She turned on him, her eyes wide with fear. "Let me go! If you won't get us out of here, I will. I can't stay in here. I've got to get out. I. . ." She stopped. Taking a deep breath, she visibly tried to pull herself together. "David, I'm sorry." She stepped away from him and grasped her arms as though forcing herself to be still.

"Nawab will come," David said. "So will Fletcher. He and Massaud will come back to camp tonight. Fletch'll know what to do."

"You told him to spend the night at Abdel's villa." Catherine dug her fingernails into her arms in an effort to control her rising panic. "He and Massaud won't be back until tomorrow."

"Even if they aren't, Catherine, Nawab will come looking for us." David put an arm around her shoulders. "Come on, let's sit down and take it easy for a while."

The wall was damp and cold against her back. "What if there's another tremor?" Her voice trembled as it climbed an octave. Catherine started to get up. "We can't just sit here and wait for somebody to rescue us. It might be too late. We might be—"

"We won't be." David pulled Catherine down beside him and turned her so that she was facing him. He saw the terror in her eyes, and because he knew he had to do something before she lost control, he said, "Grow up, Catherine! Having hysterics isn't going to do us a damn bit of good, and it sure as hell doesn't become you."

Her eyes widened. She stared at him for a long moment, then lifted her chin and turned away. She was more angry than frightened now.

For a long time neither of them spoke. Finally David said, "An earthquake can be pretty frightening. First one I was ever in terrified me."

After a minute or two Catherine asked, "Where were you?"

"In San Francisco. I'd gone there with my father." He switched his flashlight off, and she tightened her hand around the one she held, protecting it from him.

"I was seven," David said. "It was the last time I saw him."

Catherine looked up at him, her anger momentarily forgotten. "I'm sorry. He must have been very young when he died."

"He didn't die. He just went away." David leaned his back against the wall. He hadn't thought about his father in a long time, but he supposed it was the earthquake that had jarred his memory and made him think of the man who had once been the most important person in the world to him. He'd never talked about his father to anyone, but now all of the early memories came flooding back. He wanted to keep Catherine's mind off being trapped, and besides, he felt a sudden and overwhelming need to tell someone.

"He took me to San Francisco to tell me that he and my mother were getting a divorce. I remember I tried not to cry, and when I did, he said it was all right, that sometimes even men cried if something really hurt them." The hint of a smile crossed David's face. "That surprised me so much I stopped crying."

Catherine, looking at him, found herself wondering what kind of a little boy he had been and what it had been like at that age to be told that your parents weren't going to be together anymore. And it seemed to her that she could see him, with his face pinched to keep from crying.

"After a while we went down to Fisherman's Wharf and had dinner," David said. "My father told me that he was going to live in California and that I'd live with my mother in New York. I said that I wanted to live with him, but he told me I couldn't." David paused, remembering the look of anguish on his father's face when he'd told him that it wasn't possible.

The next day his father had put him on a plane to New York. He'd never seen him again.

Catherine moved closer. "What happened, David? Did he just drop out of sight?"

"In a way. There were never any letters, but every month a check arrived to pay for my schooling—conscience money my mother said. She told me that my father had a new wife and that he didn't care about us any more. I didn't believe her, not for a long time. I kept thinking that he would come back to us if I could prove to him how smart I was. I thought that if I made him proud I was his son, he'd come back for me.

"My mother and I moved around a lot, and it was difficult, always trying to get used to a new school. But I kept my grades up, because I still had this crazy idea that if I was the best in everything I did, my father would love me again.

"Mother remarried a man named Herb Gilford when I was thirteen. She changed her name and insisted that mine be changed, too. By that time I didn't care. My father didn't want me, so I didn't want his name, either."

David took a deep, shaking breath. "I was in my sophomore year at Princeton when he called me."

"Your father called you?" Catherine turned so that she could see David's face. "What did you do? What was it like to see him again?"

"I didn't see him." There was agony in David's voice. "I didn't want to."

"Oh, David." Catherine reached for his hand.

"The summer after I left Princeton, I won a grant to work on a dig in Sicily. I met a man, his name was Wade Blackford, and he'd known my father. They'd gone through college together, and they'd stayed friends." David hesitated, and when he spoke again, his voice was unsteady. "My dad had died just six months before I met Blackford. Blackford told me that my mother had kept Dad away from me. That's why we'd moved so often. That's why she'd changed my name. The checks that my father sent to the New York bank were forwarded on to wherever we were. There'd been letters, too, Blackford said, and presents that were always returned unopened."

David looked at Catherine. "My dad had tried for all those years to find me. He'd hired private detectives, he'd done everything. And when he found me, I wouldn't even talk to him."

"But you didn't know. David, you didn't know."

"But I *should* have talked to him, I should have listened to his side of the story."

For a long time neither of them spoke. Catherine held his hand and soothed his skinned knuckles with her thumb. She wanted to say something to ease the pain she knew he must be feeling. But the words didn't come, so she sat quietly, waiting.

When at last David spoke, he said, "I confronted my mother with what Blackford had told me after I got back to the States. She said—" his voice was ironic "—she said she'd done it for me, so that I wouldn't be torn between the two of them." His hand tightened on Catherine's. "I changed my name back to Pallister, and I went to see the woman my dad had been married to. She didn't want anything to do with me at first, but finally she talked to me. She told me about all the years in between, all of those years I'd lost."

"Did you have any brothers and sisters, I mean half brothers and sisters?"

"No, I was his only child. His son."

Catherine wanted to put her arms around David and draw him close, to do something, anything, to take away the hurt. But she only held his hand, and in a little while he said, "We'd better turn the other flashlight off, Catherine. There's an edge of light coming in from outside, and we'll need to save the batteries for tonight."

Catherine hesitated, then she turned it off. Darkness closed in around them. When her eyes became accustomed to the dark, she saw a small edge of light appear. But not enough light to dispel her fear. When it became too much to bear, she moved closer to David. She began to talk as he had. She told him about her mother who had been ill for so long and about her father. "I wanted to be the best for him, just as you wanted to be for yours." She looked up at David, trying to see his face in the half darkness. "Maybe they're the reason we succeeded at what we wanted to do, David."

"Maybe." He put his arms around her and drew her close. For a moment Catherine stiffened. Then, because she needed the warmth of another human being close to her, she let herself relax against him. David rested his chin against the softness of her hair, and they sat like that for a long time without speaking.

At last Catherine's eyes closed. The dimness of the tomb faded, and there was only David, the hard comfort of his chest and the arms that held her close.

She awoke to darkness and remembered terror. She cried out, and David said, "It's all right, Catherine. I'm here." His arms tightened around her.

"David?"

"Yes, Catherine?"

"It's so dark."

"Someone will come soon."

"I hate the darkness." She covered his hands with hers, holding tight to still her trembling. "Did you sleep?"

"A little." He rubbed his chin back and forth against her hair. "You make an interesting sound when you sleep, Professor Adair."

She half turned. "Do you mean I snore?"

"No, you purr."

"I purr?"

"Sensuously."

She moved away from him, not sure she liked the direction the conversation was going. She cleared her throat and said, "Would it be all right if we had a drink of water?"

"Sure." He switched on his flashlight and reached for the canteen, sorry now that he'd left the lunch Sahibzada had packed for them in the Jeep.

Catherine took a few sips and handed the canteen back to him. "Can we keep the light on?"

"For a while."

She looked around the two-thousand-year-old tomb, and because she felt the terror she'd known earlier returning, she said, "Talk to me, David."

"I talked too much before. I shouldn't have said all that, about my father I mean. I shouldn't have—"

She put her fingers against his lips. "I'm glad you did."

He took her hand, holding it to his lips, and slowly kissed her fingers.

"What are you doing?" she said softly, trying to pull her hand away.

"I'm making the darkness go away," Catherine. David put his hands on either side of her face and kissed her.

David's lips were soft against hers. She tried to draw back, but he held her, his touch so gentle, his mouth so warmly persistent that she stilled her efforts. I'll stay like this for a moment, she told herself, only a moment. But then he put his arms around her and pulled her close. She closed her eyes, and the darkness faded until there was only David and the feel of his mouth on hers.

Without conscious thought Catherine's lips softened and parted. Very gently David took her lower lip between his teeth to soothe and caress before his tongue eased between her lips to seek and find her tongue. She stiffened again, then with a sigh she touched her tongue to his and heard the quick intake of his breath.

Finally he let her go, and with his lips only a fraction of an inch from hers he whispered her name. He kissed her again and tightened his arms around her, holding her so close she could feel the beating of his heart against her breasts. His lips were more demanding now, and with a soft moan of surrender, Catherine put her arm around David's neck, holding him as he held her, lost in the wonder of his kiss.

He cupped her breast, and when she tried to pull away, he said, "Just this, Catherine. Let me just hold you."

Incandescent sparks spread through her body, weakening and warming her, making her wish for things so long forgotten. With each gentle stroke of David's fingers the flame grew brighter, the longing more intense and she whispered against his lips.

With a low cry of need he crushed her closer. The kiss deepened, consuming them both. With frantic fingers he fought with the buttons of her shirt and pushed her bra aside to feel the warmth of her skin, to kiss the sweet roundness of her breasts. The spark became a fire, and Catherine was lost in the feel of David's lips upon her.

A shout cut like a blade through the darkness. "David, Catherine—are you in there?"

He raised his head from her breast, then quickly kissed her again, stood up and pulled her to her feet. Gripping her hand, he ran with her to the blocked entrance. "In here," he shouted. "We're in here."

"Are you both all right?" Fletcher called.

David tightened his hand on hers. "Yes, we're fine."

"We're going to try to push the rocks in toward you, David, so you'd better back away."

"Okay. Whenever you're ready." David looked at Catherine. "It won't be long now," he told her as they backed away. "We might even get back to camp in time for supper if we're..." He stopped, watching as she drew her blouse together. He saw the trembling of her lips, and a wave of tenderness flooded through him. He drew her back into his arms and gently kissed her. "I'm glad they've found us," he said, "but I wish Fletch had waited just a couple more hours."

Catherine rested her head against his shoulder, then she looked up at him and whispered, "So do I," and felt hot color flush her cheeks.

She stepped away just as the first boulder thundered into the tomb. A moment later Fletcher's face appeared in the opening.

"Hello, in there," he said cheerfully. "Anybody for a hamburger?"

It was a long time before Catherine went to sleep that night. She lay on her cot in the tent and thought about the day she'd spent with David. The shuddering fear that she felt in the tomb lingered, but it was overshadowed by the memory of the sudden and unexpected intimacy she'd shared with him. Not just the intimacy of his kisses, but of the way he'd talked to her, telling her about the father he'd loved and lost, of how he'd felt when his father told him it was all right for a man to cry. It was that kind of intimacy, even more than the way she had felt in his arms, that frightened Catherine. She'd wanted to draw him close and shelter him from ever being hurt again. When he'd kissed her, she'd wanted to lose herself in him. If he'd laid her down on the cold floor of that hidden tomb, she knew that she would have welcomed him.

Catherine sat up in bed and hugged her knees. She was acting like a teenager, an adolescent with a crush, instead of a thirty-seven-year-old woman. It had to stop and it had to stop now! She would *not* make a fool of herself over a younger man. She simply wouldn't allow what had happened today to ever happen again.

At last, exhausted by all that had occurred, Catherine slept. It was almost nine o'clock when she awoke in the morning. She glanced at the clock beside her bed, muttering because the alarm hadn't gone off. She picked it up and saw that it had been turned off. There was a thermos of coffee beside it and a note that read, "I thought you'd like to take it easy this morning." It was signed D.

Quickly Catherine threw a robe on, gathered up clean clothes and ran to the makeshift shower. Standing under the cool water, she thought of David coming into her tent to turn the alarm off, of him watching her while she slept. She remembered that he'd told her that she purred when she slept, and she smiled. She closed her eyes for a moment, feeling again the touch of his lips on hers, the hands that had so gently stroked her breasts.

David, Nawab and Azan were working deep in the tunnel when Catherine appeared. Fletcher and Sahibzada were cleaning potsherds.

"Good morning," Fletcher said when he saw her. "How do you feel? Recovered from your experience?"

"I'm fine, but I wish you hadn't let me sleep so long."

"It was David's idea. He knew you needed the rest." Fletcher sat back on his heels. "I was awfully worried about you, Catherine. About both of you of course, but especially you. Thank God Massaud and I decided to come back from Edfu last night."

"What time did you get back?"

"After dark, about eight I imagine. By that time Nawab had gotten concerned, and because Massaud and I had the truck and you and David had the Jeep, he'd started walking to the tomb. He and Azan were halfway there when we ran into them." Fletcher hesitated. "I know what it must have been like for you, Catherine. How bad it must have been."

"Not as bad as I thought, Fletcher. David was very patient, very kind."

Yes, that was it, David had been kind. He'd taken her mind off her terrible fear by making love to her.

Her face burned with shame when she thought of her response. It had happened once, she thought. She'd never let it happen again.

Chapter 9

David looked at her across the table, puzzled when Catherine glanced at him, then away. She'd been doing it all day, and it bothered him, more than he liked to admit. Every time he'd tried to get her alone for a minute she'd disappeared.

As soon as dinner was finished she rose to leave, but before she could move away, David said, "I wonder if I could speak to you for a minute, Catherine?"

"Massaud has given me some more transcript pages," she said quickly. "I'd really like to go over them tonight, David."

"This won't take long." Before she could object, he took her arm and led her away from the camp in the direction of the dunes. When they were out of sight of the others, he stopped and said, "You've been avoiding me all day, Catherine. I'd like to know why."

"I haven't been avoiding you. I...we've all been busy. There hasn't been a minute—"

"There's been a minute. What is it, Catherine? What's bothering you?"

"Nothing." She walked a few steps, then turned back, because she knew that sooner or later they had to talk about what had happened between them.

But before she could speak, David said, "I thought that after yesterday we understood each other a little better. I thought we were friends." A smile softened his mouth. "More than friends, Catherine," he said, taking her hands.

"David, please..." She hesitated, not knowing how to say what needed to be said before this went any further. "We're friends," she said, "of course we're friends. I don't know what I would have done if you hadn't been with me, if you hadn't talked to me and helped me get over my fear. You made the darkness disappear, David. I'm grateful to you."

"Grateful? I kissed you and you kissed me back and it was wonderful." He put his hands on Catherine's arms, forcing her to face him. "It was wonderful," he said again.

"Because of the situation. But it won't happen again, David. It's never a good idea to have that...that kind of a relationship going on at a dig. I've seen it happen and so have you. It creates dissension, all sorts of bad feelings."

"That won't happen to us, Catherine. We're not kids. We're—"

"You're right, David, we're not kids. At least I'm not. I'm older than you are and—"

"So that's it!"

"That's part of it."

He laughed, but when he saw how serious she was, his face sobered. "Catherine, you're being silly. You're a couple of years older than I am. So what?"

"I'm six years older than you are. And I'm not interested in . . . you know."

"No, I don't know. What happened to us yesterday was something special. It meant a lot to me, and I think it meant something to you as well."

Catherine took a deep breath and forced herself to go on. "I was afraid of the dark yesterday, David. That's all it was. I'm grateful to you for helping me, but I'd like both of us to forget it."

David looked at her for a long moment. He wanted to take Catherine in his arms and kiss her with all the anger and the passion he was trying so desperately to hold back. He wanted to feel her lips part and soften under his. He wanted to hear again that soft moan of pleasure when he touched her breasts. But he couldn't force her. If Catherine ever yielded herself to him, it would be because she wanted it as much as he did.

He looked at her, his face expressionless. "If that's the way you want it, Catherine, it's forgotten." Then he turned away, while he still could, and went swiftly back to the camp.

The occasion of my mistress, Alifa's fifteenth birthday was not a joyous one, for she and a few servants would soon leave Philae and journey up the Nile to her new home.

It has been a time for weeping since the day that emissaries from the king arrived by royal barge. They came, we learned, because he had heard of Alifa's beauty and sought her for his wife. King Amonset was the great pharaoh who had united

Upper and Lower Egypt—it was a great honor to be thus chosen.

And thus it was settled and done.

Catherine pinched the bridge of her nose and tilted the light so that she could see better as she continued to read of how Alifa had wept as the barge moved slowly away from her island home. She had vowed that, if the gods were willing, she would return.

The transcript continued, describing Alifa's first meeting with King Amonset.

He is older than her father. His hair is white, and there are lines in his face like the grooves in the sand after a wind storm. When my mistress first saw him she bowed her head so that he could not see the shock on her face. But when she raised it, her face was clear and sweet. "My lord," she said, and leaned to kiss his hand.

He is not an unkind man, and I believe he cares for her, but oh, I weep because my mistress must give up her maidenhood to such as he. For she is young and fair of face, and I would that she could find a prince, one worthy of her beauty and her youth.

That was as far as Massaud had gotten with the transcript. Catherine put the pages with the others that he'd given her and switched off the lamp. Silently she undressed and lay down on her cot. She thought of Alifa, and it seemed to her that she could see the young queen, a girl barely out of childhood, forced to give herself to a man she'd never seen before, a man she didn't love and who was older than her father.

She thought of David and knew how wonderful it would be to give herself to him.

At noon the next day they uncovered the final step leading down to the tomb and stood before a stone door.

"This is it!" David's voice was jubilant. He stared at the door, his face alight with excitement.

"Congratulations, Dave." Fletcher clapped him on the shoulder and chuckled. "That old gut instinct of yours never fails!"

"Yes." Catherine put her hand out. "Congratulations, David."

"I told you we'd find Alifa here." He couldn't keep the triumph out of his voice as he picked up a tool and said, "Let's get to work."

Catherine knew she should have been happy for him. He'd made a momentous discovery, and he had the right to be proud of it. But she'd been so sure of the research she'd done, and of the instinct that told her she would be the one to discover Alifa's tomb. She'd been wrong. David had been right all along and the triumph was his.

By nightfall they'd broken through the door to a second one walled up in mortar.

"It'll have to wait till morning." Fletcher held one of the lamps high to inspect the door.

David nodded. He looked past the others to Catherine. His face was flushed from the heat, dirty from all the work he'd done. But it was filled with pride and enthusiasm. He looked very young, and suddenly Catherine thought of a small boy who had to be the best to please the father he thought no longer loved him.

For the first time in a week Catherine smiled at him. "It's wonderful, David," she said, and meant it. "You should be proud; you've made an important discovery. It's a great victory for you."

"For all of us, Catherine. This is our victory." His eyes lingered on her face, and for a moment it was as though the two of them were alone. Then she looked away.

That night Fletcher brought out a bottle of wine. "I've been saving this for a special occasion," he said, "and tonight seems pretty special." He filled the four glasses and handed them to the others before he raised his and said, "Congratulations, Dave. You've done it again."

"Allah karim," Massaud said. "God is generous, David. It is not our custom to drink spirits, but I raise my glass to you."

"Yes, David." Catherine looked at him across the rim of her goblet. "I, too, raise my glass to you."

Her face, softened by the lamplight, was clear and guileless. She meant what she said, she *was* happy for him—for all of them. He wished suddenly that they were alone, because he wanted to take her in his arms and tell her how much this meant to him, especially because he knew how much Alifa meant to her. He would tell her that it was her triumph, that he gave it to her.

David barely slept that night. His thoughts that they would soon break through the door and find the tomb that archeologists had searched for years to find kept him excited and on edge. As soon as it was opened, he would drive into Edfu and send a telegram to the Smithsonian. Then perhaps he and Catherine—no, he would have to include Fletcher and Massaud—the four of them would take a week off. They would take a Nile steamer up the river, sleep in air-conditioned cabins, drink long, cool drinks and watch the life of Egypt flow endlessly by. At night he and Catherine would stand out on the top deck. He would hold her in his arms until the hour grew late.

David's body grew rigid with longing, and he made himself think instead of the excavation and the glories he would discover.

Tomorrow.

The day was hot, the air so still and thick it was an effort to breathe. By ten o'clock David's shirt was soaked through. He took it off and wiped the sweat off his forehead. He knew they should take a break, but he didn't want to stop, not when they were this close.

The last piece of mortar fell away; he stood in front of the door.

"We're here." Fletcher took a deep breath. "This is it, Dave."

David's hands were damp with sweat. After almost two thousand years, he thought. He looked at Catherine. Her face was flushed with heat and excitement. "When we open the door," he said, "I want you to go in first."

Her dark eyes widened. The tip of her tongue came out to moisten her lips. "This is your find, David. You should be the one—"

He shook his head. "You go first."

Massaud and Fletcher were dusting the earth away from the door. "It won't be long now." Fletcher could barely keep the excitement out of his voice. "Just another minute or two." He stopped, then exultantly said, "Yes, here it is! The royal seal! By God, we've done it. We've..." He paused, frowning in confusion. "Have a look," he said to Massaud. "I don't want to be wrong on this."

"What's the matter?" David pushed Massaud out of the way. "What's wrong? What is it?"

Fletcher pointed out the seal. "I'm sorry, Dave—"

"Sorry? What in the hell...?" David brushed the dirt carefully away from the seal and leaned closer to decipher the ancient writing. "Potiphera, Pharaoh of... Pharaoh of Egypt." He looked at Fletcher, then back at the seal as though unable to believe what he was seeing.

"I'm sorry, Dave." Fletcher cleared his throat. "It's a great find though. Potiphera ruled in the last period of the Twelfth Dynasty, didn't he? He—"

"I was so sure," David said painfully. "Everything indicated that Alifa was here. It's the right distance from Amonset's tomb. This is where she should have been." He looked at Catherine. "You were right, she isn't here." He turned away, and his face hardened when he picked up a tool. "Don't just stand there," he growled at Nawab, "get to work. I want this door opened today."

But it was midmorning of the next day before they opened the tomb. David had tried hard to tell himself that night that it didn't matter, he hadn't really failed. Though Potiphera had been a minor king who'd ruled for less than ten years, the discovery of his tomb—of any tomb—was important. Tomorrow after he had a look around he would still contact the Egyptian authorities and report his find. He would let the Smithsonian know too. He would do all of the things that had to be done, and when the preliminary work was finished, he would begin again to search for the lost queen. There was still time. It was the end of May; he had until August. Two and a half months. David's hands tightened into fists. How could he have been wrong? All of his research had indicated this was where Alifa's tomb should have been. He'd never been wrong about a dig before. What had happened this time?

The thought came to him then that perhaps Catherine was right about Alifa. Perhaps the young queen had returned to the Island of Philae.

"No," David muttered under his breath. "No, dammit, that's not what she did. She's here somewhere, and I intend to find her."

The tomb of King Potiphera yielded a treasure house of ancient wonders. There were enormous gilded wooden cases, fitting into each other like Russian dolls; a small golden barge; a breastplate with solar and lunar emblems; a gilded, jewel-encrusted chest with hieroglyphic inscriptions surrounded by a row of turquoise scarabs; solid gold lances and daggers. In the burial chamber they found a wooden sarcophagus inlaid with glass and semiprecious stones.

"This is an incredible find," Fletcher said as they gazed around the treasure-filled room. "Let me get Massaud and the others, they've got to see this."

"It's really wonderful, David," Catherine said when they were alone. She wanted to help him, to assure him that this truly was a remarkable discovery, one that he could be justifiably proud of. "I know you're disappointed," she added. "I know how sure you were that Alifa was here."

David looked at her. "You were right all along, Catherine." He ran a tired hand across his face. "You still believe she went to Philae, don't you?"

"Yes, I do. But I'll go anywhere you want to go, David. I'll work with you any place you decide to excavate. You were wrong this time, but you've made a great discovery. I'll be proud to work with you for as long as we're in Egypt."

He didn't deserve this kind of loyalty from her. She'd offered him her help, and for a moment he wanted to take her into his arms and rest his head against her breast. He wanted to tell her how much it hurt him to fail. Instead he kept his distance and said, "Thank you, Catherine, I appreciate that," and turned away from her when Fletcher entered the tomb.

A week later authorities from the Egyptian Department of Antiquities arrived in Edfu and drove out to the excavation site with Abdel Moustafa. It was decided that David and his crew would stay to assist with the cataloging, which would take at least a week or ten days, then they would turn the rest of the operation over to the Egyptians. The credit for the find would be given to David and his team.

He wasn't sure which direction he would take after that. Fletcher had spoken to him at length about the warrior, Ramah, and he'd suggested to David that before they resumed their search for Alifa, they spend a few weeks searching for Ramah's tomb.

"I know finding his tomb wouldn't have anywhere near the importance of a discovery like Potiphera or Queen Alifa," Fletcher said. "But I've been interested in Ramah for a long time, and I'd like to give it a try. He was such an outstanding warrior, David, a general when he was twenty-two, only twenty-four when he died."

"I thought he was killed in the war against the Assyrians."

"He was wounded in a battle, but he didn't die right away—or at least that's the way the story goes. He was sent back to Egypt by Nile barge, and he died here. If you don't want to take the time to search for him, I'll understand and I won't belabor the point. But I may stay on in Egypt after the expedition is over and do some hunting on my own."

"If you were sure you knew where you wanted to begin looking, and if we had more time, I'd go along with you, Fletch. But the important thing now is to continue searching for Alifa, because time is running out."

But that afternoon Abdel's chauffeur arrived with a telegram from the Smithsonian that read:

> Congratulations on your find. Extending your grant to a full year, longer if necessary. Please advise location of any new projects. Good luck.

David tightened his hand on the telegram. Thank God! He had time now, as much time as he needed. They could finish up here and then begin all over again. He wouldn't give up until he found the lost Alifa.

Three days later Fletcher was stricken with a bout of malaria that was serious enough to leave him bedridden.

"You need medical attention," David said. "I'm going to have Massaud drive you to Edfu. I want you to see a doctor, Fletch. No argument. You're going and that's final."

"Not while the rest of you are working your tails off."

"Then we'll all take a week off." David looked at Massaud, who stood in the open flap of the tent. "How about you? Could you use some time with your family?"

"Yes, David, most definitely." Massaud grinned. "And with my girlfriend, Jehan. I could drive Fletcher to Edfu and go on to Cairo from there if you're sure it's all right."

"I'm sure." David turned back to Fletcher. "It's settled, Fletch. You're taking a week off."

"What about you and Catherine?"

"Maybe I'll take a Nile cruise. Catherine can go to Cairo with Massaud if she wants to. Or she can come on the Nile cruise with me. It's up to her."

It's up to her, David told himself, but if I have anything to do with it, she's coming with me. He thought of the days they'd spend together on the Nile, of quiet mornings on the deck watching the great river flow by.

And he thought of the nights.

Chapter 10

Catherine had never been a good sailor. For her tenth birthday her father had taken her to California, and one of the highlights was supposed to have been a sail to Catalina. Catherine had been sick all the way there and all the way back. That's why now it was a special delight to be able to take a cruise and relax without the worry of a queasy stomach.

The first night of the trip she stood out on the top deck and watched the lights of Edfu fade away. But there were other lights from the shore and lanterns flickering from small village homes. She'd been reluctant to take this cruise with David, but she needn't have worried. As soon as they boarded, he excused himself and went to his cabin. He didn't appear for dinner or afterward in the lounge, and Catherine knew that he was still sorting through the latest turn of events and planning his next move.

David had had little to say during the week that followed the discovery of Potiphera's tomb. He'd worked from sunup until late at night, doing the heavy work that Nawab and his crew were paid to do, besides doing most of the cataloging of the contents of the tomb.

Only when it came time to crate the contents for shipment back to Cairo had David been able to turn and walk away. Their equipment would stay where it was, at the excavation, and so would the crew, until David decided what he was going to do next.

Once they'd arrived in Edfu he made sure there was a doctor to take care of Fletcher and booked passage for himself and Catherine on the Nile steamer. He was courteous and helpful, but remote, closed into some private corner of himself. For the first time in his life he felt that he'd failed at something that meant a great deal to him.

David lay in his bunk the first night on the boat, listening to the hum of the motors, tortured by thoughts of his failure.

While two cabins down Catherine lay in her bunk thinking about him. She knew what this setback meant to David. Yet for all her sympathy, Catherine couldn't help feeling a sense of exhilaration. If David had been wrong, did that mean that Alifa's tomb *was* on the Island of Philae? Could she ever convince David to search there?

She was on the top deck the next morning when he appeared. "Everything all right?" he asked. "Did you sleep well?"

"Yes, thanks. Did you?"

"Well enough. There's an afternoon excursion to Kôm Ombo. Would you like to take it?"

"Yes, of course."

"Then let's meet in the dining room at twelve." He hesitated. "Look, I know I haven't been pleasant company for the last week or so. I'm sorry. It's just that I was so damn disappointed."

"I know, David, and it's all right." Catherine sat up in the chaise. "Why don't we not talk about it and just enjoy the cruise?" She smiled up at him. "Just imagine, a whole week of being able to sleep in air-conditioning and to eat food that Sahibzada hasn't over or under cooked. I might even have a very tall gin and tonic with ice tonight."

"I might even join you."

She made him feel better, and she was right about not talking shop. They should relax on the cruise, do some sight-seeing, get some rest. They would have plenty of time to think about work when the cruise was over.

Kôm Ombo, a strategic stop on the old Ethiopia-Nubia trade route, boasted a twin temple dedicated to the gods Haroeris, one of the solar manifestations of Horus, the falcon god, and Sobek, the crocodile god of fertility. The afternoon sun was hot. It shimmered on the golden sand in undulating waves of heat as they wandered around the temple with others from the ship. When they climbed over a pile of rubble, David took Catherine's hand and held it until it was time for them to leave.

When they returned to the boat, he said, "I think I'm going to have that gin and tonic now. Care to join me?"

Catherine was about to say that she never drank in the afternoon, but somehow this didn't seem a day for nevers, and she let David lead her into the air-conditioned salon. She took off the wide-brimmed straw hat she'd worn for sight-seeing and fanning her face said, "This air-conditioning feels wonderful."

"The heat's been getting to all of us. The next three or four months are going to be even hotter. I'm worried about Fletch, Catherine. I'm not sure he's going to be well enough to stand it."

"He'd hate to leave though." She took a sip of the cool and refreshing drink. "The doctor in Edfu was sure he'd be able to bring Fletcher's malaria under control, and the week's rest will do him a lot of good. He'll be all right, David, and perhaps when we start back to work, you can make him take it easier, put him in charge of the potsherds, out of the sun, while the rest of us do the harder work. It would be terrible to ask him to leave, David—he probably doesn't have many full-fledged digs left."

David looked tenderly at Catherine. Her porcelain skin had burned and peeled and finally tanned, and she'd lost weight. Yet here she was insisting that Fletcher take it easy while she worked along with the men. For the first time since the discovery of Potiphera's tomb David felt a surge of excitement that had nothing to do with archeology.

He looked at Catherine—really looked at her for the first time in weeks. The tan became her and her hair was a longer, more becoming length. The few pounds had made a difference, and her cheek bones were more prominent, her figure even more alluring than it had been before. He let his gaze drift over her, then blinked to attention when she said, "The ship's leaving the dock."

She turned from the window to smile at him. "I can't tell you how much I'm enjoying this, David. Except for the trip from Luxor to Edfu, I'd never been able to enjoy boats, because I'm a rotten sailor. This is a treat for me; I'd like the cruise to go on and on."

So would I, David thought as he looked at her over the rim of his glass. So would I, my dear Professor Adair.

* * *

They danced in the salon after dinner that evening. Catherine wore the green caftan and the green velvet slippers; David wore dark pants and a white dinner jacket.

Catherine rarely went to parties, and except for the celebration that Abdel had given in their honor, she hadn't danced in years. She refused to dance when the band played disco, feeling self-conscious and out of place as she watched the couples gyrating in time to music she thought of as highly unmusical.

"It's fun," David said. "Let's give it a try."

Catherine looked at him skeptically. "Maybe later," she said.

"I'll hold you to that." He smiled. And I'll hold *you*, Catherine, just like I did before. His gaze dropped to the strand of sandalwood beads resting on the soft green material against her breasts, and he felt the breath catch in his throat. She'd been so different the night in Edfu, so softly feminine, so unlike the woman she'd been these past months at the dig. How many nights had he lain on his cot and thought about her, remembering the feel of her in his arms, the haunting sweet smell of sandalwood against her skin?

David became aware then that the tempo of the music had changed and that the lights had dimmed. Dancing couples moved closer together. He stood up and held his hand out. "Come and dance with me now," he said.

Almost reluctantly Catherine got to her feet. She took his hand, and when they were on the dance floor, she stepped into his arms.

His hand was warm against her back as he gently urged her closer, and she felt stiff and awkward.

"Relax," David said as he brushed his lips across her temple. He moved his hand against the small of her back, slow movements that were barely discernible in the half light.

Catherine tried to move back, but he held her. His body was lean and hard against hers, and after a moment she rested her face against the white jacket, enjoying the comfortable feeling of being in his arms. She felt the motion of his hips close to hers, the strength of his legs and the warmth of his hand moving slowly against her back. He lifted her hand to his lips and tucked it close to his chest.

They moved as one person, and Catherine felt herself relax against him. She was caught by the music and by the man who held her so close. When he again raised the hand he held to his mouth and kissed each finger, she sighed and closed her eyes.

She knew she should move away from him, and she told herself that when the song ended, she would. But when the song ended, and another began, Catherine remained in his arms.

They danced until the music stopped and the band began to pack their instruments. "Let's go out on deck for a while," David said.

The night air was cool and soft. A moon that was almost full shone overhead and streaked the slow-moving water with golden ripples. Hand in hand they went to the bow of the ship, and when they stopped Catherine said, "There are times like tonight when I can't believe I'm really here. I'm afraid I'll awaken, and it will all have been a dream."

"This isn't a dream." David put a finger under her chin and tilted her face up so that he could look into her dark eyes. "This is real, Catherine." He brushed her lips with his.

"David..." she whispered against his lips. "I—"

But he stopped her words with a kiss so fiercely possessive that he almost frightened her. He held her, pinioned against him, her body tight to his as the kiss deepened, and only when her body softened against his, did he let her move a fraction of an inch away.

"Catherine." He spoke her name as gently as a caress. He kissed her again, softly, taking the time to savor the taste of her, the fullness of her bottom lip, the sweetness of her mouth. She trembled against him, and when he touched his tongue to hers, her arms crept up around his neck, and he felt the play of her fingers against his skin.

When at last he stepped away from her, he saw that her eyes were luminous in the moonlight. "Will you come with me now?" he asked.

Wordlessly Catherine looked at him. She wanted to say something that would distance them, that would bring them back to where they were before. But the words didn't come. She wanted David, and tonight she would be his.

They walked slowly to his cabin. He drew open the curtains and, taking Catherine's hand, led her to the bed under the wide picture window. They looked out at the moonlight on the water, and David said, "I thought about you last night."

"I thought about you, too."

He touched the side of her face. "I've wanted you for such a long time, Catherine." He slipped his hand around to the back of her neck and pulled her toward him and kissed her, slow and easy because he wanted to take the time to relish the taste of her. In a moment she would lie beside him, but for now he was content with just a touch.

But only for a moment.

He slipped the caftan over her head, then stood and took his jacket off, still moving slowly, content to look at her, pleased with the trimness of her body in her lace bra and panties. He unknotted his tie, unbuttoned his shirt. He undid his belt and slipped it through the notches of his trousers. He saw her bite her lower lip when he stepped out of his shoes and slipped his trousers down over his legs. He knelt on the bed beside her, sensing her nervousness.

"It's all right, Catherine. It's going to be all right, love." He slipped her sandals off, then eased the bra from her shoulders. He lay back against the pillows and brought her down beside him. He felt the quick beat of her heart against his chest and put his arms around her, holding her close while he stroked her back. Only when he felt the tension flow out of her did he kiss her again.

David's mouth was so warm against hers, the hand that stroked her so gentle. She sighed as slowly, slowly, the smoldering flame that had threatened to consume her up on the deck caught and flared again. He touched her breasts, and the sigh became a soft moan of pleasure. He rubbed the swollen peaks against the palm of his hand, and she whispered his name. He leaned to kiss them, and she whimpered with pleasure.

David raised himself over her and kissed her eyelids closed. He gathered her in his arms and told her how lovely she was before he began to trail a line of sweet, hot kisses down her face, her throat, against her ears, lingering until she pleaded for him to stop. Gently he bit the lobe of one ear and soothed it with his tongue before he moved again to feast upon her breasts.

Almost beside herself, unable to bear this sweet torture a moment longer, Catherine whispered, "David, please, I can't stand it. I can't..."

He tightened his hands on her hips and leaned to nuzzle a line of fire around her waist. She was naked, except for the sandalwood beads that hung between her breasts.

She heard the breath catch in his throat as she opened her legs to him, and he covered her body with his. With a kiss he joined his body to hers.

For that first frightening moment Catherine stiffened. But David held her, and suddenly her body was alive with a passion she hadn't even dreamed of. With a low cry of need she lifted her body to his and whispered his name in the quiet of the room, quivering with pleasure.

She was lost in him, consumed by him as she pressed her fingers against the small of his back and urged him closer. Everything was out of focus. She was lost, giving as he gave, wanting this never to stop, because there could never again be anything as wonderful as this. She'd never known, had never even imagined this kind of longing, this reaching. It was too much.

Suddenly her body spun out of control. She cried out and felt David's mouth on hers, taking her frenzied cry. His hands tightened on her body, and he plunged against her, exploding with a moan of pain and pleasure as he held her tightly.

Catherine lay with her body against his while he stroked her. "You're so beautiful," he said, and she felt quick tears sting her eyes—no one had ever told her that before.

He didn't speak after that, he only held her. But when she started to shift away, David said, "No, Catherine, stay with me tonight."

"I can't," she whispered. "Someone will know."

He smiled against her lips. "No one will know, love." He put his hand against the back of her head and pulled her down to his shoulder. "Go to sleep, Catherine," he said as he tightened his arms around her. "Go to sleep, my love."

Catherine awoke to the steady hum of the motors and to sun warming her naked body. She lay pressed close to David, her head on his shoulder, her arm thrown across his waist.

"Good morning." He kissed her shoulder. "Did you sleep well?"

"Yes, I..." She looked up at him, swallowing hard. "I'd better get dressed."

"There's no hurry." David glanced at the clock on the bedside table. "It's not even seven. We've got an hour before the dining room opens."

"Yes, but, if I dress now and leave maybe no one will see me." She started up out of bed, but David pulled her back down beside him.

"Don't go," he said. "Please, Catherine, stay with me."

She looked at him. His face was flushed from sleep, and his tousled hair fell over eyes as blue as the waters of the Nile. She brushed the hair back from his forehead and murmured his name.

He brought her fingers to his lips before he pulled her over him so that her body rested on his. Cupping her face between his hands, he kissed her and held her close while he caressed her. His legs pressed against hers, and his toes curled against hers as the kiss grew and deepened.

She felt the brush of his chest hair against her breasts, the whole length of him beneath her, and her body grew weak with longing.

The kiss ended. He rolled onto his side, taking her with him so that her head rested on his arm. He picked up the sandalwood beads and said, "I went to sleep with the scent of these last night." His hand tightened on them.

"They've bewitched me, Catherine, just as you've bewitched me." He took the beads between his lips and with a slight tug brought her closer so that their lips had only the sandalwood beads between them. He gave them to her lips and said, "You excite me so, Catherine. I want to hear you cry my name the way you did last night. I want to make love with you. Oh, Catherine."

He rolled her beneath him and entered her, quickly, deeply. He reached to kiss her lips and slipped his tongue into her mouth, mirroring the dance of their bodies, sliding into the moist warmth of her until it was too much to bear.

He didn't want this to end, and he tried with all the force of his body to make himself slow down. He repeated her name again and again, loving the sound of it. He kissed her eyelids and her nose. He leaned to take one tender tip of her breast between his teeth to tease and suckle, and when he did, she held the fullness up to his hungry mouth and sighed with pleasure.

Catherine's body quivered under his, and she knew she couldn't hold back any longer. She whispered his name, begging him for release, and David thrust against her deep and hard, carrying her over the edge of passion while she clung to him, sobbing his name, mindless, senseless, totally his now in this final soaring moment.

David's hands were on her body, soothing her to quietness while he rained kisses as soft as a butterfly's wings upon her face and told her how beautiful she was.

At last Catherine lay quiet in his arms. She knew she should get up. Then her eyes drifted closed, and with the sun drying the sweat from her naked body she went back to sleep in the comfort of David's arms.

Chapter 11

In the late afternoon when the boat had docked so that the passengers could visit Darau, David and Catherine hired a felucca. The tall, turbaned Nubian asked David where they wanted to go, and David replied, "Into the sunset."

With a smile that exposed large white teeth the Nubian held the tall-masted sailboat steady while they boarded. Then with his hand on the tiller, his dark blue *gelabaya* flowing around him, he turned the boat into the wind.

The sun was a large orange ball in an apricot sky. The air, after the heat of the day, was as cool as the waters of the great river. This was the hour when the farmers brought their water buffalo, their mules and camels to drink from Mother Nile. This was the hour when the barges filled with produce let down their anchors just as they had thousands of years before when they had brought cedars from Lebanon, grain, textiles and gold, incense and myrrh. Children played on the banks of the

GIVE YOUR HEART TO SILHOUETTE®

FREE!

Mail this heart today!

AND WE'LL GIVE YOU 4 FREE BOOKS, A COMBINATION CLOCK/CALENDAR AND A FREE MYSTERY GIFT!

SEE INSIDE!

IT'S A

SILHOUETTE HONEYMOON

A SWEETHEART

OF A FREE OFFER!

FOUR NEW SILHOUETTE INTIMATE MOMENTS® NOVELS—FREE!

Take a "Silhouette Honeymoon" with four exciting romances—yours FREE from Silhouette Books. Each of these hot-off-the-press novels brings you all the passion and tenderness of today's greatest love stories . . . your free passport to a bright new world of love and adventure! But wait . . . there's even more to this great offer!

COMBINATION CLOCK CALENDAR—ABSOLUTELY FREE

You'll love your new LCD digital quartz clock, which also shows the current month and date. This lovely lucite piece includes a handy month-at-a-glance calendar, or you can display your favorite photo in the calendar area. This is our special gift to you free with this offer!

SPECIAL EXTRAS—FREE!

You'll get your free monthly newsletter, packed with news on your favorite writers, upcoming books, even recipes from your favorite authors. We'll also send you free gifts from time to time, as a token of our appreciation for being a home subscriber!

FREE HOME DELIVERY!

Send for your Silhouette Intimate Moments novels and enjoy the convenience of previewing four new books every month, delivered right to your home. If you decide to keep them, pay just $2.49 per book—26¢ less than what you pay in stores—with no additional charges for home delivery. Great savings plus total convenience add up to a sweetheart of a deal for you!

START YOUR SILHOUETTE HONEYMOON TODAY—
JUST COMPLETE, DETACH & MAIL YOUR FREE OFFER CARD!

SILHOUETTE BOOKS "NO RISK" GUARANTEE

- There's no obligation to buy—and the free books and gifts are yours to keep.
- You pay the lowest price possible and receive books before they appear in stores.
- You may end your subscription at any time—just write and let us know.

FILL OUT THIS POSTPAID CARD AND MAIL TODAY!

SILHOUETTE BOOKS

FREE OFFER CARD

FREE CLOCK/ CALENDAR

FREE HOME DELIVERY

PLACE HEART STICKER HERE

4 FREE BOOKS

PLUS AN EXTRA BONUS MYSTERY GIFT

YES! Please send me my four SILHOUETTE INTIMATE MOMENTS novels, free, along with my free Clock/Calendar and Mystery Gift as explained on the opposite page.

240 CIL YACV

NAME ______________________

(please print)

ADDRESS ______________________ **APT** ________

CITY ______________________

STATE ______________________ **ZIP** ________

Prices subject to change. Offer limited to one per household and not valid for present Intimate Moments subscribers.

PRINTED IN U.S.A.

Limited Time Offer! Make sure you get this great FREE OFFER—act today!

If offer card below is missing, write to:
Silhouette Books, 901 Fuhrmann Blvd., P.O. Box 1867, Buffalo, N.Y. 14269-1867

CLIP AND MAIL THIS POSTPAID CARD TODAY!

NO POSTAGE NECESSARY IF MAILED IN THE UNITED STATES

BUSINESS REPLY CARD

First Class Permit No. 717 Buffalo, NY

Postage will be paid by addressee

Silhouette Books®
901 Fuhrmann Blvd.
P.O. Box 1867
Buffalo, NY 14240-9952

river, their voices floating on the evening air as sweet as the night birds who sang above them.

The sun god, Ra, sank lower, almost to the top of the palms, a golden reflection on the water. Soon he would disappear into the land, to rest and rise again tomorrow.

Catherine would always remember this moment as she gazed about her. She would remember how the river looked at this particular moment, how the sun turned David's skin the color of bronze and how his warm hand clasped hers.

"It's so beautiful," she said, and leaned her head against his shoulder.

"On an evening like this it's as though nothing has changed in five thousand years. The Nile goes on forever and Egypt is eternal." He raised an arm and pointed. "There on the bank you can see the silhouette of the temple."

"And the shadows of all the people who've worshipped there." In the distance they heard the call to prayer, floating like a ghostly voice over the water. The boatman turned his face toward the sound, his turbaned head bowed in silent prayer until the voice faded.

For a reason he could not explain, David felt the sting of tears behind his lids. He wrapped Catherine closer in his arms, her back toward him so she wouldn't see his face. He thought of his father telling him that it was all right for men to cry if they were sad. But it wasn't sadness he was feeling—it was an overwhelming sense of the beauty of the night and of the joy of sharing this beauty with Catherine.

He'd never felt this way before, not with anyone. There'd been other women in his life, but none who'd ever affected him the way Catherine did. Making love with her had been more wonderful than he could ever put into words, but it went far deeper than that. It seemed to him as though he had known her forever, that she was an inextricable part of him.

David brushed his face against her hair and smiled, remembering that his first impression of her had been of a coldly austere, painfully plain woman. He tightened his arms around her as he thought about last night when she'd whispered his name in the darkness, and of this early morning when she'd lain trembling in his arms. With the last rays of the sun on her face and the smooth dark wings of her hair curved against her cheeks she was neither cold, nor plain. She was as beautiful as an Egyptian goddess, but as warm and as giving as only a woman could be.

He loved her.

The breath caught in David's throat. Yes, he loved Catherine, and he knew deep down in the secret places of his heart that this love would last forever. He breathed in the scent of her hair and felt his body tighten with desire. He knew that tonight he would make love with her again.

When darkness fell, the Nubian brought the tall-masted sailboat back to shore. David paid him, adding a generous tip that brought a smile to the man's face as they said good-night. Then David took Catherine's arm and helped her up the gangplank of their ship.

"I'd better change for dinner," she said. "I'll meet you in the dining room."

David shook his head. "No," he said, taking pleasure in watching her eyes widen with awareness.

"David." His name trembled on her lips as she reached out to him.

In the near darkness of her cabin, when the silver light of the moon reflected upon the water, David undressed her. When she stood naked before him, he cupped her face between his hands. He murmured her name and he kissed her so tenderly that she felt tears sting her eyes, and when they streaked her cheeks David kissed the saltiness away. Then he put his arms around her and held her, loving the womanly press of her breasts against his bare chest.

"I love you," he said, kissing her again before she could respond. Because he was afraid of the sudden alarm he saw in her eyes. He picked her up and laid her down on the bed. He touched her face and brushed the dark bangs back from her forehead so that he could trace the line of her brows and her nose, down to the indentation that led to her parted lips. "Your skin is the color of golden sand," he said as he leaned to kiss her.

Catherine lifted her arms to encircle his neck and bring him down closer to her. She touched the soft hairs at the back of his neck and ran her fingers lightly over his shoulders and down his back. He turned on his side to kiss her breasts, and she murmured her pleasure.

"Touch me, Catherine," he said softly, and she trailed her fingers slowly down his stomach. She heard his indrawn gasp of breath as she touched the silken shaft and felt her heart swell with the knowledge that she was giving him pleasure.

David rolled onto his back, taking Catherine over him. The dark wings of her hair caressed his face as he drew her close and kissed her. "I wonder if you know what you do to me," he said. "I look at you across a room, I watch you walk, I touch your hand, and the wanting becomes so strong that I have to look away. You're a beautiful, sensual woman, Catherine. I've wanted you since our first morning at Edfu when you'd gone down early to swim at Abdel's villa. I came out on my balcony and saw you standing there with your face raised to the sun. I thought that you were the most beautiful, the most desirable woman I'd ever seen."

"That was months ago," she said.

"Yes, months." He kissed her again. "Make love with me now," he said, setting her upon his thighs.

Her sherry eyes widened for a moment when he entered her, then feeling him inside her, she shivered with pleasure and began to move slowly against him. David reached for her breasts, teasing the small buds with his fingertips while his body moved under hers.

Her movements quickened, and small cries of pleasure tumbled from her lips. David watched her through half-closed eyes. Her lips were parted, her eyes hooded with passion. He grasped her hips and brought her closer, rubbing the thick mat of his chest hair against her breasts. She cried out and writhed wildly against him, lost in almost unbearable excitement as she whispered his name again and again.

David clasped her to him. She sought his mouth, as frantic as he was, caught up in a maelstrom of passion that seemed almost too much to bear.

"Now," he whispered urgently against her lips. "Oh, Catherine..."

"Yes, oh, David, yes." With a strangled cry Catherine buried her face against his shoulder as ripple after ripple of heat surged through her body. She felt a hand, flat against the small of her back, holding her so close that their bodies merged into one as their hearts raced in unison.

"You're mine, my Catherine, my beloved." The words were muffled, indistinguishable against her throat. He told her all that he felt, how dear, how precious she was to him. He wanted to tell her that he loved her, and that he would never let her go, but he remembered the alarm he'd seen in her eyes when he'd told her earlier of his love. He'd told himself that he would take it slowly, that he would wait until he knew she wanted to hear the words—until she was able to say them back to him. But she felt so good in his arms. He wanted to hold her forever and make her a part of him. She was his love, his darling love.

The days flowed past as endlessly as the Nile. They made no pretense now of being in separate cabins. They went to bed together and woke together, and it began to seem to Catherine as though it had always been this way—as though David had always been a part of her life.

Each time they made love, Catherine told herself it would never be this good again, but it always was. She held nothing back from David; for these few perfect days on this ancient river she was completely his. She followed where he led, giving and receiving as she learned to let go and let her body soar to heights she'd never dreamed possible.

David was a wonderful lover, at times so tender she wanted to weep with love. At other times he was so wildly fierce she trembled with fear, a fear that dissipated with her rising passion, which grew and grew until she became as fiercely demanding as he was.

Afterward, when their passion had been spent, when they lay close in each other's arms, David would stroke her to calmness and tell her how lovely she was, how good she made him feel. He told her that he would never let her go.

But Catherine knew what would happen when the cruise was over. They would go back to Edfu to renew their search for the lost tomb. These days she was sharing with David were the most precious of her life, but they couldn't last. Soon they would be back with Fletcher and Massaud, back to the reality of life. And to the stark reality of the difference in their ages. Nothing could change the fact that she was thirty-seven. David needed someone his own age, a woman who would give him children.

Catherine tried not to think about what it would be like to have a child of David's, a blue-eyed boy with a stubborn set to his chin and a smile exactly like his father's. Or a girl. How she would love to have a little girl.

There was to be a party for the passengers on their last night on the ship, and Catherine went shopping in the ship's boutique. Brows furrowed, lips pursed, Catherine looked at the lovely clothes on the rack. At last she decided on a long straight skirt in a pale shade of lilac and an ivory satin jacket trimmed with gold brocade. The first button was daringly low, and when she tried it on, she realized that her bra showed. She shook her head at the woman waiting on her and said, "I don't think this is right for me."

"Without the bra it looks as though it's made for you," the woman said, smiling. "All you need to wear under it is a bit of perfume."

It was Catherine's turn to smile. She hesitated only a second, then said she would take both the skirt and the jacket.

"Would you like to look at a cartouche?" The woman pointed to the display in the glass case in front of her.

Catherine shook her head, for although she admired the quadrangular pieces inscribed with Egyptian hieroglyphic writing, she couldn't afford to buy one. A gold cartouche would be perfect with the ivory jacket, but it simply wasn't in her budget. The gold loop earrings she'd bought in Edfu would have to suffice. And perhaps she would even do her eyes with kohl from the small pot that Safa had placed in her hand when she'd left the villa.

That evening Catherine showered and dressed in her own cabin. Before she slipped into the ivory satin jacket, she touched a bit of kohl around her eyes and mascara to her lashes, and with a final flourish she put perfume between her breasts. When that was done, she put on the jacket and stared at herself in the mirror.

Slowly Catherine shook her head, and suddenly the words to the song "If They Could See Me Now" danced crazily through her head. Was this really her? Professor Catherine Adair, who could intimidate her fellow professors with one raised eyebrow and send her students into a panic with the words, "There will be a test tomorrow."

For a moment she was tempted to take the revealing jacket off. But before she could decide what to do, someone knocked at her cabin door. "Who is it?" she called out.

"Your room boy, *madame.*"

Catherine opened the door. "I'll be gone in just a few minutes," she said. "You can fix the bed then."

"It is not the bed, *madame.* I was told to give you this." He handed her a small beribboned box, bowed from the waist and turned back into the corridor.

Catherine closed the door and with a puzzled frown opened the box. Inside, on a piece of black velvet, rested a gold cartouche surrounded by tiny chips of sapphires and rubies. She held it in the palm of her hand and, taking it to the light, studied the symbols that spelled the one word—*Forever.*

She closed her hand around the cartouche and stood there in the center of the cabin, thinking of the fates that had brought her David.

Abdel Moustafa was on the dock waiting for them when the ship arrived at Edfu the next morning.

"Sabah el kheir," he called. "Good morning, how was your trip?"

"It was wonderful," Catherine said. "How nice of you to come to meet us. How's Fletcher?"

"Completely recovered. He has spent the last three days in my library poring over books. He has much to tell you." Abdel signaled for his chauffeur to take their bags. "You look splendid, David. I can see that the rest did you good."

"Yes, it did." David smiled at Catherine. "I feel like a new man."

She blushed and quickly looked away, remembering last night after the party when he'd opened the ivory satin jacket and, pulling her down on the bed, had knelt to kiss her breasts. She'd threaded her fingers through the thickness of his hair, holding him close against her, and her breath had quickened with the sure knowledge that in a few moments their bodies would be joined in love.

Later, when they lay drowsy and satiated, when his body still covered hers, he'd tightened his fingers around the cartouche and repeated the word inscribed there, "Forever."

But it couldn't be forever; he had to understand that. The magic they'd shared had been wonderful, but now, of necessity, it was over. They could hardly continue their affair once they returned to the camp. David had said that he loved her. It was dear of him to have said the words, and she would always cherish them. But words fade away.

But when Catherine looked at him, sitting across from her in the car, when she looked at the mouth that only a few hours ago had whispered her name in the throes of passion and at the hands that had played so tenderly upon her body, her throat constricted with pain and she wondered how she would ever let him go.

Fletcher was waiting for them in the patio when they arrived. He rushed up to greet them, kissed Catherine's cheek and shook David's hand. "I've got great news," he told them. "Great news! I know where Ramah's tomb is."

"Ramah's tomb?" David frowned. "We hadn't definitely said we'd look for it, Fletch."

"I know, David, but it'll be so easy it would be a shame to pass it up. Come on into the library, both of you. Let me show you what I've found."

What Fletcher had found among the many books that were spread out on the desk and tables and the floor was incontrovertible evidence that there had indeed been a warrior by the name of Ramah who'd lived in the time of Amonset II. Both a scholar and a warrior, Ramah had been as handsome as he was good. He'd been brought to the pharaoh's attention by one of the priests—the man who'd seen to Ramah's education—and he soon became a favorite of Amonset's.

"Had the king married Alifa then?" Catherine asked. "Or was Batsira still alive?"

"Batsira died somewhere around this time, but Amonset hadn't married Alifa yet. He married her a year after Batsira's death, so I suppose Alifa and Ramah met shortly after that. Why do you ask?"

"I'm interested in every phase of Alifa's life. Ramah couldn't have been much older than she was, could he?"

"Only three or four years I should imagine."

"I wonder..." Catherine paused, and a strange expression crossed her face. "I wonder what it was like for her, being married to a man much older than she was, I mean. And suddenly having a man her own age appear on the scene."

"Even if she thought about it, there was very little she could do. At least while the king was alive." David grinned at her. "If you're trying for a love story here, Catherine, I'm afraid you're going to be disappointed. From everything I've read, Alifa was a faithful wife. And after Amonset died, Ramah spent most of his time off fighting for Egypt. Besides, Ramah was the king's devoted subject, he wouldn't have done anything to hurt Amonset or his memory."

"That's right," Fletcher said. "Ramah was like a son to the king. According to the transcripts I've been reading, Amonset even protested when Ramah went off to fight. Like a father he wanted his son to stay by his side. But Ramah did go off to war, and while he was gone, Amonset constructed a temple to his honor. It was completed before the king died."

Fletcher looked at Catherine and David, his face showing all the excitement he felt. "The temple is here, Dave, close to Edfu. Not too far from where we were digging."

"Now wait a minute," David said. "We agreed to begin searching for Alifa."

"I know, Dave. And I know finding Ramah's tomb wouldn't be as great a discovery as finding her's would be, but I don't think it would take us long. The Smithsonian has extended our stay in Egypt; we've got time. Let's go for it."

David looked at Fletcher, then at Catherine. Almost imperceptibly she nodded. "All right," he said. "One month. If we don't find Ramah's tomb in a month, we give it up. Agreed?"

"Agreed." Fletcher clapped David on his back. "I think I know just where to look, Dave. I've made a sketch." Fletcher pushed aside some of the books and papers on the desk. "Here it is." He jabbed a finger at a spot on the map he'd drawn. "This is where we'll find Ramah."

The three of them spent the remainder of the day going over the papers and the maps that Fletcher had laid out. As Catherine looked at all the information he had, she began to feel a growing sense of excitement. She was still disappointed at not continuing the search for Alifa immediately, but she was sure that Fletcher was right and that they would find Ramah's tomb exactly at the spot he'd pinpointed on the map. Perhaps when they found it, they would find another clue to Alifa's disappearance, because if Ramah had been a favorite of the young queen's husband, then he must have known her. It was entirely possible that when they found Ramah's tomb, they would find something that would lead them to Alifa.

Catherine was glad to have something to take her mind off David—at least for today. Sooner or later they had to talk, but she wanted to put that off as long as she possibly could.

Massaud arrived from Cairo in time for dinner. Abdel had his servants prepare a sumptuous meal, and afterward the five of them sat out on the terrace with after-dinner drinks. Tomorrow they planned to return to the site of the recent excavation, pack up all of the equipment and move on to the place where they would begin their search for Ramah's tomb.

Catherine leaned her head back against the chaise, drowsing and lazy as she let the conversation go on around her. She was very conscious of David in the chair next to her. She wanted to touch him, but knew she couldn't, not with everyone here. With a painful catch in her throat she thought about the long months ahead and knew they would be difficult.

This was her fault. She'd broken the unwritten law about never romancing a co-worker. She should have had more sense than to have become involved with David. Involved! Such an unimportant word to describe the immensity of the emotion she felt for him.

When the hour grew late, Catherine excused herself. "If we're going to get an early start in the morning, I'd better get some sleep," she said. She looked at David, then quickly away.

Safa greeted Catherine in the corridor outside of her bedroom. *"Ahlan wa sahlan,"* the woman said in greeting. "It is good to see you again. I have come to assist you to bed."

"That's not necessary, Safa, but thank you," Catherine said with a smile. "I'll see you in the morning."

"I will bring you tea then."

"That would be very nice. Seven-thirty would be fine."

"*Massaa el kheir, madame*, goodnight."

The room was warm. Catherine undressed, then went into the bathroom to shower. For a moment at least she was cool, but when she lay down on the bed, the satin sheets seemed too warm. She closed her eyes, willing herself to sleep, but when sleep didn't come, she got up and, pulling her robe on, went to stand out on the balcony. The men had retired, and the gardens were quiet.

There was no moon tonight, and everything was hushed and still. She could barely make out the swimming pool, and suddenly she found herself thinking longingly of how cool the water would be. Quickly she threw the robe aside and reached for her bathing suit.

Barefoot, Catherine slipped quietly from the room, down the silent corridors, out to the patio. For a moment she found herself thinking that this was a first for her. She smiled, because everything this past week had been a first. Tomorrow she would become the serious Professor Adair again. But tonight she could still dream.

Above her in the trees Catherine heard a lark singing, and she stopped to listen to the song that was sweeter than any music she'd ever heard. Then it seemed to her as though she could hear voices from the river. She listened. No, not from the river, but beyond from some distant, unfathomable place she could not see.

Then the voices faded. The song of the lark stilled, and the night became silent once again.

Catherine lowered herself into the water. The coolness covered her, and when she looked up at the infinity of the stars, it seemed to her that they were so close she could reach up and touch them. She lay motionless in the water, enveloped by the night, suspended somewhere in time.

She didn't know how long she floated that way, but suddenly she heard a sound, and when she looked up, she saw David standing beside the pool. As she watched, he dropped the robe he was wearing and stood motionless, naked.

"Catherine," he said, so softly that only she could hear, and came into the pool beside her. Before she could speak, he put his arms around her. His mouth covered hers as they slid slowly beneath the surface of the water.

He tugged at her suit, pulling it down over her body, catching it before it fell to the bottom of the pool. When they surfaced, she, too, was naked, and he brought her back into his arms.

His mouth was hungry against hers. "I want you," he said. "Oh, Catherine, I want you."

"David, we can't. Not here."

But he was past hearing as he ran his arms over her shoulders and down to her breasts, cupping them, urging her closer. "You feel so good," he whispered as he wound his legs around hers and took her with him below the surface of the water again.

David's hands were cool against her breasts, but his mouth was as warm as the blood that pounded through her veins. Catherine felt the thrust of his masculinity against her legs, and she began to tremble with anticipation. "We can't," she whispered again, even as her hands slipped over his wet buttocks to press him closer.

He kissed her again, and she was lost. Lost, as he led her to the side of the pool and lifted her so that her legs were around his waist. With a low cry of need he joined his body to hers.

David's lips ground hard against hers, deeper, closer, as she began to move against him in a frenzy of passion that matched his own. He left her mouth to find her breast, to take a cool bud between his teeth to bite, as he had bitten the olive a lifetime ago. She cried out, not in pain but in joy and offered it to him gladly, proudly, shivering with unimaginable pleasure when he soothed it with his tongue.

She whispered his name as she tightened her legs around his back and dug her fingernails into his shoulders.

He kissed her mouth while he plunged hard against her, holding her as she clung to him, clung because she knew if she didn't, she would spin away, up to the stars.

Then the stars shattered and fell and covered them, and they sank beneath the water, mouths and bodies clinging, until not even the larks could hear their murmured words of love.

Chapter 12

The place that Fletcher had decided upon and that David agreed was a good point to start their excavations lay just on the other side of the sand dunes from their first site.

"You're probably right about this," David told Fletcher as he surveyed the site, strategically located between Amonset's tomb and Batsira's. He grinned wryly at the older man. "Next time you take a week off maybe you'll come up with the location of Alifa's tomb."

"Or perhaps Catherine will." Fletcher looked fondly at her. "You're still sure we'll find her in Philae, aren't you?"

"Yes, but I don't suppose I'll ever be able to convince our fearless leader."

"Your fearless leader has just had a lesson in humility," David said. "One of these days I might just give in to that idea of yours."

Not that he believed they would find the queen's tomb there, he thought as he saw the sudden look of excitement in Catherine's dark eyes, but it wouldn't hurt to let her have a look around. Maybe after this next excavation, if they were successful in finding Ramah's tomb, they would plan to take another couple of days off and go to Philae. The island was a beautiful spot, and he would enjoy showing it to her. David repressed a sigh, thinking of all the places he would enjoy going with her.

It had been three nights ago that they'd made love. He still remembered how cool Catherine's body had felt against his, how softly pliant and yielding. She'd been so beautiful afterward, her eyes still dazed with passion, her breath coming fast against his cheek. She'd whispered his name in the stillness of the night, and he'd thought his heart would burst with loving her.

He didn't think he could stand another day or night without touching her. It might very well be a couple of months before they would be able to take any time off again to be alone together; he didn't intend to wait that long to make love to Catherine.

David looked at her. He thought what a complex woman she was and of how she had changed from the woman he'd first met in Cairo. She'd built barriers around herself, and although he'd managed to break past some of them, others were still there. He knew that it would take every bit of his willpower to get her to move in with him, but he thought that she would—with a little persuasion—if he could just get past that proper Puritan attitude of hers.

He watched her as Fletcher explained where they would begin the dig. Her dark hair fell about her face and when she leaned forward to look at the sketches Fletcher had made, David saw the outline of her breasts. He wanted her with an ache that was painful in its intensity, an ache that went beyond a physical need.

Not since he was a child had David felt the need to be close to anyone. His relationship with his mother these last few years had been little more than polite. He had friends whose companionship he enjoyed, and there'd been women he'd been fond of. But never before, except with his father when he was a child, had he felt such a strong bond with another person. Not until now.

With Catherine David felt complete for the first time in his life. He wanted to be with her, to make love with her, go to sleep with her and wake up with her. He wanted to do all the things that two people in love did. He wanted to sit beside her in a movie and share a box of popcorn. He wanted to walk on a beach in the rain with her, listen to a symphony with her, argue politics with her. He wanted to share his life with her, because she was his life and because he knew deep down in his soul he would never feel about another woman the way he felt about Catherine.

Before they went to the new location, the archeologists returned to their first excavation site. The Egyptian antiquities people were still there, but the cataloging had almost been completed. The artifacts and all of the other things they'd found in Potiphera's tomb had been packed up and sent to Cairo. The sarcophagus would be shipped the following week.

"We had a robbery here a few nights ago," the man in charge told David.

"Didn't you have a guard posted?"

"Of course, sir, but the thieves knocked the poor man unconscious before he could cry out. He's in the hospital in Edfu with a fractured skull. They carried off whatever gold they could get their hands on and some very good artifacts. I suggest that if you plan to begin excavations near here you post an extra guard once you get into the tomb."

"I will," David said with a frown. Tomb robbers had been common enough in Egypt since the time of the pharaohs, which was why today there were always guards posted at archeological sites. Thieves rarely tried the well-known tombs at Luxor, in the Valley of the Kings or even the temple of Edfu. But theirs would be a remote camp, he would have to take extra precautions.

It took Nawab and his crew more than a day to move all of the equipment to the new site beyond the dunes and almost a week to set up the generator, the platforms, winches and the detection equipment.

Unlike the other site, there was a small oasis there, and that's where they set up the tents. With the temperature over ninety by midmorning, they would need whatever protection they could get from the sun. But as fierce as the heat was, it was nothing compared to the flies. They were the scourge of an Egyptian summer, and the only way to keep them away was to carry a fly whisk and keep it in constant motion. The Egyptians didn't bother. Except for an occasional flick of a hand they kept on doing whatever they were doing while flies crawled around their eyes, their noses and their mouths.

"My idea of hell would be to be in Egypt this time of year without a fly whisk," Fletcher told David one hot afternoon. "How in the devil can these fellows let the rotten things crawl all over their faces that way?"

"They're used to it, I guess." David flicked the horsetail whisk and, looking at Fletcher, asked, "Feeling all right these days?"

"Sure, I'm fine. Abdel's doctor took good care of me. Fixed me right up. Did you and Catherine have a good cruise?"

David nodded. "Yes, it was fine."

"Uh huh." Fletcher raised an eyebrow. "She's changed, hasn't she? Really quite beautiful these days. She's lost some of that aloofness and seems more at ease with herself." Fletcher grinned at David. "The two of you seem to be getting on better as well."

"We're getting along. She's a remarkable woman. Extremely capable."

"Capable?" Fletcher grinned. "She's a hell of a lot more than that, Dave. She's an extremely desirable woman. If I were ten years younger... But I'm not, so I'd damn well better get back to work."

Fletcher turned away, and for a moment David felt a flush of anger at the thought of another man finding Catherine desirable. Without stopping to think, he hurried over to where she was standing talking to Massaud and said, "I'd like to speak to you for a minute, Catherine."

She looked at him, startled at his tone. "I'll be back later, Massaud. I can't wait to read what you have."

"Read what?" David asked.

"More of the transcript. Massaud worked on it while he was in Cairo. He'll give it to me tonight to read."

"You're going to be too busy tonight to read anything."

"What do you mean?" Catherine stopped and faced him.

"You're moving in with me, Catherine."

"I'm what?"

"You're moving in with me. I want you, and I can't stand being away from you like this."

"But we can't do that, David. What would the others think?"

"I don't give a damn what anybody thinks."

"But I do!" Catherine shook her head. "I'm sorry, David, but it's quite impossible."

"No, it's not! Dammit, Catherine, we're not children."

"Then stop acting like a child." Angrily she shooed some flies away. "I won't have everyone in camp knowing that you and I . . . that we . . ."

"That we're lovers?" David took her hands. "I can't just turn off the way I feel about you, Catherine. What's happened between us, what we shared on the boat has been one of the most important things in my life. Doesn't it mean anything to you?"

"It means a great deal to me." She stepped away from him. "But it's over, David."

"What . . . ?" His face went white. "What in the hell are you talking about?"

"What happened between us shouldn't have happened. You're a young man, David. You—"

"Oh, God," he growled. "Not that again."

"Yes, that again," Catherine said firmly. "Whether you like it or not, David, nothing can change the fact that I'm older than you are." Her chin came up. "I don't have affairs, casual or otherwise. What happened between us was wonderful, and it's something I'll always treasure. It was an idyllic dream, but this—" she swept her hand out over the desert "—this is reality, David. We're going to be working together for the next six or eight months, possibly longer. It's better to end this—whatever it is between us—now."

"This . . . whatever it is?"

Catherine put her hand on his arm. "When you get married, it should be to someone your own age or younger, David, someone who can give you children."

"I didn't know we'd discussed marriage."

"We hadn't." Catherine felt her face flush. "I only meant—"

"Would it make a difference if I proposed?"

"David, please." She averted her face. "Don't make this any more difficult than it already is."

"Is that what you want?" he insisted. "Do you want me to ask you to marry me?" He turned her to face him. "Do you, Catherine? Because if you do, then I will."

"David..."

"Will you marry me, Catherine?"

"You don't mean that," she whispered.

"Don't I?" His hands tightened on her arms. "I'm waiting for your answer, Catherine. *Will* you marry me?"

She looked at him, her eyes bright with unshed tears. Slowly she shook her head.

"I see." David took a deep, painful breath. "We could have had something special," he said. "I don't think the fact that I'm a few years younger than you has anything to do with your wanting to put an end to this, Catherine. I don't think you have the courage to make a commitment."

"David..."

But he'd already turned away.

Catherine told herself that it was better this way. If it had to end it was better now before either of them was hurt too badly.

But oh, could anything ever hurt this much again? She looked at David's retreating back, and more than anything in her life she wanted to run after him. She wanted to tell him that she loved him, that she would marry him, that she would do anything he wanted her to to save their love.

But Catherine remained where she stood. She only waited until he disappeared into his tent, then she went slowly back to the camp.

Catherine switched the lamp on and opened the pages Massaud had translated. She looked down at the words written there, but she didn't see them; all she saw was David's face when he had turned and walked away from her. She'd hurt him—she knew that now, she'd known it then. But this . . . whatever it was they felt for each other would pass. There'd been women in his life before he had known her; there would be women in his life when she was gone.

Catherine put her head down on the desk. He would get over her. But would she ever get over him?

Finally she sat up and dried her eyes. Then she turned the lamp on the pages in front of her and began to read:

> The ceremony where the king took to his wife the fair Alifa was an opulent one. She became his property, his most valued chattel, to be cherished as the consort to a god, accorded the most exceptional privilege of physical contact with him.
>
> On the day she was wed her skin was oiled and perfumed, her almond eyes were traced with kohl. She wore a fine linen gown of the purest white with a draped and pleated robe. Her hair was covered by a heavy wig upon which a circlet of gold was placed. A jeweled pendant hung around her neck, and she wore a golden bracelet upon which a scarab beetle was carved.

It was I who wept when she knelt before the king. Her face was pale but serene when he placed his hand upon her head and said, "Arise, my queen."

Again when it was time to help her into the bridal chamber I wept, and it was she who comforted me. "Do not weep, my dear friend," she whispered. "This is my destiny, and I cannot refuse it any more than I can refuse my death when it comes. Go now, for my king must not see your tears."

In the morning I found her standing by a window, looking out toward Mother Nile. "Is it done then?" I asked. She turned to me, and I do not think that ever again will I see such sadness on another's face.

"It is done," she said.

Tears blinded Catherine's eyes and fell upon the manuscript. She wept, as the handmaiden had wept, for the young queen who had yielded herself to a man she didn't love. She wept for herself, because she loved David and had lost him.

Catherine put the transcript aside and turned off the lamp. When she'd undressed and lay down on her bed, her thoughts turned to Alifa. Had the young queen ever longed for a lover to whom she could respond with her whole heart? Or had she gone to her tomb never knowing the joy of love?

Catherine closed her eyes thinking about the joy of love. It was a very long time before she went to sleep.

At the end of the first week the archeologists found the first stone steps.

"This is it!" Fletcher's face was alive with excitement. He hugged Catherine, picked her up and swung her off her feet. "We've found it. We've found Ramah."

"Congratulations, Fletcher." David shook Fletcher's hand. "Now let's get back to work."

"Sure, Dave." Fletcher wiped the sweat off his forehead and looked at Catherine with a puzzled frown. She knew that he'd expected more of a response from David, but David hadn't been big on responses this past week. He'd had little to say to any of them and almost nothing to say to her.

Catherine blamed herself, because she hadn't behaved in a professional manner. If she hadn't begun the affair with David, none of this would have happened. She understood his anger, but she didn't know how to handle it. All she could do was go on being pleasant and throw herself into the work ahead of them.

The Egyptians, sure now that they would find another tomb, were enthusiastic workers. They forged ahead in spite of the heat that became more intense each day.

By the end of the fourth week they'd uncovered five steps and found the entrance to the tomb.

Catherine lost more weight, and there were times when she felt as though the sun were sapping every bit of strength out of her body. Her skin burned over the tan. She covered herself with sunscreen lotion, but the lotion attracted the flies, and the flies almost drove her to distraction.

But the biggest distraction was David. He'd lost weight, too. His body was as lean and as hard as his face, his skin tanned the color of copper. He worked harder than any of them, driving himself mercilessly under the broiling sun. There were dark patches of fatigue under his eyes, hollows in his cheeks, lines that hadn't been there before. A hundred times a day Catherine wanted to tell him that she was sorry, that perhaps she'd been wrong. A dozen times every night, lying awake on her cot, she was tempted to go to him. But she didn't.

Not until the night of the robbery.

She'd finally fallen asleep when she heard a shout, followed by the sound of gunfire. She sat up, startled. There were more cries. She pulled a robe on over her pajamas and ran from the tent.

Men raced into the night, shouting as they ran. Catherine heard Fletcher yell, "They're taking the Jeep," then saw the beam of headlights stabbing through the darkness. Nawab ran forward, his son, Azan, right behind him.

Catherine saw the Jeep, the four men in it, the spit of fire from their rifles. Suddenly David sprinted forward, firing as he ran. Shots split the night. She heard the splintering of the windshield. The Jeep swerved, righted itself, accelerated. She saw David, gun raised, almost in front of the Jeep, firing. The Jeep swerved again, heading straight for David. With a terrible sound it hit him and hurled his body backward.

Catherine ran forward, screaming, not even aware that the Jeep had stopped and that guns were blazing on both sides.

David lay facedown in the sand. Catherine knelt beside him. She touched his shoulder, and her hand came away wet with blood. She gasped, then carefully rolled him over and saw that he'd been shot just below the shoulder. Blood ran from the wound, his face was white and still.

"Is he...?" Fletcher knelt beside her. "Good God, Catherine, is he dead?"

"No!" she cried. "No, of course he isn't dead!" Forcing herself to be calm, she put her fingers on the side of David's neck and felt the slow, steady beat of his heart. "He's unconscious, Fletcher. We've got to get him into his tent where there's some light."

"Right. Just as second, I'll get one of the boys." He stood up and called out, "Sahibzada, Yahya, over here."

The two men ran over, and with Catherine cautioning them, carried David to his tent. She switched the light on and had to bite down hard on her lower lip to keep from crying out. She knew little about bullet wounds, but this one looked serious. She grabbed a clean towel to try to stem the flow of blood and held it as tightly to the wound as she could.

"David?" she said, and when he didn't respond, she told Fletcher to apply pressure to the wound while she wet a cloth and placed it on David's forehead. There was a knot over his left eye that frightened her almost as much as the bullet hole in his shoulder.

"David? David, please. Please open your eyes," she pleaded.

"S'right." His eyelids fluttered open. "Damn thing hit me."

"It sure as hell did," Fletcher said. "Take it easy, Dave. We're going to get you into Edfu to a doctor."

"Don't need..." He tried to sit up, but a hiss of pain whistled through his teeth, and he fell back on his cot.

"The Jeep's probably out of commission." Fletcher secured the towel around David's arm. "I'll bring the truck around. Several of our men have been wounded, we'll take them in, too."

"I'm going with you," Catherine said. "Please have someone get a pair of jeans and a shirt from my tent."

Fletcher nodded, and when he left the tent, David said, "The Jeep hit me?"

"You hit *it*! What were you trying to do, stop the Jeep with your bare hands? You could have been killed. You almost were! What happened? Who were they? What—"

"Take it easy."

"Take it easy? You were almost killed, and you're telling me to take it easy?" Tears ran down her cheeks. "Oh God, David, if anything happened to you . . ." She couldn't go on.

"You'd what Catherine?" He reached out and touched the side of her face.

"I wouldn't want to live," she said.

"Love..." He closed his eyes. His hand dropped from her face. "Head hurts," he mumbled.

"I know, David. Rest now. I'm here. I'll take care of you."

Two of the workers entered the tent with Fletcher. "Handle him carefully," she cautioned them. "You drive, Fletcher, I'll hold David steady."

Catherine was calm now. She told the men what to do and how to place David in the back of the truck. She crawled in beside him and cradled his head on her lap. There were other men in the truck and two bodies covered with canvas. She recognized Azan, who sat with his bandaged leg stuck out in front of him, and said, "Does anyone have any idea who the thieves were?"

"We know who one of them was." He kicked a canvas-covered body. "Gamal," he said. "The man Mr. David fired."

Catherine closed her eyes. Why? she thought. Dear God, why did this have to happen? Gamal was young. He had his whole life ahead of him. Why did he have to die like that?

She held David close, and when he groaned and muttered, "Where we going?" she soothed the hair back from his forehead and quieted him.

"To Edfu. There's a hospital there. You're going to be all right, David. You're going to be all right, darling."

"You called me darling."

"Shh." She bent and brushed his lips with hers, then held him as the truck sped over the rocky road that would take them to Edfu.

Chapter 13

All that night and the following day Catherine stayed by David's side. Not until she was sure that he was out of danger did she allow Fletcher to take her back to the camp. She returned to the hospital the next morning to find David sitting up in bed trying to feed himself with his left hand.

"Let me help you," she said.

"I can manage."

"No, you can't. The doctor said you shouldn't do anything strenuous for a few days."

"Strenuous! What's strenuous about eating scrambled eggs and ham?"

"You can't cut the ham."

"I'll eat it with my fingers."

Catherine sat down on the bed beside him. "Please let me help you, David. You might hurt your shoulder or your head. You have a concussion. You have to be careful."

David started to say no again, but he saw on her face the same anxious expression she'd had ever since the night he'd been wounded. He only vaguely remembered being brought to the hospital in the back of the truck and Catherine holding him in her arms. Through the blur of pain and ebbing consciousness he'd been aware of the softness of her body and of the strength of her arms. He remembered drifting off with the knowledge that when he opened his eyes again, Catherine would still be with him. And she had been, all through that long and painful night and the following day.

He covered her hand with his and said, "I'm all right now, Catherine. The doctor says I'm going to be fine. Don't worry."

"I'm not worried." She tried to smile, but her smile faded, and her hand tightened on his, because she felt again the same terrible surge of fear she'd known when she heard the thud of his body against the Jeep and had seen him slam to the ground. Tears stung her eyes, and she looked away.

"What is it, Catherine?"

She swallowed hard and, visibly pulling herself together, said, "I'm sorry, David. It's just that I... I was so afraid. When I saw you run in front of that Jeep—"

"I didn't mean to run in front of it. I just wanted to get close enough to wing the guy driving it." He hesitated. "Fletcher told me that Gamal was one of them and that he was killed when he jumped from the Jeep. It's such a damn waste, Catherine. He was only a kid."

"He was twenty-five years old, David. Old enough to take responsibility for his actions."

"Yeah, I know, but..." He shook his head. "Did they try to take anything besides the Jeep?"

"Some of the equipment." She put the tray on his lap. "You've got to eat," she said, and picked up the fork.

"No one's ever fed me before."

"Not even when you were a baby?" She smiled and gave him a forkful of eggs. When he finished it, she cut the ham up in small pieces. "How's your shoulder this morning?"

"Sore. The doctor said it'll be okay in a day or two." He paused while Catherine fed him. "He said my head would be, too. I hope he's right."

"Still have the headache?"

"Yeah. A million guys playing a Sousa march with drums." He shook his head when she offered him another forkful of eggs and slumped down in the bed. "I can't eat any more, Catherine."

"All right." She picked up the breakfast tray and put it on the bureau. When she came back, she sat beside him again and said, "Would you like to rest?"

"I guess so." He reached for her hand. "If you'll stay for a while."

"I'll stay."

He looked up at her. "I thought I'd lost you," he said.

"David—"

"No, don't say anything now. We'll talk about it later. It's enough that you're here." He closed his eyes, but there was a pucker between his brows, and Catherine knew he was in pain. Very gently she smoothed his unruly hair back from his forehead and began to massage his temples.

"Yes, do that," David said sleepily. "That's nice, Catherine. Nice."

In a little while his breathing evened, and he slept. He looked so vulnerable lying here, Catherine thought. His face was scratched and pale under the tan. His hair was sun streaked, and his light brows bleached almost white by the long hours in the sun. She studied his face, the planes and the hollows, the strong nose and the jutting chin, the full and kissable lips. She knew that if anything had happened to him, something would have died within her. She didn't know where their relationship was going, she only knew that David had become the most important person in her life and that she loved him. She was relieved that she'd finally let her mind form the words her lips had been unable to say. She loved him.

Four days later, in spite of the doctor's objections, David insisted on leaving the hospital.

"I want to get out of here," he fretted. "The headache's gone, and except for the arm feeling stiff and a little sore, I'm okay."

Catherine drove him back to camp in the Jeep. She tried to be especially careful when they turned off the highway onto the dirt road leading to the excavation site, but it was difficult not to jar the vehicle. She gripped the wheel and glanced at David each time she slowed for a bump. Finally he said, "It's okay, Catherine, I won't break."

"I'm so afraid of hurting you." She rested her hand on his thigh to reassure herself that he was all right. Their relationship had changed during these past few days. It wasn't quite where it had been before they'd returned to the excavation, but some of the tension between them had eased. They hadn't spoken about their relationship, but she knew that sooner or later they would have to. There would be little chance for them to be alone once they returned to the camp, and after a moment of indecision Catherine slowed the Jeep and stopped. "I think we'd better talk," she said.

"Yes." David turned on the seat so that he could look at her.

"About us, about the way things have been between us these last few weeks. I know you've been angry with me, David." She looked at him, and her eyes were troubled. "Maybe angry isn't the word. You offered me your love, and I turned away from it because I was afraid. Because I'm older..."

"Damn it, Catherine—"

"No, please, David, let me finish. I *am* older than you are. Maybe six years isn't all that much, but if we married and you wanted children, it might be difficult."

Catherine wanted to touch him, but she knew if she did she wouldn't be able to say all the things that needed to be said. "I've read so much about you these last few years, David. I resented your success, because the things that came so hard for me came so easily for you—your work, the grants, the successful digs. I read all the articles you published, and even when I admired your brilliance I gnashed my teeth, because you were doing all the things I wanted to do."

She reached for his hand. "I read about the women you dated, too, David." She caressed the back of his hand with her thumb and didn't look at him. "I don't know when you found the time or the energy to work."

"The press has a way of exaggerating, Catherine," David said defensively. "But we're both old enough to have had experiences."

"Experiences?" She hesitated. "I had my first, my only experience when I was twenty-one, David."

"Your only...?" A look of disbelief crossed his features. "Come *on*, Catherine. You're a passionate woman. I can't believe that, not unless your first affair lasted for fifteen years."

"It didn't, it lasted for one week." She'd never told this to anyone, but suddenly she felt the need to tell David, to try to make him understand how it had been for her for all those lonely years.

"I was twenty-one, in my first year of my master's program, when my father insisted I take the summer off," she began. "He bought me a ticket to Jamaica and made a reservation for me at a hotel on the north shore. I met someone there."

She told him then, about Ron Palmer and his friend and about what had happened that day on the skiff.

"I felt so used, so dumb," Catherine said when she'd finished. "And guilty. God, David, I felt so guilty. I used to lie awake nights thinking about what a terrible thing I'd done, what a fool I'd been."

David took her hand. "But you hadn't done anything except trust some slimy kid who got his kicks out of seducing somebody as naive as you were." He tightened his hand on hers. "I know how you must have felt, Catherine, how hurt and disillusioned and yes, all right, foolish. But I can't believe you'd let something like that affect your whole life."

"It wasn't just that, David. I was gun-shy for a while, but I got over it in a year or two. But by then I was so involved with getting my Ph.D. that I didn't have time to think about anything else. After that there was the job at the university and trying to prove myself in my profession. I was just too busy. Archeology was, is, my life. A long time ago I told myself that it was all that mattered—I didn't need anything else.

Catherine looked at him, wanting with all her heart for him to understand. "When I came to Egypt, everything started to change," she said. "I became aware of things I'd never been aware of before. I felt things I'd never felt.

It was as though in some way I couldn't even begin to understand I was changing, becoming someone different, someone I didn't even know." She hesitated, uncertain now whether or not to go on. "I began having dreams, David."

"Dreams? What kind of dreams?"

"About Alifa. They're so real, David, so vivid that sometimes it seems to me that I'm Alifa and she's me, and when I wake up I'm not sure where she ends and I begin."

David's brows drew together in a frown. "What are you talking about, Catherine? I don't understand."

"Neither do I. Maybe it's the heat. Maybe it's my obsession with Egypt. With Alifa." She touched his face. "Maybe it's you, David, the way I feel about you, the way you touch my heart. When you and I became lovers, you taught me things about myself that I'd never suspected were there. I felt so alive, so *electrified* with love." Tears misted Catherine's eyes, and for a moment she couldn't go on. "That frightened me as much as my dreams about Alifa," she said.

David didn't speak. Wordlessly he put his good arm around Catherine and drew her close to him. He was glad she'd told him about her first sad experience with love. He understood better now why she'd held herself so aloof, even why she dressed the way she did.

But he didn't understand about the dreams or her strange obsession with Alifa.

David remembered the first time he'd ever seen Catherine. It had been at the Pyramid of Gizeh when she'd been so frightened, so vulnerable. But once her fear had passed, he'd seen only the self-possessed, coldly professional woman. It hadn't been until that early morning at Edfu when she'd stood beside the swimming pool with her arms raised to the sun that he'd glimpsed another side of her. He still remembered how he'd felt that morning, the sudden heat that made his body tighten with need. The certainty that before this dig was over he would possess Catherine Adair.

But he hadn't counted on falling in love with her.

He kissed her now, his lips gentle and undemanding on hers. "What do you want to do about us, Catherine?" he asked when he released her. "You know that I love you, and I think that you love me."

"David..." His name trembled on her lips. "Yes," she said. "Yes, David, I love you. But I need time. I've never been in love before, I have to get used to the feeling. Can you be patient with me? Can we, for now, just be friends?"

"Friends?" He raised an eyebrow in disbelief.

"Yes. Please."

David hesitated. At last he said, "All right, Catherine. If that's the way you want it, I'll play things your way." He cupped her chin and kissed her. For a moment she resisted him, then her lips softened under his, and she sighed with pleasure.

When the kiss ended, David looked at her. "You'd better get going before I change my mind and haul you off behind one of those sand dunes," he growled.

And felt a wonderful flare of hope, because for a moment she looked toward the dunes, and there was regret in her eyes.

Three days after David returned to camp the crew broke through the door to expose a tunnel leading downward. He pulled the sling off and tossed it aside. It might have been the job of the Egyptian workers to clear the rubble away, but this was David's dig, and he wanted to be a part of every phase of it. So did Catherine and Fletcher. Once a six-foot passageway had been cleared, they began dusting the walls of the tunnel.

"Absolutely amazing." Fletcher held his flashlight up to the walls. "Look how vivid the colors are." He pointed to the figures. "See here? Armies marching, men with daggers, bow and arrows, scimitars and swords. Look, Catherine, the chariot at the head of the column and the warrior with the breastplate and headpiece, that has to be Ramah."

"You're right!" David said, as excited as Fletcher now, pleased that he'd let himself be talked into going ahead with the search for Ramah's tomb. This would be something, along with the discovery of Potiphera's tomb, to please the Smithsonian committee. The two finds were certainly worthwhile, and he was excited at the prospect of the work ahead as they probed deeper toward the burial chamber. For a moment he could almost forget that he still wasn't any closer to the real reason he'd come to Egypt. He still hadn't found the tomb of the young queen.

David and Catherine had talked about Alifa last night, and he had agreed to read the transcripts. He didn't give much credence to them, but Catherine still believed they would find the answer to the young queen's disappearance there.

Two weeks had passed since their discovery of wall paintings, paintings that continued as the archeologists delved farther and farther along the corridor, hoping to find the sealed door leading to the burial chamber.

David's headache was gone. His right arm was still stiff, but not enough to slow him down. Every morning he and the rest of them started work just before daylight, because by ten in the morning the temperature was well over a hundred degrees. By one o'clock, even below ground in the passageway, the heat was almost past bearing. That's when they usually broke for lunch. From then on, until four when it began to cool off a bit, they worked cleaning the potsherds in the shade. Only when the sun began to go down behind the dunes did they resume their work on the tomb.

At night the desert slowly cooled, but still heat rose from the sand, and the canvas tents were hot and uncomfortable. Night after night David lay awake, cursing the heat and wishing he had the courage to go to Catherine. He'd promised her he would wait, but the waiting was difficult. Sleep was almost impossible, and when it came he dreamed of her, and he would awake with a start, his body covered with sweat and aching with need.

On one such night, when the thoughts of Catherine were so strong that David knew if he didn't do something he would go roaring into her tent, he switched on the light and began to read the transcript that Massaud had translated for Catherine.

As he read he began to form a picture of the young queen in his mind. He saw her as she was at fifteen when she bade farewell to her island home, when she'd stood silently on the barge as Philae faded from view. He imagined her being led into the bridal chamber and thought he understood how terrible it must have been to have given herself to a man who was older than her father, even though that man was a king.

> Two years have passed. My queen has adjusted to her life. The king is a good man, and he appears to be fond of her. Even though she has borne him no children he has taken no other wife, but he spends more and more time with his favorite concubine, It-

un-hab. I do not know if this hurts my mistress, or if she is relieved that she seldom must perform her wifely duties.

There is much talk now of the war with the Assyrians. Often I have seen warrior chieftains arrive to confer with the king and his counsel. Only last week a noble warrior whom I had not seen before arrived to confer with King Amonset. He was young and fair of form and face. As it happened, Alifa was with the king when the warrior appeared. He bowed low before them as is the custom, then I saw him look upon Alifa, and it seemed from where I stood that I saw the breath catch in his throat.

Alifa smiled, for she is always gracious, but suddenly her smile faltered. She looked at him, and it was as though the king and all who were in the room were not there. There was only Alifa and the warrior, caught and held in each other's eyes.

I scarcely dared to breathe until the moment passed and Alifa excused herself and left. When we were alone, her step was unsteady and her face was flushed. "Are you not well, mistress?" I asked.

"I am well," she replied, "but for a moment a strange feeling overcame me, a feeling I have never before experienced."

I think I knew then what had changed for her. And I was right, of course, for after that first meeting nothing was ever the same.

David stared at the words before him. So it was true, there had been another man in Alifa's life, just as Fletcher and Catherine had suggested. But who had he been? The transcript referred to him only as a noble warrior, a *nameless* warrior.

He stood up and looked out from the open flap of his tent. The camp was dark but for the single light in front of the excavation site where a guard was on duty. For a moment David was tempted to go to Catherine's tent and ask her for other pages of the transcript she had so that he could read more of the story. But he knew that if he went to her it would be for her.

With a sigh David turned back into his tent where he snapped the light off and lay down once again on his cot, unaware that Catherine, sleepless on her own cot, had seen him standing at the entrance to his tent. For a moment her heart had beaten fast with anticipation. She wondered if she would have the courage to refuse him if he came and wasn't sure whether she was relieved or disappointed when he turned back inside.

Catherine lay for a long time after David's light had gone off, picturing him stretched out on his cot. She thought how it would be if she were lying close to him, her head resting in the hollow of his shoulder while he caressed her back.

Finally Catherine fell asleep and dreamed of a time when love was new and anything was possible.

Dreamed...

...the memory of him and of the way he had looked at her stayed with her in the days that followed. She had but to close her eyes to recall him. How handsome he was! How strong his body, how straight and tall. How young. Her face burned with shame, because she could not help but compare him with her lord and husband.

She should not think such thoughts. The king, in his way, was kind to her. He treated her with courtesy, and he took no other wife. At first she had been ashamed when it became common knowledge that he had taken It-un-hab to his bed, but her relief had been greater than her shame because now Amonset rarely called for her to attend him in the night.

This evening she went alone to her favorite spot overlooking Mother Nile. As the shadows of evening fell the birds came to roost in the willow trees and on the other bank she could see farmers coming from the fields, leading their oxen and water buffalo to drink from the river.

She stood there, silent and alone, while the god of the night drew his cloak about him. She was about to turn back to the path she had taken when she heard a sound coming from the path behind her. "Who is there?" she asked.

"It is I, my queen." He knelt on one knee before her.

"No, don't . . ." Her voice quivered like the song of a frightened bird. "Don't kneel before me."

He stood then, splendid in his linen kilt. His chest, except for the golden collar, was bare. His feet were clad in leather sandals. His legs were strong and straight.

"I did not mean to frighten you," he said.

"You did not."

"Do you come here often?"

She nodded. "It is quiet here and I am alone."

"If you prefer to remain alone I will leave."

"No." She held up a hand to restrain him. "You may stay."

"The king does not mind that you come here alone?"

"My lord is . . . otherwise occupied this evening." She did not add what everyone at court knew, that her husband had retired to his chambers with It-un-hab.

"Would my queen like to walk a bit?"

She looked at him, barely able to see his face in the darkness. "Yes," she said, "I will walk with you."

He rested his hand on her arm, and it was as though she had been touched with fire. "Come," he said. "Let us go this way."

The shadows closed about them as they stepped into the silence of the night.

The silence.

The sky was still dark when Catherine awoke. She lay for a moment, wondering where she was, where he had gone. She opened her mouth to call his name, but before she could, she became aware that she was here in a tent, alone, not walking along the banks of the Nile—and she didn't know whose name to call.

Catherine sat up and ran her hands through her hair. She'd been dreaming again, but this time the dream had seemed so real.

Morning sounds interrupted her thoughts as she swung her legs out of the cot and pulled her robe on over her pajamas. She smelled the aroma of fresh-brewed coffee and knew that she should hurry to the shower and dress for breakfast. But she stood where she was, looking around her as though she'd never seen this place before.

Chapter 14

On a Sunday morning, when the desert air was so hot and still that it seemed as though everything stopped and waited, they uncovered the wooden door that led to the tomb.

Triumphant and excited, Fletcher clapped David on the back. "This is it, Dave!"

"Let's get some of this dirt away so we can find the seal," David said. "Hand me the brush, will you, Massaud. The seal should be about there."

While Massaud and Fletcher held the lamps, Catherine helped David dust the door.

"Have you found it?" Fletcher asked impatiently. "Let me try. It has to be there."

"I've found it! Yes, here it is." David brushed the dirt away.

Fletcher leaned over his shoulder to read aloud the hieroglyphic writing: "This tomb is a gift from King

Amonset II, ruler of Upper and Lower Egypt, to his noble warrior, Ramah of Thebes."

David clapped Fletcher's shoulder. "You were right, Fletch. Congratulations. It's Ramah's tomb all right."

"No." The word that Catherine uttered was so low that only David heard. He turned quickly. In the pale light of the cavernous passageway her face was puzzled, doubtful. She stared at the seal, her lips compressed, and shook her head.

David frowned. "What's the matter?"

"Nothing. I don't know why I said that. It's just that I...I have a feeling that something's wrong." She glanced quickly at Fletcher, glad that he was too occupied to have heard her, then knelt on the floor to better study the seal.

It took them almost all of that day to completely uncover the door. They stopped in midafternoon for a sandwich, but returned to work as soon as they had finished eating. By dark they were all hot and exhausted, and David called a halt.

"We can finish in the morning," he said. "Let's have our showers and something to eat."

"You go ahead." Fletcher mopped the perspiration from his face with a bandanna and took a drink from the canteen fastened on his belt. "I want to stay with it a little longer."

"No, Fletch, you're as tired as the rest of us. It's better to get some rest and tackle this tomorrow."

"But—"

"No buts, Fletch. Come on. What you need is a good cold beer."

And a week's rest in air-conditioning, David thought as he followed the older man out of the passageway. Fletcher didn't look good. His color was bad, and like the rest of them he'd lost weight these past few weeks. David hoped it wasn't the malaria again, but he suspected that it was and that Fletcher hadn't told him. He decided to keep an eye on his friend, and at the first sign of another attack he'd send him to Cairo for treatment.

But David didn't speak of that when the four of them sat at the dinner table that night. The talk was excited, jubilant, for they knew that tomorrow they'd break through the door to Ramah's tomb.

And after that? Catherine wondered as she looked across the table at David. After all the work inside the tomb, the cataloging and all the things that went with a fresh discovery? Would she be able to convince him to go to Philae when this was over, or would he persist in resuming the search for the missing tomb here?

Once they got into the burial chamber, it would take them at least a month, even with the assistance of the Egyptian Antiquities people, to do everything that needed to be done. The Smithsonian had extended David's grant, but her sabbatical would be over at the end of summer, and she would have to be back in Arizona for the fall term unless they found Alifa's tomb. If they did she would stay in Egypt, with or without a sabbatical. If they didn't find the tomb... but she wouldn't allow herself to even think that.

None of them slept very much that night, so eager were they for morning to come when they could move aside the great door and enter the tomb.

What had Ramah been like? Catherine wondered as she lay sleepless on her cot. They knew so little about him, only that he had served under King Amonset, that he'd been a courageous warrior, a favorite at court and that he'd died when he was only twenty-four.

Had he known Alifa, or had he served the king before Amonset had married her? What if Ramah had been

Alifa's lover? Catherine smiled to herself. The idea was farfetched but nice to think about. Perhaps tomorrow they would find the answers to a lot of questions, even questions about the young queen.

The four of them were dressed and having coffee the next morning when the sun rose over the desert dunes like a brilliant, glowing ball of fire that turned the sand to gold and shimmered in heat waves above the desert floor.

"Let's get to it," Fletcher said as he pushed his chair back. He pointed to a line of Egyptian workers passing along basket after basket of earth from the tomb. "Nawab and his crew are hard at it. Time we got to work."

"Right." David grinned at Catherine and Massaud and picked up his hard hat. He called a greeting to the men hauling dirt and rubble from the tomb and, when he entered the passageway, saw that most of it had been cleared. He hadn't particularly wanted to do this dig, because he was so intent on finding Alifa's tomb, but now he was just as excited as Fletcher. This was by far the easiest and fastest dig he'd ever undertaken, and while the tomb of a warrior wasn't a spectacular find, everything and anything they uncovered added some knowledge of Egypt's glorious past. It wouldn't be long now, he thought as he set to work on the door, they would be in Ramah's tomb by midmorning.

It was just as David had predicted; at exactly ten-thirty they pushed back the door of the tomb. A whoosh of hot, dry air rushed out, and David said, "Wait! Stand back! Let's get some fresh air in there before we go in."

"By God, I can hardly wait. Turn your light in there, Dave. Let's have a look."

David grinned. "All right, Fletch, it's all yours. This is your discovery, so you go in first."

"Thanks, Dave." Fletcher squeezed past, bending down to pass through the opening, careful of the rocks and debris still piled there. David came behind him, then Catherine and Massaud.

"It's big," Fletcher said jubilantly. "A bigger room than where we found Potiphera." He beamed his flashlight around. "We need more light," he said. "Have one of the fellows get a lamp down here."

"I'll take care of it," Massaud said and turned quickly back into the passageway to call to Nawab and Azan.

David beamed his flashlight over the walls. "The paintings are here, and the colors are still good." He brought the light down to the floor. "The sarcophagus must be on the other side," he said. He paused, frowning as he looked around. "But where are the funerary furnishings? There should be a chariot, scimitars and swords, the usual things they buried with a warrior as distinguished as Ramah."

"They're here someplace. They have to be." There was a note of panic in Fletcher's voice. "Where's the sarcophagus? Let's have a look at the other side of the room."

"Why don't we wait for more light?" A feeling he didn't like or understand gripped David. Where in hell were all the appurtenances usually found in a tomb? Had grave robbers gotten into it? But they couldn't have. The door had been sealed. And if they had somehow gotten in, there would have been pieces of pottery, some evidence of the man who'd been entombed here.

"Where's that light?" Fletcher snapped. He looked around for Nawab, and when he saw him he said, "Here you are. Give me the light, will you?"

Fletcher took it and held it above his head. "That's better. Now we can see..." His voice faded. "My God," he said. "My *God*, the tomb is empty!"

For a long time no one spoke, then Fletcher cleared his throat and in a strained voice said, "This has to be an antechamber, Dave. The burial chamber must be farther on."

"I don't think so, Fletch. I'm afraid this is all there is."

"But it can't be! This room, the passageway, the seal on the door. It's Ramah's tomb!"

"But Ramah isn't here." David put his arm around the other man's shoulders. "I know how disappointed you are, Fletch. We all are. I'm sorry. I don't understand it any more than you do. But the tomb is empty. There's no use going any further with it."

Fletcher stared at him in disbelief. "Not go any further? How can you say that after all the work it took to get here? We've got to keep on."

"Why don't we rig up the lights and take a look at the wall paintings?" Catherine said. "Maybe they'll give us a clue to what happened to Ramah. Maybe there's a reason why he wasn't buried here." She looked at David. "We could use the magnetometer on the walls, couldn't we? Maybe there really is another room."

"Sure, we'll do that," David said. "But not today. I think we ought to take the rest of the day off and start first thing in the morning. Is that all right with you, Fletch?"

"Yes, I...I guess so." Fletcher looked around him. "I can't believe it," he murmured. "I just can't believe the tomb is empty."

He spent the remainder of the day either alone in his tent or walking about the dunes. Catherine watched him, wanting to help, but knowing Fletcher needed this time alone. Today had been a terrible disappointment for him. She suspected, as David did, that there would be no other chamber, but she hoped they would at least learn something from the wall paintings.

That afternoon when she and David sat under the canvas shade drinking a cold beer she said, "What do we do now?"

"Tomorrow we'll rig up more lights, use the magnetometer and tap the walls to make sure there isn't another chamber. We'll study the wall paintings too, maybe they'll tell us something. After that? I'm damned if I know, Catherine." He shook his head. "It's the strangest thing I've ever encountered. Why would King Amonset have gone to all the trouble of building an empty tomb?"

"Because he didn't know it was going to be empty?" Catherine made circles on the table with the cold bottle. "It would have taken years to build a tomb like that, David. The king probably started it when Ramah first began to distinguish himself as a warrior."

"The king died before Ramah did. If Ramah was killed in the battle against the Assyrians, maybe his body was never returned here."

"But according to what little is known about him he wasn't killed in that battle," Catherine said. "He was wounded and his men brought him here." She leaned back in her chair. "But if they brought him back, why isn't he buried here?"

"I don't know." David shook his head. "Poor Fletch. I know how he feels—just the way I felt when we found Potiphera instead of Alifa."

"David..." Catherine hesitated, then began again. "David, I know you're as disappointed about Ramah as Fletcher is, but there's still Alifa's tomb. The Smithsonian has given you all the time you need. We both know there's no use excavating here further, so we've got to decide where we're going to look next."

"I thought we'd move closer to Amonset's tomb." He saw the expression of doubt on her face and said, "You still want to go to Philae, don't you?"

"Yes, David. I do."

"Philae's a small island, Catherine, but unless we had a pretty definite idea of where we were going to excavate, it could take years to find Alifa's tomb there—if indeed it is there."

"It might take years to find it here, as well," she said defensively. She saw the sudden flash of anger in David's expression, but she plunged on. "I think I know where to begin looking, David. We could use the magnetometer to measure the intensity of the magnetic field and—"

David glared at her. "How *could* you know where to look? You've never even been to Philae!"

"But I've been researching Alifa since I was in high school. I know all about her, how she felt about the island and—"

"How could you possibly know how she felt?"

Catherine stared at him, then stammered, "From... from the research I've done. From the transcripts. They tell about the day Alifa left Philae, how she stood on a rise of land above the shore and looked out over the Nile. That's where I think she is, David, somewhere where she'd see the river. If I could only go there—"

David slammed the bottle of beer down on the table and pushed his chair back. "Look," he said, trying to remain calm, "we all want to find the lost tomb, but this has become an obsession with you, an obsession that worries me, because I love you. You told me the day we drove back from the hospital that you'd been dreaming about Alifa. Yesterday you knew somehow that Ramah's tomb would be empty."

"No, I . . . I didn't *know*."

"Didn't you?" His blue eyes looked into hers as though he would find an answer there. This feeling Catherine had about Alifa bothered him. He'd meant it when he said Alifa had become an obsession with her. Perhaps if he took Catherine to Philae, if she could see for herself what an unlikely place it was for a tomb, she might get it out of her system.

Once they finished here, perhaps they would go.

The Department of Antiquities in Cairo was notified that Ramah's tomb had been uncovered and discovered to be empty. Two officials from that office arrived, and when they saw the empty tomb, they were as stunned as the others had been.

When they'd studied and photographed the wall paintings, they returned to Cairo. Before they left, one of them, an older man by the name of Ahmed Hussan, said, "It is an incredible mystery, is it not? Why would a tomb as elaborate as this one be empty?" He looked at David. "Nonetheless, this is a most interesting discovery, Dr. Pallister, one that I am sure will have archeologists all over the world shaking their heads."

When the two men returned to Cairo, David and his crew took their own photographs. Fletcher spent hour after hour in the tomb, studying the figures on the walls and trying to make sense out of their mystery.

There was no doubt in any of their minds that King Amonset II had built this tomb for Ramah at least three years before the young warrior's death. The paintings, in still-vivid colors of yellow, blue, sienna, black and white, depicted his life and battlefield adventures. He was shown relaxing under the protective eye of the god Horus, facing other gods and goddesses who would sit in judgment of his soul. Osiris and Isis were depicted, as well as Anubis, the jackal-headed god of death.

There were other scenes that traced the battles Ramah had fought and his bravery in facing the enemy. In the paintings he was very young. His handsome face was clear and unlined, his body strong and straight.

Catherine was as fascinated as Fletcher with the paintings. She stayed behind after the others had finished, lingering over the art that depicted the young hero's life. What had there been about this man that separated him from other warriors who'd gone before? What made him different?

She'd come alone this day at dusk to look at the paintings again. By the light that Nawab had rigged and with the aid of her flashlight, Catherine moved slowly around the room. Finally she stopped before a series of pictures that showed Ramah taking his ease upon a gold chair while a serving maid offered him a goblet.

Catherine beamed her flashlight directly on the paintings. What was it? she wondered, that had made this man so special?

Suddenly in this dry and arid tomb it seemed to her that she heard a voice say, "He was a man unlike all others."

The small hairs rose on the back of Catherine's neck, and for a moment she felt a chill of fear. Then the fear passed. She shook her head as though to clear it and moved on to another section of the wall to study the lower pictures. She paused before one that showed Ramah with a spear raised over a jaguar, then knelt on the floor of the tomb to study it.

Next to the painting of Ramah and the jaguar there was a study of Ramah with the god Min. Catherine smiled, for there was no mistaking Min, the lewd one in the divine family of gods. There were many legends about this god of fecundity and virility, but the most popular one was that the gods once departed from Thebes, leaving it under Min's protection, and when they returned they found all the women pregnant. Why had he been depicted here next to Ramah? Had Ramah possessed the power of Min?

Catherine sat down facing the wall and looked at the paintings until it seemed to her that Ramah had become as real today as he'd been almost two thousand years ago. He was a man who lived and breathed, but a man unlike all others.

It was very quiet here in the empty tomb. Catherine leaned her head back against the wall and yawned. Slowly, slowly, her gaze fixed on the painting of Ramah and the jaguar, her eyes began to close.

His eyes, as dark as the night that surrounded them, lingered on hers. "I knew from that first moment that I must touch you or go mad," he said. "Since the night I walked with you beside the Nile, I have been obsessed with thoughts of you. Whenever I go walking you are with me. Every step your hand is in mine. I feel the softness of it whether I am awake or asleep."

She let him lead her back among the willows. He brought her hand to his lips, and she began to tremble, because it was as it had been that first time, a touch of fire. His tongue caressed her fingertips, licked and tasted each one as though it were a delicate fruit.

Warmth flowed through her body, weakening her so that she feared she might faint. Her body became soft, and he drew her to him and kissed her lips as slowly as he had kissed her fingers. Sampling, tasting, he took her bottom lip to suck as he would a ripe mango.

Her lips parted to welcome his tongue while incandescent heat ran through her body. For a moment she was not even aware that he had touched her breasts, so lost was she in the magic of his kiss. Only when she began to quiver and burn with pleasure and the heat between her legs drove her to weakness did she whisper a protest. But he took her words into his mouth, and when she swayed against him, his fingers sought her nipples through the thin white fabric, and she moaned with a pleasure she had not thought possible.

One hand slid down the roundness of her belly to cup her there in that forbidden place. Her hands came up against his chest to push him from her, but lingered to caress his own hard nipples until he moaned against her mouth and said, "Now, my love, it must be now."

He laid her down among the ferns. He gazed into her eyes and eased the linen gown above her hips.

She lay, her heart beating wildly in her chest. As she looked up at him he unwrapped his kilt and stood like a god before her.

Slowly then he knelt beside her. He brought her hand to his lips and turned it so that he could kiss her palm before he brought his naked body down to hers.

He breathed her name against her ear.

Her arms, as though of their own volition, came up to encircle his neck. In a moment he would bind her to him in ecstasy. He would . . .

"Catherine?"

"Yes," she whispered. "Oh, yes."

David knelt beside her. "Catherine?" he said again.

She looked at him. Her lips were parted, swollen as though from dozens of kisses. Her eyes were passion-dazed and languid. He touched her hand and she trembled.

He drew her to her feet. "Darling, what is it?"

She began to tremble, and David put his arms around her. He meant only to comfort her, but she raised her face to his and kissed him with lips that were on fire. Her body was soft, and when his arms tightened around her, she moaned with pleasure.

He spoke her name against her lips and felt his body catch fire against hers. He reached under her T-shirt to caress her breasts, and at his touch she dug her nails into his shoulders, and the breath hissed in her throat.

"I thought I'd die with wanting you," David said hoarsely. "You don't know the nights I've lain in my tent wanting you. How many times I've been tempted to come to you. Oh, Catherine. Catherine, love."

Her body stiffened. "David?" Her eyes went wide with shock, and she stepped away from him. She looked at him, dazed, bewildered, then a shudder ran through her body. She covered her face with her hands. "Oh, my God," she whispered. "What's happening to me?"

Then, before he could speak, Catherine turned and ran from the tomb.

Chapter 15

Catherine told herself that it was the heat that had caused her to act so strangely. She protested when David suggested she go to stay with Abdel Moustafa while the rest of them finished cleaning up the tomb. But David had insisted, and this morning he'd driven her into Edfu.

Before they reached the villa he stopped the car and turning to her said, "You'll feel better in a few days. I want you to get a good rest and stay out of the sun."

"I'm not tired and I'm not crazy." Catherine glared at him.

"Then how do you explain what happened yesterday?"

"I fell asleep and you startled me."

"There's much more to it than that, Catherine. You were disoriented. I don't think you even knew who I was or who you were. You kissed me, then you looked at me as though I were a complete stranger, and you burst into tears."

David gripped her hands. "You've been working too hard, Catherine, and besides, this heat is enough to do anyone in." His voice softened. "Take it easy for a few days, swim and rest and stay out of the sun. I'll be back for you at the end of the week."

He wanted to put his arms around her and hold her close, because he was afraid, and he didn't know why he was afraid. He couldn't explain, even now, the way he'd felt yesterday when he'd walked into Ramah's empty tomb and seen Catherine staring at the wall paintings. There'd been an expression on her face of such love and longing, of such unbearable sadness, that for a moment he was frozen where he stood. He spoke her name several times, and when at last she heard him, she looked at him as though he were a stranger, someone she'd never seen before. Then she'd kissed him, deeply, passionately. Her body had been molten fire against his, and he'd known that she wanted him to take her there on the floor of the tomb. He would have, he wanted to, but suddenly she'd broken away from him and run away weeping.

David didn't understand it, he only knew that he loved her. He put his hand behind her head now and drew her to him for a brief kiss. Then he let her go and drove to the villa. He spoke to Abdel only a few minutes, then he put his arm around Catherine and said, "Have a good rest. I'll see you in a few days."

She was stiff and unyielding, her face expressionless as she watched him drive off.

Safa took her to the room she'd had before. "Too skinny," Safa said, frowning at Catherine. "It is the heat. You must eat and you must rest. I run bath, then you sleep. Yes?"

"Yes, thank you." Catherine undressed and put her robe on, and when Safa left, she went into the bathroom. Before she got in the tub, Safa returned with a frosted glass of lemonade.

This was the first bath she'd had in weeks. The perfumed water was cool, and she lay back in it, sipping the lemonade. She wanted to stay here forever and not think about anything. Certainly she didn't want to think about yesterday when she'd run weeping from Ramah's tomb.

David had said it—whatever the *it* was that had happened to her—was because of the heat and because she was exhausted.

Now as she lay back in the water Catherine admitted to herself that she was frightened by what had happened. She didn't know what had come over her, she only knew that there was a space between the time she went in the tomb to study the drawings and when she found herself in David's arms. He'd been kissing her, and she knew it shouldn't have been him, it should have been someone...someone else. Catherine closed her eyes. Dear Lord, what was happening to her?

She rubbed the cool glass against her forehead. Maybe David was right, maybe it was the heat. She needed a few days off to sleep and swim and not even think about where the next dig was going to be. David was in charge; he would pick the next excavation site, and it would be close to Amonset's tomb. She had nothing to say about it. At the end of August her sabbatical would be over. She would go home and try to forget Egypt and David. She would forever put away all the hopes she'd had of finding Alifa's lost tomb.

During the next few days Catherine rested. She swam in the early morning before the sun was up and at dusk when the air had cooled. Every evening she went to stand on the bank of the Nile, watching the farmers bringing their oxen and their mules and water buffalo to drink.

She listened to the songs of the birds who came in to roost in the trees that lined the banks.

At night she lay alone on her bed, reading from the new pages of the transcript that Massaud had given her. When she turned the light off, she watched the circular fan go slowly round and round until at last her eyes grew heavy and she slept.

David didn't come on the weekend as he'd promised, but on the following Tuesday he arrived in time for dinner. "We've finished the work of cleaning up," he said. "The gear is packed and ready for the next move."

Catherine took a sip of her tea. She didn't ask where the move would be—she already knew. She barely listened while David and Abdel talked, and when dinner was over she excused herself. "I'd better pack so I'll be ready to leave with you in the morning."

But David said, "Let's walk a bit, Catherine. I'd like to discuss some things with you."

"Yes, yes." Abdel waved his ringed fingers. "It's a lovely night for a walk. Follow the path through the gardens. It leads to a walk along the river. It should be beautiful tonight, because there is a breeze and a new moon is starting. I will see you in the morning before you leave."

David thanked Abdel, and taking Catherine's arm, he led her out through the French doors into the terraced gardens. "What have you been doing?" he asked.

"Resting, reading." She shrugged. "Not much of anything."

"What have you been reading?"

"The manuscript. Massaud gave me more of the pages before I left."

David frowned. "I brought you here to Abdel's to relax and to forget about Alifa." When Catherine averted her face and didn't answer he slowed his steps. "I've decided where we're going to begin excavating," he said.

"Fine."

"You don't want to know where?"

"Near King Amonset's tomb, that's where you decided, isn't it?"

"I've changed my mind."

"Oh?" Catherine looked at him, waiting.

He reached for her hand. "We're going to Philae, Catherine."

Her lips parted in surprise. "Philae?"

"That's what you want, isn't it?"

"Yes, but..." Tears sprang to her eyes. "Oh, David, are you sure?"

He shook his head. "No, Catherine, but I know how strongly you feel about it, and I have to give you your chance."

Catherine looked at him for a long moment. Then she rested her head against his shoulder. "I don't know what to say," she whispered.

"You don't have to say anything." David put his arms around her. He still didn't know whether or not he'd made the right decision. He only knew that he loved Catherine, and that somehow, in a way he didn't understand, she was convinced they would find the missing tomb on the Island of Philae. There'd been a lot of times on a dig when he'd trusted his gut instinct, now he was going to trust Catherine's.

He rested his face against her hair, and they stood there, under the willows on the banks of the Nile, with only a sliver of golden moon to see when she turned her face up for his kiss.

Catherine knew that for as long as she lived she would never forget that first sight of Philae. The Nile waters were bluer here, and there was a freshness to the air. As the motor launch drew close to the rocky shore, she could see the granite rocks, the palms, the sycamores and the ancient temple pylons that dominated the landscape.

Beside her in the motor launch David said, "It's a fantastic sight, isn't it?"

Unable to speak, Catherine only nodded. It was more, so much more than she'd even dreamed it would be. For as long as she could remember, she'd read everything she could find about this island. She'd looked at pictures and listened to her father tell endless stories of its beauty, and she'd dreamed of the day that she, too, would see it. Now the dream had become reality.

When the launch touched shore, David took her hand to help her alight. Catherine stepped out of the boat, and a shiver of excitement ran down her spine, for she was here at last.

Two other launches, loaded with equipment, followed theirs, and in the next few hours Catherine was too busy helping unload the equipment to spend any time looking around.

Two Egyptian officials and a dozen or so workers were already there waiting for them. After everything had been unloaded, the officials took them to a rise of land overlooking the Nile where they could put up their tents.

"It's going to be good to be near the water," Fletcher said as he looked around him. "I like the desert well enough, but I have to admit that I was getting damn sick of the sight of sand. It's cooler here, and a man can breathe." He looked at David. "You have any idea where we're going to begin excavating?"

David shook his head. "I'm leaving that up to Catherine."

She looked at him, her eyes widening in surprise, but before she could say anything, David said, "We'll take our time, get the feel of the place and pretend we're tourists for a day or two. Then we'll let Catherine decide where we're going to begin."

He was leaving it up to her. He was giving her this chance to prove her theories about Alifa, to find out once and for all if her conviction that the lost tomb was here on Philae was fact or fantasy. He was staking a lot on his belief in her, and she didn't know whether it was because he believed in her or because he loved her. Whatever the reason, she didn't want him to ever regret the decision.

At twilight, when at last the tents were up and all of the tourists had left, they sat drinking cold beers, looking out over the river that was flat and still in the last golden rays of the sun. The generator hadn't been set up, and Catherine didn't miss its steady hum. The smell of the dinner that Sahibzada was preparing over a charcoal brazier wafted on the evening air.

"If we had any lights, I would give you the rest of the transcript," Massaud said. "I finished translating it last night. I think you may be right, but I will leave that for you to discover." He smiled at Catherine. "But the transformer will be ready in a day or two."

"A day or two!" Her eyes sparkled with excitement. "I don't care whether we have lights or not. I'll use a lantern to read."

"Very well then, I will give it to you right after dinner."

Catherine could hardly wait. She finished eating before anyone else, then sat impatiently, drumming her fingers on the table until Massaud finished.

When at last he did, she told the three men good-night and hurried to her tent, where she lighted the lantern and began to read.

Three years have passed. The king is dead. Gravely ill for many months, he was daily attended by the court physicians. They listened to his heart speak and advised him to rest. They also prescribed herbs, charms and incantations. But each day the king grew weaker. Alifa stayed always by his side, and when the king grew worse, she summoned It-un-hab, hoping that his beloved concubine would help him to rally.

The season of the harvesting of crops came to the land. One day, in the early-morning hours when the land was still and the gods spoke quietly, the breath was taken from the king. He died in Alifa's arms and whispered her name as he set forth on his voyage beyond the beyond.

They prepared his body for burial, laid it in the sarcophagus and carried it to the tomb. The priests led the procession, and they were followed by the lords and nobles, the queen, then the concubines and the people. Their keening cries rang shrill and loud, and they flung dust upon their heads to mourn the passing of the king.

Thus it was that at nineteen Alifa became Queen of Upper and Lower Egypt.

Catherine paused in her reading. The camp had grown quiet, and the only sound was the occasional call of a night bird and the soft slap of water against the rocks. She closed her eyes, wondering what it had been like for one so young to be in a position so great. Then she adjusted the light and read on.

The High Priest of Amon, along with the Vizier of Upper Egypt and the Vizier of Lower Egypt took charge after the death of the king, for although she held the title of queen, there was little for Alifa to do.

It has been a time of trouble for Egypt, of wars with the Syrians, the Anatolians, the Dardanians, the Sardinians, and the Assyrians. The finest of our country's warriors have gone from here to fight and die in those alien lands.

One such warrior was he of whom I have spoken before. A year after the king died, the warrior returned to Egypt from fighting the Dardanians, and he was called to court to receive his honors. My queen was present when he came, and again I saw them look at each other with barely disguised longing. I knew that soon my queen would find joy and love in his arms.

The warrior, as good as he was brave, brought a smile to her lips and a light to her eyes. Soon they began meeting secretly for walks along the river, while I followed a discreet distance behind. One night he led her to a quiet place under the trees. I stayed where I was so that I might warn them if anyone approached, and my limbs trembled for I knew that on this night they would become lovers.

Thus it was in that quiet place, with only the whisper of the wind and the soft splash of water against the shore to break the stillness of the night, that their love was consummated.

They met often after that first time, sometimes in that bower of trees, sometimes in her chamber. Always I watched nearby, ready to warn them lest someone should come.

I knew in my heart their love could last but a season, and I was right, for one day the priests and the viziers called upon Alifa in her chambers and told her they were arranging a marriage for her with a noble from Hermoúpolis. Two days later they sent her lover to fight against the Assyrians.

My mistress became ill with grief and worry. She begged the high priest to allow her to return to Philae. He was reluctant, but fearing for her health...

Catherine looked up from the manuscript. She'd been right! Alifa had come home.

The next few pages of the manuscript dealt with the joy of Alifa's return to Philae. Her father had met the royal barge at the shore and welcomed her with gifts and flowers. Then there was mention of war and finally the news that the queen's lover had been wounded.

With trembling fingers Catherine turned the pages of the manuscript and read of Alifa's determination to bring him to Philae.

She has offered a fortune in gold to the men who will bring him here. Each day now she stands on the shore watching for the barge that will bring him back to her.

Catherine turned to the last page.

At last he came, alive but so sorely wounded that I wept, because I knew that soon, and forever, he would leave the queen. For four days and four nights she stayed with him. On the morning of the fifth day he opened his eyes and looked upon her face for the last time. "*Ana ohebok*, I love you," I heard him whisper. Alifa kissed his dying lips, and thus it ended.

The priests prepared his body for burial. Alifa, anguished with grief, did not leave her chambers. She saw only her father and a few of her most trusted servants.

When the day of entombment came, she followed the line of keening mourners, so swathed in black that none could see her face. She was silent, but she did not weep. The next day she met with those closest to her, and when they had gone, she asked her father to come.

That night when it was time to sleep, I prepared her for bed, and she said, "Leave me, dear friend, for tonight I must be alone."

"No, mistress," I pleaded. "Let me stay."

She kissed my forehead. "My trusted friend," she said. "Go now, for it is time."

I wept as I kissed her fair head, for I knew that I would never see her again.

That night my mistress disappeared.

The words swam before Catherine's eyes. She read them again... *That night my mistress disappeared.* What did it mean? Where had Alifa gone?

Catherine turned the lantern down and went to stand in the opening of the tent. The other tents were dark, the night was still. "Where are you?" she whispered into the night. But there was no answer, only the whisper of the wind against her face.

Chapter 16

It was almost like coming home, Catherine thought the next morning when she stepped out of her tent into the bright sunlight. The temples were golden in the sunrise, the water of the Nile an unbelievable shade of blue. The soft air played against her skin; it was a day full of promise.

When she heard movement, she looked and saw David coming out of his tent. "Morning," he said as he came toward her. "Did you get any rest last night? Your light was still on when I went to sleep."

"Yes, I'm fine. But I'm starved. Do you suppose Sahibzada has started breakfast?"

"Let's go see." She looked different this morning, David thought, more relaxed. Her eyes were clear and bright, and there was an expression of eagerness in her face. The uncertainty and confusion that he'd seen these past days had vanished; she looked happy and self-assured.

Catherine linked her arm through his and said, "Thank you for bringing me here, David, and thank you for trusting me. I know you're taking a risk, believing in me like this."

"Not too much of a risk," he said with a smile. "You're a brilliant archeologist, Catherine, a professional who's done her homework. We wouldn't be here if I didn't think there was some validity to the way you feel about Philae." David put his hands on her shoulders and looking into her eyes said, "I know how much finding the lost tomb means to you, but there've been times these past few weeks when I've been worried about you. You've been so intent about finding Alifa that it's become an obsession. You scared the hell out of me that afternoon in Ramah's tomb, Catherine."

"I can't imagine you afraid of anything, David."

"You don't really remember what happened, do you?" He tightened his hands on her shoulders. "When I lifted you off the floor you kissed me—I knew you wanted me to make love to you. And I knew that if I did, it would have been the most violent explosion of passion either of us has ever known. I ached with wanting you, Catherine, but suddenly you looked at me as though you'd never seen me before, as though I were someone else—someone you didn't even know."

"I . . . I don't believe you."

"Don't you?" He let her go. "It wasn't a great feeling, Catherine."

Catherine stared at him and knew that what David was saying was true—she had no recollection of his coming into the tomb. With a great effort of will she met his gaze. "I don't understand what happened that afternoon, David. There's a time lapse between when I went into the tomb and when I found myself in your arms. Maybe I fell asleep and dreamed..." Her face flushed. "Maybe I dreamed that you and I were making love."

"It wasn't me that you were kissing, Catherine."

Her eyes widened with shock. "What are you saying David?"

"I'm not sure I know. I only know that when you realized it was me, you panicked." David cupped her face with his hands. "If anything like that ever happens again, I'm going to take you away from Philae, from Egypt."

"No!" The cry was torn from her soul. "No, David, please." She gripped his arms. "That was a dream, you're the reality. I love you. I..." Her voice broke, and she buried her face against his shoulder. "Only you, David. Only you."

He held her for a few moments. Then he let her go. But he didn't kiss her. He took her hand, and together they went to find Sahibzada and their breakfast.

The workmen fixed the generator that day and finished setting up the camp. Because there was little she could do to help, Catherine made a tour of the island.

She went first to the ancient Columns of Nectanebo and to the colonnade on the left that was inscribed with the cartouches of Augustus, Tiberius, Claudius and Nero. From there she moved to a pylon decorated with scenes of prisoners being massacred. The king depicted there was Ptolemy Auletes, the father of Cleopatra, and Catherine stood, looking up at it, thinking of that young queen whose beauty had bewitched so many men.

From there Catherine went to the funerary temple of Osiris, husband of Isis, and she wondered if Alifa had come here to pray after the death of her lover. For legend had it that Isis had discovered the secret of resurrection.

Later in the day Fletcher joined her as she stood out on an overlook of land. "Not getting too much sun, are you?" he asked.

"No. It doesn't seem as hot here by the water as it did in the desert. Besides I've burned and peeled and tanned so many times that I think my skin is impervious to the sun." She smiled at him. "It's wonderful here, isn't it?"

"Wonderful," Fletcher agreed. "I was your age the first time I came to Philae. I felt about it then just as you do now. It's like a small jewel set in the Nile. I like it best in the evening when the tourists have gone and only the gods remain." He took his pipe out of his shirt pocket, filled it from a small pouch of tobacco, and when it was lighted he puffed contentedly for a few minutes, then said, "I'm very glad to be in Philae, Catherine. I hope we'll find Alifa's tomb here."

"So do I." Catherine looked around her. "This is what I've always hoped for, Fletcher, but I didn't really expect it to happen. I certainly never thought David would agree to it. Actually, I'm not sure why he did."

"Aren't you?" Fletcher raised his shaggy brows. "You know he's in love with you, don't you?"

"Yes, but I... I didn't think anybody else knew."

"One has only to see him looking at you," Fletcher said with a grin. "What about you, Catherine, if you don't mind my asking? Are you in love with David?"

She took a deep breath. "Yes," she said, "I'm afraid I am."

"Why afraid?"

"Because of the difference in our ages. I'm older than David."

Fletcher laughed. "I thought I was the old fogy and you were a modern woman. I can't believe you'd let a few years keep the two of you apart. That's utter nonsense.

David's a fine man. If you let him get away from you, you're not the woman I think you are." He turned from her to stare out at the water and puff on his pipe.

Catherine felt as though she were six years old again and being reprimanded by her father. She didn't answer Fletcher until finally he said, "Sorry. None of my business. I shouldn't have spoken up."

"Of course you should have. You're David's friend, and mine, I hope." She hesitated. "I have a lot of thinking to do, Fletcher, and this seems like a good place to do it."

They strolled back to the camp then and sat with David and Massaud to watch the sunset. It had been a good day, a satisfying day. Soon she would have to begin looking for an excavation site, but for now all Catherine wanted to do was familiarize herself with the island.

When she finished her drink, Catherine excused herself and went to the public rest rooms to bathe before dinner. In a few days they'd have shower facilities rigged up, but for now they made do with what was available. She splashed water over her body, then washed her hair in the sink and dressed in a short peach sarong and a matching bandeau she'd bought on an impulse while they'd been aboard ship.

Catherine looked at herself in the mirror and knew that she'd changed. Her skin had tanned the color of copper, and her dark hair had grown almost to shoulder length. But those weren't the things that had changed her. Rather it was something in her face, an expression in the eyes and a softness of the mouth that hadn't been there before. Egypt had changed her, she thought, and so had love.

After a dinner of chicken, fresh vegetables, fruit and yogurt, they lingered over coffee, easy and unrushed, for until Catherine decided where the excavations would begin, there was little for them to do.

David watched her as she chatted easily with Massaud and Fletcher. She looked very different tonight, a modern-day Cleopatra with sherry eyes and long brown legs. His gaze lingered on her legs, moving slowly up to where the sarong came to midthigh. Her midriff and her shoulders were bare, only her sweetly rounded breasts were covered.

It had been an achingly long time since they'd made love. Except for that day in the tomb there'd been no opportunity, even if she'd been willing. He'd promised not to force the issue and to wait for an answer to his proposal of marriage. But he wasn't a patient man.

He'd never asked a woman to marry him before, but he wanted to spend the rest of his life with Catherine. He would like to have a child with her, and it seemed to David as he looked at her now that he could almost see a boy or a girl with her dark eyes and serious expression. Suddenly his throat ached with longing for that child and for Catherine, and he knew that he would never give up trying to convince her that they belonged together.

The shadows lengthened, and the blue of the sky was streaked with patches of flamingo and orange and gold, then slowly faded to a lavender darkness. As it faded the moon came out, bright and fat and yellow, to outline the ancient temples, like ghostly remnants of the past, against the endless horizon of the night.

At last Fletcher rose and with a yawn said, "I think I'll call it a night."

"Yes, so will I," Massaud said. "I have to finish the paper I've been writing on the projects we've done." He looked at David. "I'm glad we've come to Philae and am truly sorry that in a few weeks I must return to school."

"Yes, I know." David smiled at the young student. "But you'll come back when we find the lost tomb, won't you? I'm sure your professors would want you to."

"Yes, of course I will come back."

Massaud bade them both good-night. When they were alone David said to Catherine, "What about you? When's the sabbatical up?"

"The end of August."

"You're going to extend it, aren't you?"

"Yes! I don't intend to let school or anything else interfere with this. I'll stay here until we find Alifa." She stood up. "I'm going to take a walk. Would you like to come?"

David nodded and took her hand as they strolled toward the shore.

"It's so quiet." Catherine paused, listening. "All you can hear is the splash of the water." She led him toward the Temple of Isis and out onto an empty rock-terraced promontory over the water. "I've never seen a place as beautiful as this," she said. "I feel as if I've come home."

David looked at her lovely profile that was lighted only by the moon that shone above. He wanted to take her in his arms, but he held himself back. When Catherine came to him, it had to be her decision, and it would be him she offered herself to, not a ghost of centuries past.

After a little while, Catherine said, "I found a path along the water today, David. Let's walk a bit."

All that could be heard were their footsteps and the gentle slap of water against the rocks as they made their way through the trees along the rocky path. When at last Catherine stopped, she said, "Yes, this is the place. See how beautiful it is, David? On one side you can see the outline of the temples through the trees. On the other side the Nile." She breathed in the night air. "Mother Nile with the moon shining on the blue water." She smiled. "On a night like this anything seems possible."

He waited.

"It's a night made for lovers, David," she said softly.

"Is it?"

"Yes." She took his hand and led him farther into the bower of trees. When she stopped she looked up at him, barely able to see his face in the light of the moon that filtered through the trees. She wanted him to make love to her, but she didn't know how to begin, how to tell him. If only he would say something, if only he would take her in his arms.

But still he waited until she spoke, and his name was a trembling sigh on her lips.

David took her into his arms and pressed the length of her body against his while he rested his face against her hair and breathed in the scent of her. He thought about kissing her and laying her down on the cool earth and joining his body to hers. But for now it was enough to hold her, for there was joy in the waiting when he knew that soon they would join in love.

Catherine raised her face for his kiss. He looked at her, then gently brushed his lips against hers. "Catherine," he murmured and crushed her to him. His mouth found hers again, hard and demanding, for the hunger was building in him. He kissed her greedily, nipping the corners of her mouth and felt his body strain with need. Her lips parted. Her tongue sought his, and she cupped his head, holding him while their mouths devoured each other.

David slid his hands down her bare shoulders around to her back, almost groaning aloud in the pleasure it was to touch her. He circled her bare midriff and reached under the swath of cloth to touch the softness of her breasts.

"Wait," Catherine whispered, and reached around her back to remove the bandeau. "Touch me, David," she begged. "Touch my breasts."

They were cool against the fire of his hands. He held them, cupping the roundness before his fingers found the hard peaked tips. And all the while her mouth moved hungrily against his.

With his hand against the small of her back David pressed her closer. But it wasn't enough. He unfastened the sarong skirt, and when it fell to the ground, he put his hands inside her silky panties and cupped her buttocks.

"Catherine," he whispered against her mouth.

"Yes," she said, slipping her cool hands inside his shirt, pulling it out of his trousers so that she could encircle his back. She rubbed her face against the mat of his chest hair and fumbled with the buckle of his belt.

David held her away from him, his hands on her shoulders as he looked at her. Her eyes were sleepy with desire. Her lips were swollen, and she was breathing quickly. He thought his body would burst with wanting her when he let her go so that he could pull his clothes off, and he groaned with pleasure when he heard her whispered response as their bodies touched.

Quickly David pulled Catherine down with him and laid her under the bower of trees. He knelt beside her and brushed her dark hair back from her face. "This is me, Catherine," he said. "I'm David, not a ghost or a fantasy from the past." He cupped her breasts. "These are my hands, Catherine. *My* hands that arouse and please you."

"David...?"

He heard the uncertainty in her voice, but he wouldn't stop, he had to go on, he had to make her know who it was who claimed her.

She lifted her hand to stay him, but he pressed it down across his belly and said, "Touch me, Catherine, and know that this, too, is me."

Her hand trembled on his flesh, and he sighed with pleasure. "More," he said. "I want more."

When he knew that it was too much, that if she didn't stop, his body would explode, he lifted himself over her. "Look at me," he said in a strangled voice. "Look at me, Catherine, and say my name."

"Please..." Her body quivered with desire.

"Say my name," he demanded.

Catherine looked up at him. "David," she said. "Oh, David."

He thought he would die with loving her.

He moved against her, slowly, deeply as her warmness closed about him, held him. They kissed, their mouths as close and loving as their bodies. With every thrust she lifted herself to him, offering as he offered, demanding as he demanded.

Their cadence changed, quickened. David bent to kiss her breasts, and her fingers tightened around his back. Consumed with passion, wild and fevered, she bit his shoulder, then licking it, urged him on with words of love.

He cupped her buttocks and rocked her closer, her name a strangled cry upon his lips. He felt her body quiver, and he said, "No! Not yet. Make it last. Wait, Catherine, wait." Even though his own body screamed for relief.

Catherine's body shook with passion as she moved wildly, mindlessly against him. She heard his strangled cry of pleasure, and it was too much. Weeping, exhausted, she lifted her body to his, at one with him in this final shattering ecstasy.

She opened her eyes and saw the moon, and then moon and earth came together, and she was crushed between them, crushed in the heaven of David's arms. Forever and always David. Only David.

"I love you," she said against his lips, and her body shook with the reaction of what they had shared as he tightened his arms around her.

David tasted the salt of her tears and felt a surge of tenderness and love unlike anything he'd ever felt before, because he knew that Catherine belonged to him. He held her and told her that he loved her, and he caressed her to calmness. When finally she raised her moon-streaked face, he kissed her and whispered, "Tell me," against her lips.

"I love you." Catherine rested her face against his shoulder and thought that for the first time in her life she knew what true happiness was.

It was a long time before she spoke. "I suppose we should get up and go back to camp before somebody misses us."

"Everyone's asleep." David kissed the top of her head and, leaning on his elbow, looked down at her. "You're so beautiful, Catherine." He kissed her lips, lingeringly, tenderly. "I want you again," he said.

"Yes." That's all, a simple yes that spoke of love and acceptance and of a desire that matched his.

Their bodies came together more gently this time. They made love slowly, looking into each other's eyes, tasting each other's mouths while they whispered words of love. When David leaned to lick her breasts, she offered them up to him, a feast for his pleasure. She felt the earth, still warm from the sun, under her back, and a laugh grew somewhere in the back of her brain, because she was the proper Miss Catherine Adair and she was making love on the ground of an Egyptian island and it was more wonderful than she'd dreamed anything could ever be. Because it was love. Because the man was David.

When at last they reached that high plateau of pleasure, they whispered their final sighs into each other's mouths.

Their bodies calm, they lay looking up at the moon and the dark silhouette of the ancient temples. "I'll always love you," Catherine said. "Not just in Egypt, but wherever we are. In Arizona or New York, in Afghanistan or Pittsburgh."

"Pittsburgh?" David smiled and brought her back into his arms again. He knew in his heart that at last Catherine belonged to him.

Three days later Catherine stood on the same spot where she and David had made love. She stood there for a long time, looking out at the sparkle of water on the river and at the rubble of nearby rocks. She closed her eyes, not moving, scarcely breathing, and felt the breeze on her face and the gentle rustle of the leaves above her head.

She thought of how it had been the other night with David, of the love they'd shared and of the beautiful joining of their hearts and bodies. She thought of Alifa waiting here on the banks of the river for her lover's return.

Catherine opened her eyes and looked again at the rubble of nearby rocks. Suddenly it seemed as though the world stilled. Heart beating fast, she walked toward the rocks. When she stopped, her legs were trembling so violently she didn't think they would support her, and it was difficult to breathe.

Minutes passed and still Catherine stood, spellbound, unable to move. At last, with a sigh, she nodded to herself, then turned and hurried back to the camp.

When David saw her, he waved his arm in greeting. "What is it, Catherine?" he called.

"I know..." She had to stop to get her breath. "I know where to begin the excavations," she said. "Oh, David, I know."

Chapter 17

David stared at Catherine. Her face was pale under the tan, and when he put his arm around her shoulders, he felt her trembling.

"Easy," he said. "Take it easy, Catherine."

She looked up at him, an expression of excitement and joy on her face. "I've found the place where we should begin the excavation, David. I know where to start."

"You're sure?"

"As sure as I've ever been about anything in my life."

"Take me there," he said, and when she took his hand and led him to the place, David stood without speaking. He'd told Catherine he would let her select the site, but now that she had he was assailed by doubts. There was no indication of any kind that a tomb lay below the surface of the ground.

"Why here?" David tried to keep his voice noncommittal.

"Why not?" she asked, and laughed aloud with a feeling of exhilaration too big to contain. "I just know this is the place. I feel this is it."

"That's not much to go on, Catherine."

"Of course it is. You've said yourself that you'd made some of your best finds with pure instinctive gut feelings. So have I."

"But we've both had something to back up those feelings." David shook his head. "I don't know, Catherine. I just don't know."

"Don't know what?" she challenged. "You said I could select the excavation site, and I have." She pointed down at the rocks at her feet. "This is where I want to begin." Her whole body was tensed, waiting.

David didn't know what to do. He'd expected the site Catherine chose to be closer to the other temples, not here on this rock-strewn piece of land overlooking the Nile. It would take days just to clear away the rubble to begin the excavations. If she had any basis of fact to indicate this might be the place, it would be a different matter. All she had to go on that Alifa had returned to Philae were the transcripts that Massaud had translated, and they seemed cryptic at best. Now she wanted to begin the excavation in this spot because of a *feeling*.

But a promise was a promise—that was the bottom line. He'd given his word, he had to go with it.

"All right, Catherine, we'll try it here. I gave Fletcher a month—it's only fair that I give you the same. If we've uncovered enough evidence that there's something here, we'll continue with it. If we don't, we call a halt."

"But a month might not be long enough," she protested.

"It'll have to be. If we don't find anything by then, we go back to Edfu. Understood?"

Catherine looked at him without answering. Finally in a crisp, businesslike voice she said, "Yes, understood. If that's all the time we have, I'd like the men to begin clearing the area this afternoon."

David nodded. "I'll get them started on it right away." He moved to touch her, but she stepped back away from him.

"Look," he said, "what I feel as a professional doesn't have anything to do with the way I feel about you as a man. We have to keep our work and our personal feelings separate."

"I'm not sure I can do that, David."

"Catherine..." He hesitated, trying to find the words to convey all that he felt. "What happened with us last night and all the other nights that we've shared is something very rare and precious. But this dig is my responsibility, and in spite of how I feel about you I can't put that responsibility aside. You're a professional, Catherine, I expect you to understand that."

"I understand." She turned to walk away from him, but David put a detaining hand on her arm. "There's something else," he said. "After last night I don't see any reason why we shouldn't be together. I want you to move into my tent. We're adults. We're in love, and we're going to be married. There's no earthly reason we shouldn't be together."

"There's a matter of propriety, David. I wouldn't feel comfortable in that kind of a situation."

David wanted to grab her shoulders and shake her back to the woman she'd been that night by the Nile, because suddenly she'd changed, she was once again the thoroughly proper Professor Catherine Adair, and he didn't know how to reach her. "Dammit, Catherine..." he said, then stopped. This wasn't the time for a discussion about their personal lives. She was too defensive about the dig to talk about their love life, and he knew that while they were two separate things to him, they weren't to Catherine. He would wait a day or two, and everything would be all right between them again.

It took the native workers almost a week to clear the site that Catherine had chosen. All day long the line of men filled and lugged away huge baskets of rock and rubble. The work was hard, and the sun beat down upon their backs with merciless intensity.

The four archeologists worked almost as hard as the natives. In the evening after supper Catherine and Massaud went over the manuscript pages. It wasn't that David was jealous; he knew there wasn't anything between Catherine and the student, but he wanted Catherine to spend her resting hours with him.

At night David lay on his bunk, his body tense with anger and longing, tempted to go striding into her tent, throw her over his shoulder and haul her off, caveman style. In spite of the ache in his body, David grinned at the thought of Catherine screaming and kicking and of how Fletcher and Massaud would look when it happened. He tried not to think of what would happen once he got her to his tent.

When the land had been cleared, they used the magnetometer. Slowly, carefully, they measured every inch of the surface in the area. Day after sweltering day Catherine paced back and forth over the site, watching the men work the apparatus. They were into the second week now. If David held to his one month ultimatum, she had only two weeks left. She knew she was right, but she needed time. And time was running out.

Then, on the twentieth day, while Fletcher was monitoring it, the magnetometer recorded a distinct dip.

"Hey!" he yelled in an excited voice. "I've got something!"

"What is it?" David called as he ran toward Fletcher. "What've you got?"

"Something here."

"Let me see." Catherine hurried over to Fletcher just in time to hear David's shout of excitement. Then he grabbed Catherine and swung her up off the ground. "We've got something all right," he said, and not caring that anyone was watching, kissed her hard and fast and set her back on her feet.

"Well done." Fletcher grinned. "Now let's get back to work."

Three days later they uncovered the first step. That night David opened a bottle of champagne. "I've been saving this for a special occasion," he said as he raised his glass. "To Catherine. To—" He paused. "What . . . ?" he started to say, then felt the earth move beneath his feet. "Earthquake!" he cried as he pulled a startled Catherine into his arms.

The earth lurched. Glasses slid off the table. The bottle of champagne overturned. The Egyptian workers began to shout, and Fletcher went down to his hands and knees.

When at last the earth steadied, David said, "That was a tremor and a half. Everybody okay?"

"More or less," Fletcher said as he picked himself up off the ground. "What about you, Massaud?"

"I am okay, professor." Massaud adjusted his glasses. "I'd far rather be here during a tremor than in my apartment in Cairo. If a jolt like this happened there, half the apartments in the city would fall down. I hope my family's all right."

"Take a felucca in to Aswan and call them," David said. "You'll feel better if you do."

"Thanks, I think I will."

David picked up the spilled bottle of champagne. "So much for the toast, Catherine. We'd better check to make sure there hasn't been any damage to the equipment."

Everything proved to be all right, but David felt a nudge of worry that he didn't mention to the others. Tremors like the one they'd just experienced could prove deadly during an excavation. Walls could cave in and ceilings could collapse. They would have to be extra careful shoring up once they got farther into the ground. He would tell Nawab to make sure his men took every precaution as they went deeper. If there were any more tremors, the men might even refuse to continue working.

But there were no more tremors. For the next few days everything was quiet, and the work went smoothly.

The only problem for David was not being able to make love to Catherine. They couldn't even retreat to the bower of trees where they'd made love when they first came to Philae, because now that the generator was working there were spotlights all around the area and two guards constantly on watch.

The heat was unbearable, and it was beginning to take its toll on everyone. But Catherine never complained, never slowed down, and she continued to work as hard as any of the men.

As much as David worried about her, he worried even more about Fletcher. The older man had lost an alarming amount of weight, and there were times when he sweated so profusely that great beads of perspiration ran down his forehead into his eyes. Time and time again when he wiped his face with a big red bandanna David saw his hand shake. He hardly touched his food. He drank enough water and fruit juice to flood a camel, but it never seemed to be enough to satisfy him.

Every evening after pushing the food around on his plate to disguise the fact that he wasn't eating, Fletcher excused himself and went to his tent. On one such night David said to Catherine, "I'm worried about Fletch."

"So am I. Do you think the malaria's flared up?"

"It could be that—or else just the stress of this type of work at his age, but he hasn't said anything. I'm going to talk to him tomorrow. I'd like to talk him into going into Aswan for a checkup."

"I don't think he'll go."

"Neither do I, but I've got to try."

However the next day Fletcher seemed better, and when David suggested he go into Aswan to see a doctor, Fletcher refused. "I'm all right," he said. "It's just the heat. I'll take it easier for a few days, Dave. Don't worry about me."

Because there were so many other things to worry about, David let the subject drop.

They had uncovered three steps, and though they continued digging, that seemed to be the end of it. There were no more steps. There wasn't anything.

"I don't understand it." Catherine took off her straw hat and fanned her face with it. "There has to be something there. We've got to keep on until we find it."

David shook his head. He'd been dreading this moment. Very carefully he said, "I'm afraid we've reached a dead end, Catherine. There's nothing else here. We've got to give it up."

"Give it up! We can't do that. We can't just abandon this. Why would anybody go to the trouble of building steps that didn't lead anywhere?"

"I don't know. Maybe to throw off anybody looking for the tomb." David's sun-bleached brows came together in a frown. "Maybe it was started and abandoned because whoever wanted it built changed his mind and decided to build somewhere else. I don't know, Catherine. But we can't waste any more time on it. I think it would be better if I went into Cairo and talked to the antiquities people there. They aren't as patient as the Smithsonian group. If we don't get results pretty soon, they'll send their own team back to Edfu to start work."

"But I know this is the place," Catherine insisted. "I don't have any idea why the steps have suddenly stopped, but I'm sure this is where we'll find the tomb."

"You don't know that," David said. "I've gone along with you on this, Catherine. I said I'd give you a month, and I have." He looked at her, then away. "I said you could pick the spot where we'd begin excavating, and you did. I wanted you to be the one to find Alifa's tomb. I know how much it means to you, Catherine, but it didn't work out, so we're going back to Edfu."

He saw the expression on her face and hated himself for having to hurt her this way. But he didn't have any choice, this dig was too important to all of them.

"Massaud's going back to Cairo at the end of the week," he said. "I'll go with him. I'll see the antiquity people and call the Smithsonian group while I'm there. I've got to tell them our plans about moving back to Edfu. They've said they'd go along with us because of the Potiphera find and Ramah's tomb, even though it was empty."

David waited for a response, and when Catherine didn't answer he said, "I'll call your university about arranging an extension of your sabbatical."

"I'm not sure I want an extension."

"Yes, you do, Catherine. You're a part of all this and of me. It doesn't matter which one of us is right or which one of us finds Alifa's tomb, because when we find it it'll be for both of us. We're together in this, not just because we're archeologists on the same team, but because we love each other."

David cupped her face, forcing her to look at him. "I know you're upset," he said, "but don't you see, it's the finding of the tomb that's important. And being together when we do."

Catherine's face softened. "I know I'm behaving badly," she said. "I'm sorry, David. It's just that I'm so sure the tomb is here on Philae."

"But we can't excavate the entire island, Catherine." David let her go and shaking his head he said, "I'm sorry. I've made a decision, and I'm sticking with it."

"That's it then?"

"That's it. I'll probably be gone a week. You and Fletcher clean up the operation here. We'll leave for Edfu as soon as I get back from Cairo."

Catherine averted her face. "Very well," she said stiffly. "Is there anything else?"

Yes, David wanted to say. Yes, there's everything else. I love you, Catherine. I don't want to hurt you. But he knew that he had, that she felt he'd robbed her of her dream. Whatever happened when they left Philae, he had to convince her that her dream hadn't ended. They would find Alifa together; and they would share the dream, just as they would share their lives.

"There'll be other digs after this one," David said. "We'll spend the rest of our lives living and working together to discover the secrets of the past, Catherine. I won't let you go, not now, not ever."

But Catherine didn't answer him. Instead she turned away and walked back toward the camp.

She had little to say to David until the morning that he left for Cairo. Just before he was to leave, he asked her to walk with him. When he saw that she was about to refuse, he said, "Please, I have to talk to you."

"I don't want to leave with this misunderstanding between us," David said when they were alone.

"There's no misunderstanding." Catherine looked at him. "I understand perfectly."

"No, you don't." David put a finger under her chin and lifted her face. "I love you, Catherine, that's what I want you to think about while I'm away." He kissed her, but her lips were cool under his, and he let her go. "We'll talk when I come back," he said, knowing he couldn't force the issue now.

"Whatever you say."

"Dammit, Catherine..." Helpless with frustration, David turned away and started back to the camp.

"David, wait." When he hesitated she said, "I'm sorry. You're right. This shouldn't have anything to do with the way we feel about each other." She reached her hand out to him, and when he took it she said, "I was so certain we'd find the tomb here. I'm mad at myself for not finding it, and I'm mad at you for wanting to leave. I wanted it so much, David."

"I know, love." David put his arms around her and pulled her close. "But it just isn't practical to stay here any longer, Catherine. Try to understand."

"I'm trying." She raised her face for a kiss, and when at last he let her go, she put her head against his shoulder. "I've missed you, at night I mean. There were times when I've wanted to go to your tent and tell you that I didn't care what anyone said, I just wanted to be with you."

"Now you tell me!" His arms tightened around her. "Lady, you'll never know how many times I almost came charging into *your* tent." He grinned at her, feeling suddenly that a load had been lifted from his shoulders, that after all he and Catherine were going to be all right.

"I'll be back in a week," he said. "We'll leave for Edfu, and when we get there, we're going to be together. Agreed?"

"Agreed." She looked up at him. "But how do you make love on a cot?"

"We'll find a way," David said with a chuckle. Then he kissed her again until they were both shaking with need. When at last he let her go, he held her away from him. "I know you're disappointed about leaving Philae," he said. "But I promise you, we're going to find Alifa's tomb, Catherine, and when we do it will be a victory for both of us."

They walked to the dock where a felucca waited to take David and Massaud to Aswan to catch their plane. Catherine hugged Massaud, then she kissed David and stood with Fletcher, waving until the tall-masted sailboat faded from view.

"I think I'm going to get in out of the sun for a while," he said. "We can begin clearing up this afternoon."

"All right, Fletcher, you go ahead. I'm going to walk a bit."

Catherine stood for a few minutes looking out at the water before she turned and went toward the temple. Because of the heat there were few tourists this time of year, and she strolled alone through the vast courtyard looking up at the tall lotus-shaped columns of the corridor.

The sky was very blue, and she stood before the temple studying the tall figures carved on either side of the entrance. She turned and looked back at the broad plaza, struck once again by the beauty of the configuration, the way that each structure complemented the other. There was a lovely symmetry of plan, and she marveled at the genius of the men who'd built here.

It reminded Catherine of Monte Albán in Oaxaca, Mexico, where the *ciudadela*, the plaza, had been laid out in a perfect quadrangular shape. And of the way the pyramids had been laid out in Teotihuacán near Mexico City. The seven square miles of that sacred city were dotted with pyramids, temples and courts that were designed so that each part seemed to make up the whole.

Catherine closed her eyes trying to picture the layout in her mind. The Avenue of the Dead led from the Pyramid of the Moon past the Temple of Agriculture of the Plaza of Columns, down to the Pyramid of the Sun, then to the Temple of Tlaloc and the Temple of Quetzalcoatl. Everything symmetrical, everything planned with a beauty of purpose.

Catherine opened her eyes. With a beauty of purpose.

She stood stark still, looking at the avenue of columns and the massive temple in front of her. She began to step backward toward the site of excavation. When she reached it she frowned, then still keeping her gaze on the distant temple, she moved twelve paces to her left and stopped. From where she stood the large temple was on her right, and the smaller temple was on her left. The columns were directly in front of her, making an almost perfect square with where she was.

Catherine stood there a long time, unmindful of the sun beating down upon her. If there had been any kind of a structure on this spot, these ruins would have been laid out almost exactly like Monte Albán and Teotihuacán—in perfect symmetry.

Suddenly Catherine's mouth went dry. What if there *had* been something here? A temple or a monument as small as the one that stood overlooking the Nile? Or a tomb placed with a clear view of the water and of the columns and the majestic temple.

This would have been the perfect place, in order to conform with the way everything had been laid out, for a loving father to build a tomb for a daughter that he hoped might some day return to her island home.

Catherine didn't know why steps had been started, then abandoned so close to where she stood, but she was sure that this time she was right, that somewhere beneath her she would find Alifa's lost tomb.

Her first thought was to tell David. But David was gone, and she wasn't sure, even if he'd been there, that he would listen to her now. She'd been wrong once; he was bound to think she was wrong again. But she wasn't, she thought as she began to run toward the camp. This time she knew she was right.

Chapter 18

That afternoon, under Catherine's direction and with Fletcher in complete accord, Nawab and his men began excavating on the new site that Catherine had selected.

Catherine had expected opposition from Fletcher, but when she showed him the location and its relation to the plaza and the other buildings, he said, "I think you're right, Catherine. It makes sense, beautiful, structurally perfect sense. Too bad David isn't here. Are you going to call him tonight in Cairo?"

"I'd rather not, Fletcher. I was wrong about the other spot, and I'm afraid David would think I'm wrong about this one. If we can find something in the week he's gone, some concrete evidence that the tomb is here, he'll go ahead with it. But without that kind of evidence I don't think he will."

"Then I'm with you, Catherine. If we've only got a week, we'd better get going."

The next day they found the first step, then another and another. Nawab and his workers, as excited as Catherine and Fletcher, worked almost nonstop without complaint. The heat didn't matter—there was an excitement of discovery in the air.

On the morning of the fourth day they discovered the door. By the end of the day they'd cleaned the debris away, and Catherine, palms wet, her heart beating so fast she could scarcely breathe, brushed away the last of the dust.

"There it is," Fletcher said in a hushed voice. "There's the seal."

"I'm almost afraid to look." Fingers trembling, Catherine touched the hieroglyphic symbols. The bird for *A*. The lion for *L*. Tears almost blinded her, and she wiped them away so that she could trace the rest of the symbols, one at a time, to spell the name Alifa.

Fletcher knelt beside her and beamed his flashlight on the hieroglyphics. He looked up at Catherine. "Incredible," he murmured and began to read, "Alifa, Queen of...Upper and Lower Egypt, Daughter...Daughter of Philae." He sat back on his heels. "It's her tomb," he said in an awestruck voice. "You've done it, Catherine. You've found her!"

"Yes." The word trembled on her lips, then she burst into tears.

With a laugh Fletcher got up, wrapped his arms around her and kissed both her cheeks. "Cry later," he joked. "Right now let's get to work on the door."

All that day, while Nawab and the Egyptians continued carrying out the rubble, Catherine and Fletcher worked on the door. It was a careful, exacting job, and Catherine had to force herself to go slowly. But all the while her mind raced with what she'd find when the door was opened.

At one point she considered going into Aswan to telephone David and tell him the news. But she decided not to. By the time he returned she and Fletcher would be deep in the tomb. Perhaps they would even have found the burial chamber. She smiled to herself and imagined the look on David's face when she said, "Come with me, professor. I've got a little surprise for you." She wouldn't do it in a gloating way, but rather she would be presenting David with the gift of a find whose worth was beyond measure. A gift of love.

So intent was Catherine on the excavation that she paid little attention the next afternoon when Fletcher said, "If you don't mind, I'm going to take a break."

"Sure, go ahead," she said, not really looking at him.

"You don't want to rest a while, have a cold drink?"

"No, thanks. I'll just keep on here."

Catherine worked on. Fletcher didn't return, but she barely noticed, so intent was she on the door. She didn't stop until her back began to ache and her fingers trembled with fatigue.

"I want an extra guard posted here tonight," she told Nawab when she left the excavation site. "Mr. Fletcher and I will start work as soon as it's daylight tomorrow."

Only then did Catherine begin to wonder why Fletcher hadn't returned to work, and she said to Nawab, "Where is Professor Garson?"

"In his tent. I think he is not well."

"Not well? Why didn't someone come for me?" Before the Egyptian could answer, Catherine turned and hurried back to the camp. The flap of Fletcher's tent was open, and he lay on his cot under two blankets.

"What is it?" Catherine asked.

"Nothing much. Flare-up of malaria. Be all right by morning."

She knelt by Fletcher's cot and put her hand on his forehead. He was burning up; his body was racked with chills.

"Why didn't you send one of the men for me?" Catherine asked.

"I didn't think...anything should...tear you away from...the door," he said, trying to smile in spite of the chills.

"Did you take the medicine the doctor in Edfu gave you?"

"S...sure. I'll be okay by tomorrow. Don't...don't worry."

But Fletcher wasn't okay. Catherine stayed with him most of the night while the fever worked in cycles. First his body was racked with uncontrollable chills. Then suddenly he was too warm and began to sweat. When he did, Catherine, over his murmured protest, got him out of his pajamas, dried his body and put clean pajamas on him. Toward morning the fever broke, and he fell asleep.

Catherine stayed with Fletcher all that night, dozing in a camp chair at his side. She knew that he was ill, that probably he'd been ill with chills and fever all along and hadn't let them know. If he didn't get treatment, the attacks would go on until he was too weak to get out of bed.

When she finally left Fletcher the next morning, he was asleep. His forehead was cool to the touch, and the terrible chills had stopped. But she knew the chills and fever would return. He had to get to a hospital.

Before Catherine went to the excavation site she spoke to Sahibzada, explaining that Professor Garson was ill and that when he awakened Sahibzada was to take tea to him. Then she looked for Nawab.

He and his son, Azan, had already started work. "The professor is ill," she told Nawab. "He must go to the hospital in Cairo for treatment, and I would like you to go with him."

"But then you would be here alone, Miss Catherine."

"I'll be all right. Mr. David will be back in a day or two. The important thing now is to get the professor to a hospital."

"There is one in Aswan, Miss Catherine," Azan said.

"Yes, I know. But I think the professor would get better care in Cairo."

"I do not like to leave." Nawab scratched his chin, looking troubled. "Azan is a good boy, but he needs supervision. So do the other men. I do not know how they would feel about working for a woman."

"It'll only be for a day or two. Please don't worry. I'll be just fine."

Still the Egyptian hesitated. "Are you sure Mr. David will return soon?"

"Yes, Nawab," Catherine said. "There's an afternoon plane to Cairo. I want you and Professor Garson to leave for Aswan right after lunch."

Catherine went to work on the door, but she stopped in two hours to check on Fletcher. He was up and sitting in a chair in front of his tent when she returned.

"Good morning," she said. "How're you feeling?"

"Much better. Sorry about last night. Thanks for helping me. I'm fine now. I'll finish my tea and join you in a few minutes."

Catherine shook her head. "You and Nawab are going in to Aswan right after lunch," she said. "He'll accompany you to Cairo."

"Cairo? I'm not going to Cairo. What are you talking about? Look, Catherine, I had a bit of fever last night, but I'm okay now. You can see for yourself I'm perfectly all right."

"No, you're not all right. I think you haven't been feeling well for a long time, and you haven't said anything." Catherine pulled up a chair beside him. "What we're doing here is important, my friend, but not as important as your health."

"But dammit, Catherine, I want to be a part of the dig."

"You will be, Fletcher, just as soon as you're feeling better."

He ran a hand across his face. With a sigh he said, "All right, I admit it. I do feel like hell, and I promise you I'll go to Cairo just as soon as David returns."

"Nope. You're going this afternoon. End of discussion."

But it wasn't the end of the discussion of course. Fletcher protested while Catherine packed his bag, and he was still protesting three hours later when he and Nawab boarded the felucca to take them to Aswan.

"You'll be back in a week or two," she said as she waved goodbye. "I'll see you then. Take care."

"*You* take care," Fletcher called out. Then Nawab held his arm and led him to a seat.

Catherine stood at the water's edge, waiting until the sailboat was far down the river before she turned and went back to the tomb.

It seemed strange to be alone with only the Egyptian workers, but David would be back tomorrow or the next day. She would show him Alifa's tomb, and after he'd seen it they would open a bottle of wine and toast their success. Later, when the air was cool, they would go to David's tent to celebrate their love.

When David returned.

But David didn't come. Instead a note from him was delivered to Catherine the next morning. He wrote that one of the officials, a Mr. Frank Quinn from the Smithsonian, had decided to fly to Cairo to talk to him. It would be a couple of days before Quinn arrived. In the meantime David was having meetings with the Egyptian Antiquities people. They wanted to meet with Quinn when he got to Cairo, and very likely after that Quinn would return with him to Philae.

"It will be at least a week before I get back," David wrote. "I miss you, Catherine, and I love you. I know you were upset when I left, but believe me, this is all going to work out. We'll find Alifa's tomb and..."

Catherine smiled. She was disappointed that David had been delayed in Cairo, but at the same time she was excited because now she would have a chance to get more accomplished before he returned.

She thought about Fletcher and wondered if she should let David know that Fletcher was in Cairo. But if she did, David would worry about her being here in Philae alone. David had important things to take care of in Cairo, and in the meantime she could progress in the dig. When Quinn came, the two of them would come to Philae, and she would have a wonderful surprise for them.

The next morning Catherine and Azan pushed open the door at the bottom of the steps.

"The lights," Catherine said breathlessly. "Bring the lights." She showed her flashlight into the dark cavern behind the door, so excited she had to grasp the door to steady herself.

In a moment Azan was back. He held the light above his head, and one step behind Catherine, went through the door. For a moment she couldn't see anything, then her eyes adjusted to the fetid darkness.

"I wait," Azan whispered. "I do not like this place."

Catherine raised a questioning eyebrow and took the light from him. "All right," she said. "You stay here, but hold one of the lights up high so that I can see."

She stepped into a broad hall-like antechamber and beamed her light up and around. There were three openings in the chamber, tunnels apparently, that led in different directions. Puzzled, she studied them uncertainly, feeling like a child faced with making a decision.

Catherine held the light in front of the narrow, rubble-covered openings, muttering under her breath, because each one would have to be dug out before she could enter. If the other men behaved like Azan, she was going to have a real problem.

In her best, most intimidating classroom voice, Catherine called, *"Wen-Nabi!"* to the workers that waited behind Azan. "Get to work. I want this antechamber cleaned out and the rubble in front of the openings cleared by tomorrow morning. There will be extra *baksheesh* if any of you want to work all night."

There was a bit of grumbling before a couple of the men stepped forward with picks and shovels. *"Yala, yala,"* one of them said, and began to throw rocks into a large wicker basket.

Catherine stood over them while they worked. This was her project, and she was in charge. If she had to be a Simon Legree to get the job done, then that's what she would do.

By ten o'clock the next morning the first opening, the one on the far left, had been cleared enough for her to enter. She touched the webbed belt around her waist to check the extra flashlight batteries and squeezed through into the tunnel. She held the flashlight in front of her as she moved cautiously through the narrow passageway. She didn't know why there were three passageways, she only knew that each one, separately, had to be opened and followed.

Catherine came to steps, rubble-covered but passable. The tunnel veered to the right and except for the beam of light from her flashlight she was in total darkness. She went on, inching her way cautiously until the tunnel became too narrow to pass. Only then did she turn back. She would need to send some men in to clean it out while the others worked on the two remaining tunnels.

Catherine kept at it all day. She gave orders. She searched and dusted the walls for paintings or hieroglyphic writings, but none appeared. By nightfall she was so tired she could barely stay awake long enough to eat the meal that Sahibzada had prepared.

"You order the men," he said when he placed a bowl of stew in front of her. "They do not like that. You are a woman. Women do not tell men what to do. It is better to wait for the return of Mr. David. He is the one the men work for, not you."

"When Mr. David is gone, I'm in charge," Catherine said firmly. "I will give extra *baksheesh*, but the work must go on."

"They say it is difficult and dangerous."

"It is difficult, but it's not dangerous. I'm not asking the men to do anything I'm not doing myself."

Sahibzada acceded the point. "They say you work like a man." He shook his head. "That does not make it right, for you are not a man."

Catherine banged her cup down on the table. "Nevertheless I will continue to work," she snapped. "And so will they."

During the next few days Catherine redoubled her efforts. She worked from dawn to dusk, until her arms ached and the muscles in her back and her legs were sore and strained. But she kept on, afraid if she didn't, the men would slack off. All she could think about in the long hours of toil was that each minute of each hour she was moving closer to Alifa's tomb. And that when David returned, he would acknowledge her find.

For while the finding of Alifa's tomb was a personal triumph, it was also a triumph to be shared.

It took the workers a week and a half to clear the entrance to the three passageways. When the work was done, they gathered outside the tomb. Their faces were grimy from working all day, their *gelabayas* were sweat stained.

"You've done a good job," Catherine told them. "You may take tomorrow off. Go to visit your families. Rest and relax."

"Shoukran," they said, "Thank you."

"Is it permitted to go to Aswan?" one of them asked.

"Of course," Catherine said with a smile. "Go anywhere you like, only be back by the day after tomorrow."

By morning most of the men had left the island, and the others were preparing to go. She waved them off, called a greeting to the guard, then went down the few steps to the tunnels. She decided to work in the tunnel to the right.

Ten minutes later Catherine came to a dead end and started back toward the entrance, beaming the pinpoint of light ahead of her. It was an eerily uncomfortable feeling to be alone in the tomb, and just for a moment Catherine felt a rising panic. Her teeth clenched and her palms were slippery. She tried to go slowly but her steps quickened. Once she stumbled and instinctively her hand tightened on the flashlight, because she knew if she lost it she would be in total, enveloping blackness.

When she got out of the tunnel, she headed back to the camp. She fixed herself a soft drink and rested in the shade. But twenty minutes later she was back in the tunnel.

By late afternoon most of the workers had left the island. The others would leave in the morning. Only Sahibzada and the guard would stay behind.

Catherine had a solitary dinner that night. She slept well and awoke at daybreak. Sahibzada was nowhere to be seen when she came out of her tent, so she fixed a cup of coffee and ate an orange. Then she filled a canteen and put it in the web belt she wore around her waist. By that time the sun was up, so she was on her way to the excavation.

Today Catherine decided to try the middle tunnel. The workers had cleared most of the rubble away, and it was wider than the tunnel she'd explored yesterday.

When she went into it, she saw that the walls were narrower and the roof was lower. Her uneasiness grew as it became more and more like the passageway in the pyramid. But she tried not to think about it as she went on down the tunnel, probing the darkness with the beam from her flashlight. Once she thought about going back to tell the guard where she was, because he hadn't been there when she went in. But it was going so well this morning she decided to press on.

She came to a step, then another, and put one hand on the wall to help guide her way. Common sense told her that maybe she should wait until she had one of the men with her. But the men wouldn't be back until tomorrow, and she didn't want to waste the day. If she didn't find anything in another five minutes, she'd turn back and try the remaining tunnel.

Catherine tightened her hand around the flashlight and moved slowly forward into the darkness. At last she stopped. The five minutes were up. But when she turned to start back she beamed the light across the wall and gasped in surprise.

There were paintings on the wall, bright, vivid paintings all along this section of the passageway. If there were paintings, there was a tomb. She'd found it!

Catherine beamed her light on the wall as she moved forward, scarcely daring to breathe, overwhelmed at the wonder laid out before her. The paintings depicted Anubis, the jackal-headed god of death; Thoth, the god of wisdom, who wore the head of an ibis; and Maat, the goddess who represented truth, justice and equity. Then there was Nephthys, the sister of Isis, and Hathor, the goddess of love and happiness. Catherine's heart beat fast. The figures on the wall were leading her to the tomb. She was almost there.

She went on, beaming her flashlight on the wall, intent on the paintings, not on the rocky ground.

Suddenly, without warning, the path slanted sharply down. Catherine cried out. She tried to stop, tried to hang on to the walls, but the path was too steep, and she fell, slipping and sliding down, down into the darkness.

The meetings with the Egyptian Antiquities people had gone better than David had expected. This morning they'd approved of his returning to Edfu and had offered whatever help he might need. He'd been away for almost ten days, and he was anxious to get back to the camp and to Catherine. Frank Quinn would arrive the day after tomorrow. Then the two of them would catch a plane to Aswan and go on to Philae.

He didn't like being away from Catherine this long, especially when she'd been so unhappy before he left. But when they moved on to Edfu, things would be different, he told himself. This time they would find Alifa's tomb, and when they did, maybe they would take a week off and fly to Madrid. Maybe he could convince Catherine to marry him there.

Today, because he had time on his hands, David had decided to go to the Egyptian Museum, a place he'd been many times but never tired of. He was standing in front of the Micerinus Triad when someone said, "Ah, Mr. David, it is a wondrous thing, is it not?" He turned to see Nawab standing behind him.

"Nawab?" David stared at the older man. "What are you doing in Cairo?"

"I came with Professor Fletcher, Mr. David."

"With Fletch? What are you talking about? What's he doing here?"

"He is in the hospital, Mr. David. He became ill with the fever, so Miss Catherine insisted he come here and that I accompany him. Today he was much improved, so he told me that I must see the museum."

"Miss Catherine is alone on Philae?"

"No, sir, she is not alone. Sahibzada and the other men are with her."

David frowned. "Look, Nawab," he said. "I'm going to the hospital to see Professor Garson, then I'm going to fly back to Aswan. Are you all right? Do you have a place to stay?"

"Yes, Mr. David, I have a room near the hospital."

"Okay, good. You stay on here in Cairo then and return with the professor."

With a few more words to Nawab, David hurried out of the museum. He took a taxi to the hospital and found Fletcher in a room on the second floor.

Fletcher looked up from the magazine he was reading. "Dave? Dave! What are you doing here?"

"That's my question," David said. "How long have you been in Cairo?"

"Over a week I guess. I'm not quite sure, because I was pretty sick when I got here and I think I lost a couple of days." He looked concerned. "I thought you went back to Philae days ago. Catherine told me you were arriving the day after I left."

"I'd planned to, but I was delayed." David pulled a chair up to the bed. "I don't like her being there alone all this time."

"Neither do I. I wouldn't have left, no matter how sick I was, if I hadn't thought you'd be arriving in a day or so. I don't like it, Dave. I think we'd better get back to Philae."

"No, Fletch, you've got to stay till you're better."

"I'm okay now. The doctor said I could get out of here tomorrow."

"Fine. Then what I want you to do is go back to the hotel and wait for a man by the name of Frank Quinn from the Smithsonian. When he gets here, the two of you follow me to Philae."

"You're going back then?"

"Just as soon as I can get a plane."

"I'm sorry, Dave. This is my fault. I shouldn't have left Catherine alone, especially when she was so excited about the new excavation. She..." Fletcher hesitated. "I wasn't supposed to tell you about that."

"About what? What are you talking about?"

"A few days after you left Catherine found something." Fletcher shook his head. "It was so simple, right there in front of us all the time, and we didn't see it."

Fletcher went on to tell David how Catherine had discovered the site of the new excavation. "We found the steps, then we found the door with the seal. It's Alifa's tomb. Catherine found it."

David's eyes widened. "She found the tomb!" He shook his head in disbelief. "Are you sure? Why didn't she tell me? She should have called me right away. Why in the hell didn't she let me know?"

"Catherine wanted to surprise you, Dave. She knew how much it meant to you, to all of us." Fletcher ran a hand nervously over his face. "I shouldn't have left her, not with that kind of an excavation going on. She was so excited about it, about going deeper into the tunnels. I'm afraid she might do something reckless."

"To prove that she's been right all along." David got up. He rested a hand on Fletcher's shoulder. "Catherine's been on digs before," he said. "She knows how to take care of herself."

But when David left the hospital his face was tense with worry. He took a taxi back to his hotel, packed and found out there wasn't a plane leaving for Aswan until tomorrow morning.

He spent most of the night pacing up and down in his room, and the next morning he was at the airport two hours before the plane was scheduled to leave.

All he could think of was Catherine as the plane raced down the runway, and he tried to quell the panic that gripped him in the pit of his stomach.

Chapter 19

Catherine awoke to darkness. Her knees were scraped and her right shoulder hurt. She sat up and tried to choke back the terrible sense of panic that gripped her. The thought that she was alone in this impenetrable darkness along with the awareness that she'd dropped the flashlight when she fell was almost unbearable.

Frantically, on her hands and knees, she began to search for it, not even aware that she whimpered in pain or that she repeated David's name over and over in a litany of fear. When she couldn't find the flashlight, her fear became a palpable thing that threatened to push her over the edge of hysteria.

Breathing hard, she sat hunched, arms gripping her legs, and tried with every bit of her will to force herself to be calm. She took deep breaths and tried to think of something, anything, to replace the fear that threatened to overwhelm her.

She thought of David, whom she loved, and of her father, who had always been there when she needed him. She needed him now, to take her hand and lead her out of the darkness as he had that time in the cave near the Hopi Indian village.

Afterward he'd said, "Whenever you're afraid, Catherine, whether of the darkness or of anything else you don't understand, you must look for a secret place inside yourself. When you find it, go there and block everything out until you find peace and calm, until your spirit is free." He'd kissed the top of her head and raised her face to wipe her tears away. "There's a verse in the Bible that reads: 'Be still and know that I am God.' It's the same thing, Catherine. Do you understand what I'm talking about? You have to look for the calmness within yourself."

Catherine hadn't understood then, but she did now. Slowly, slowly her panic ebbed, and she began to look for the flashlight again. At last her hand closed around it. She flicked the switch, praying it hadn't been broken when she fell.

Light illuminated the empty chamber, and she sobbed with relief. She stood up and beamed the light to the place where she had fallen. The incline looked difficult, but she could manage it.

But as Catherine started toward the exit she saw another opening in the chamber wall. It was perhaps three feet from the ground, directly across from where she'd come in. She went to it, climbed on a cluster of rocks so that she could peer inside and beamed the light into the opening.

For a moment Catherine stared unbelieving at the sight before her eyes. Then she uttered a cry of wonder and disbelief, for through the opening she beheld a bedazzlement of riches—an alabaster boat, a golden chariot, a harness with golden buckles, swords and scimitars and jewel-encrusted chests.

She'd found the burial chamber!

Quickly Catherine climbed up and squeezed through the narrow opening. She jumped down into the room, and her eyes were wide with wonder as she looked around, scarcely believing all that she saw. There was the golden chariot, a chair set with semiprecious jewels, perfume and unguent jars, gold bracelets and necklaces, a golden crown.

Tears streaked Catherine's face as she beamed the light around the chamber, looking for the sarcophagus. Yes, it was there! She moved toward it and saw not one, but two sarcophagi.

A puzzled frown crossed Catherine's face. *Two* sarcophagi? She turned back to look at the chariot, at the swords and the scimitars.

And she understood.

She went to the sarcophagi and gently laid her hand upon first one, then the other. She knew that all of the things she'd read had been true—Alifa had loved the young warrior, loved him enough to follow him to the tomb.

Catherine beamed her light upward to the walls, and again she gasped in wonder. The walls were covered with paintings, and she knew they would tell the story of Alifa and the man she had loved.

Suddenly, without warning, the ground moved under Catherine's feet. She whirled around. The opening in the rocks! She had to get to it! For a moment she was too frozen to move, then she ran toward it, staggering with the movement of the floor.

But before she could reach it, there was another jolt, stronger than the first, and she was thrown to the ground. After what seemed an interminable length of time the earth steadied. Catherine looked around her. Her eyes went wide with shock. The rocks had shifted, the opening had closed. She was trapped here in the tomb, with the ancient ghosts of Alifa and her lover.

The felucca that David hired arrived in Philae a little before noon. When the boat stopped, he jumped out and hurried toward the camp, wondering at the unexpected quiet. Where was everybody? Where was Catherine? Even Sahibzada, who at this time of day would be preparing lunch, wasn't here.

David threw his suitcase in his tent, whipped his jacket off and ran toward the excavation site. But the men, only a few of them, weren't at the old site, they were gathered a short distance from it.

"Hello!" David called. "What's going on? Where's Miss Catherine?"

Sahibzada stepped forward. "She is not here, Mr. David. She has disappeared."

"Disappeared?" The word hit David like a physical blow. "What in the hell are you talking about? Where are the rest of the men?"

"Miss Catherine gave everyone a day off when we discovered the chamber and the tunnels, sir. I stayed behind, as did one of the guards. But yesterday morning at daylight the guard and I went to the dock when the boats came in with the food. When we returned, Miss Catherine was gone."

"Gone?" David shouted. "Gone where?"

"I do not know, sir. Perhaps to Aswan, perhaps into the excavation."

"Into the excavation? Here? You're telling me that she disappeared yesterday?"

"We fear so, sir. But you see, the guard and I were alone. The rest of the men had gone. We did not know what to do. We went partway in, sir, but there was a strong tremor, and we were afraid to go farther. There are three tunnels—"

David's face went white. "There was a tremor?"

"Yesterday afternoon, sir."

"And you didn't try to find her? You didn't think that she could be trapped somewhere in there, unable to get out."

"I am not an experienced workman, sir. I am a cook."

David wanted to grab Sahibzada by the throat. He whirled around to the others. "When did you all come back?" he roared.

"Last night," Azan said. "That is, some of us did. The others have not yet returned."

"Did you attempt a search last night when you discovered Catherine was missing?"

Azan shook his head. "We thought she had gone into Aswan."

"Idiots! You knew damn well that if she'd gone to Aswan she would have left word. You knew she was somewhere down there, and you were too damned afraid to try to find her. Get the lights. Torches. We're going in."

David felt as though someone had slammed him in the solar plexus. The thought of Catherine, somewhere deep inside the darkness of one of the tunnels made him almost physically ill. He wanted to hit somebody, to yell and rage and slam his fist against hard rock, because he remembered her terrible fear when they'd been trapped in Amonset's tomb. What was she going through now, alone and perhaps in darkness? She must be wild with fear.

David tried to get control of himself—he wouldn't be any help to her if he didn't. He had to be calm, to think clearly. He had to find her. If anything happened to Catherine... No, he wouldn't allow himself to think about that. He would find her. He had to.

Catherine stared at the now narrowed opening. Her body rigid with tension, she moved like a sleepwalker toward it. It was too small for her to squeeze through, she would have to move the rocks away. It might take a little time, but she could do it.

She propped the flashlight up against a pile of stones so that the opening was illuminated, then grasped the biggest rock at the top of the heap. That had to be dislodged before she could get to the others. She tried to jiggle it loose until her knuckles were scraped and bleeding. It wouldn't budge.

Catherine was close to exhaustion. She looked around for something, a tool, anything that might be useful. At last she chose a jeweled dagger. She wedged it under the rock and tried with all her strength to lever the rock up. But it was no use, the rock didn't budge. It was wedged in tightly, too heavy for her to move.

For a moment she felt her fear returning. She took deep breaths to steady herself. She thought of what her father had told her, trying to make herself accept where she was and allow her spirit to be free.

"Free," she repeated over and over again. "My spirit is free."

Her fear slowly ebbed away. Someone would come looking for her, she thought. She would be all right, she had enough water for a day or two. A day or two...

Catherine gripped the flashlight and, forcing herself to calmness, began to move around the room. The treasures were beyond belief. The necklaces were of ornately carved gold, and so were the beautiful collars. The alabaster boat, meant to carry the lovers into the beyond, was intricately designed.

She opened one of the chests and gasped at the glitter of precious stones and the mound of gold and silver jewelry. On the top of the glittering treasures lay three strands of sandalwood beads. With trembling hands Catherine drew them out of the chest. Their scent was as strong as it had been almost three-thousand years ago when someone had placed them in the chest.

Catherine put the sandalwood beads around her neck and breathed in the aroma. Knowing that they had belonged to Alifa brought a feeling of calmness over her. With renewed strength she began to move around the chamber to study the paintings that covered the walls.

Almost forgetting that she was trapped, Catherine began to study the wall paintings that told the wondrous story of Alifa and her lover.

It began when the warrior was a young man. Strange, Catherine thought as she gazed up at the first paintings, there was something familiar about him. He... The breath stopped in her throat. She'd seen him before—in the empty tomb at Edfu where they'd expected to find Ramah.

Ramah! Of course! That's why his tomb had been empty. He was here.

Excited now, Catherine moved on to the other paintings, which showed Ramah as a young warrior with a javelin raised over his head. There was another of him kneeling before his king. Another with Min, the god of virility—similar to the one at Edfu.

Next there was a painting of Ramah with a young woman of exceptional beauty, the same young woman Catherine had seen on the wall of Amonset's tomb. Sloe-eyed, fair of face and form, a coronet of gold encircling her head, Alifa's arms were outstretched to Ramah. Hathor, the goddess of the more erotic aspects of love, looked on.

The rest of the paintings were only of Alifa and Ramah. The first told the story of that first meeting in the palace of the king. That was followed by one of Ramah seated with Alifa kneeling before him offering a golden cup. In another, Ramah's hands were on Alifa's breasts. There were other paintings like that, paintings so sensual they made Catherine gasp in wonder.

Slowly she moved around the room, forgetting that she was trapped, so immersed was she in the unfolding story of the two lovers.

A painting at the far end of the chamber depicted Ramah in a ritual battle with another soldier. His scimitar was raised, but before he could strike, a sword pierced his side. Next to that was a picture of a Nile barge and of Ramah, prostrate, one arm hanging down.

In the next he lay upon a bed of myrrh. Alifa knelt beside him. She held his hand, she kissed his lips.

The second from the last painting showed weeping servants and Osiris, god of resurrection, looking toward an alabaster boat upon which Alifa and Ramah sat. Then the last painting. The lovers, hands joined, arriving together on the shores of the land beyond the beyond.

For a long time Catherine stood looking up at that last painting. So many questions had been answered, so many remained unanswered. The transcript had said only that the young queen had disappeared. Had she died of natural causes, or had her death been by her own hand?

What trusted servants had placed her here, at Ramah's side, where she would rest with him through all eternity?

All through that long and lonely day Catherine studied the paintings and the hieroglyphics that told the story of two young lives. She tried once more to move the boulder, and when she couldn't, she didn't panic as she had before, but sat down to rest and wait with her back against the wall. She knew that she should turn the flashlight off. She had extra batteries in her belt, but she didn't know how long it might be before someone found her. Still, it took every bit of her courage to click the switch.

The tomb was dark and so quiet that it seemed to Catherine as though she could hear the beating of her heart. She fingered the sandalwood beads, strangely comforted by their touch, and at last she slept.

David stood before the three tunnels. By now Catherine had been somewhere deep inside one of them for almost a day and a half. He ordered the men to be quiet, then he called out, "Catherine! Catherine, can you hear me?"

Again and again David called. But no one answered. He directed two men to take the tunnel on the left and two men to take the tunnel on the right. He would go into the middle tunnel alone. He had an extra canteen of water over one shoulder, and he carried two strong flashlights.

A little way in the tunnel narrowed, and the ceiling became so low he had to walk with his head bowed. For a moment David was tempted to go back and take one of the other tunnels, so convinced was he that a place like this would remind Catherine of the Pyramid of Gizeh and that she would have retreated. He actually stopped and started back, then he stopped again. The workers had told him that she'd already tried the tunnel on the left. He'd sent them on anyway, because there might be something farther down. But if Catherine thought that was a dead end, she might have pressed on here in spite of her fear. Just as he would press on.

It amazed David that Catherine had been right all along about finding Alifa's tomb here on the island. He should have listened to her, should have tried to help her instead of being so sure that he knew better than she did. He'd only come to Philae in the first place because he was in love with Catherine and he wanted to make her happy. But he'd never really believed they would find the lost tomb there.

But Catherine had found it, and when he found her he would tell her how proud he was. When he found her...

A knot formed in David's throat, and he bit his lips to keep the tears back. Dear God, he prayed, please let her be safe. Please let me find her.

He went on, careful of his steps now, flashing a light on the path before him and on the walls that closed him in. Then, ahead of him on the walls, he saw the paintings, and his heart leapt, because he knew the paintings might lead to the lost tomb and if they did, that's where he would find Catherine.

David started to run, then abruptly his steps slowed. No, he couldn't run, he had to go cautiously. The path was treacherous, and tombs like this, like the tomb of Seti I, could be dangerous.

He flashed the light ahead of him as he moved slowly forward and saw that the path seemed to drop away. Carefully David inched his way along the path. He saw it slanted sharply down, and his throat went dry. It was dangerously steep here. If Catherine hadn't seen the dip in the path, she would have fallen. Was that what happened? Had Catherine fallen? Was she hurt?

Slipping and sliding, David made his way down the incline. Yes, he saw it now, a room, a chamber of some sort, and he called out. "Catherine? Catherine, are you down here?"

Quickly David scrambled down into the chamber. He flashed his light around the floor and cursed aloud. The chamber was empty.

He turned the flashlight on the walls, hoping against hope there might be a door, an entrance that she could have taken. But there was nothing, only a pile of rocks against the opposite wall. He went closer and flashed his light over it. There was an opening above, and he stepped up on the bottom rocks so that he could see how big it was. Maybe Catherine had climbed over the rocks, maybe she had squeezed through. But when he saw how small the opening was, his heart sank.

All he could do now was go back the way he'd come and join the others in searching the remaining two tunnels. But he'd been so sure when he saw the paintings on the tunnel walls that Catherine was here.

David's disappointment made him careless when he stepped down, and suddenly one of the rocks slid out from under him, and with a great clatter of stones he fell.

He lay where he was for a moment, then cursing his clumsiness, he got up and dusted himself off. He'd just turned to leave when he thought he heard something. He froze, straining to listen. "Hello? Is someone there? Hello?"

"Catherine?" Her name was a scream on his lips.

David scrambled up to the rocks. He flashed the light through the narrow opening. "David?" he heard. "Oh, David, is it you?"

"Catherine! Are you all right?"

"Yes, I'm all right, but I feel like I've been in here forever. The opening in the rock was wider when I came in, but there was a tremor, and some rocks fell and blocked the entrance. I couldn't lift them."

"It's all right, Catherine. I'll do it. Stand away from them, sweetheart."

The adrenaline flowing through David's veins helped. With a great surge of effort he lifted the top rock, pushed and jumped aside as it thudded to the ground. "One more," he said, and dislodged another rock. He flashed his light through the opening and saw Catherine. Her face was pale, but she was all right.

"I'm coming," he said, and squeezed through to gather her in his arms.

Catherine held him as though she would never let him go. Weak with relief, she sobbed his name while David tightened his arms around her and held her close.

"David," she said, her face against his. "Oh, David, I thought you'd never come."

When at last David let her go, he cupped her face and kissing her said, "I'll never leave you again, Catherine. Wherever we go now we will go together."

"Yes, David, together." Catherine stepped away from him. She took a deep breath to steady herself for what she wanted to tell him, then she took his hand. "I've found them," she said. "I've found Alifa and Ramah."

"Ramah?" For the first time since he'd stepped into the burial chamber David looked around him. He saw the golden chariot, the swords and the scimitars. "This is Ramah's tomb?"

"He's here with Alifa," Catherine said. "See? Over there. The two sarcophagi are side by side, David. I don't know how she managed it, but I suspect Alifa took her own life so they could be together."

Catherine took David's hand and began to show him all of the wonderful things that were in the tomb. And when he'd marveled at them, she led him to where the paintings began.

David studied them, too moved to speak until they reached the one of Ramah on the barge. "This was after he was wounded in battle," he said.

Catherine nodded. "Alifa had him brought to Philae and was waiting for him here. I imagine the tomb had been prepared for her years ago by her father. He'd promised her before he sent her to Edfu to marry Amonset that some day she would return to rest forever on the island she loved so much."

"You've been right all along." David put his arm around Catherine while they gazed up at the story unfolding all around the walls of the tomb, the story of a love that had lasted even into eternity.

Others had searched for Alifa's missing tomb, David thought, but it had taken Catherine to find it. Catherine, whose heart and mind had somehow been attuned to the young queen who'd died so many centuries ago.

"I love you." David took Catherine in his arms and kissed her. When he let her go, they drank from the canteen and looked again at the treasures the room held. "It'll take us months to catalog everything," David said, "even years. We'll have to excavate the other tunnels, too." He hesitated. "I know you want to return to the university, Catherine, but I don't want you to go. This is your discovery, it belongs to you."

"It belongs to us." She smiled at him. "I won't leave. I'll stay for as long as it takes. Forever, if you still want me."

"If I want you..." David folded her in his arms. "Catherine," he whispered against her lips. "Forever won't be nearly long enough."

Epilogue

The little girl with the exotic sherry eyes sat on the floor amid scraps of colored paper and ribbons, two dolls, a bright red wagon and a collection of stuffed animals.

"It's time for bed, Alifa," her mother said.

"No!" Clutching a sad-eyed camel with unbelievably long eyelashes, the child said, "More presents."

"You've opened all your presents." David smiled down at his daughter. "It was a great birthday party, sweetheart, but you've got to go to bed now."

She tightened her arms around the camel. "Can I sleep with Mohammed?"

Catherine ruffled the silky blond hair. "Yes, you can sleep with Mohammed," she said.

"Leave it to Fletch to send her a camel." David put his arm around his wife. "I can't believe she's two already."

"Neither can I." She looked at David. "I'm so happy," she whispered. "I never knew anyone could be this happy."

David kissed her, then looking at their daughter said, "Come on, Alifa, I'll carry you up to bed."

But Alifa didn't answer. Instead she held up an oblong box that was wrapped with blue tissue paper and tied with a pink ribbon. "Present," she chortled, and began to rip the paper off.

"I thought she'd opened everything," Catherine said. "But I guess there was one we missed." She slid down off the sofa and knelt on the floor beside her daughter. "What is it, Alifa?" she asked.

Small fingers reached into the box and pulled out a single strand of beads. Instinctively she brought them to her nose and sniffed. Then she held them out to Catherine. "See my beads, Mommy."

"They're...they're beautiful, darling." Catherine picked up the empty box. "There's no card," she said to David.

"There must be." His brows came together in a frown. "They're probably from Fletch."

"The camel's from Fletcher."

They looked at each other. Then at their small daughter, who sat amid the ribbons and bows, the scattered pieces of colorful paper and the toys, holding the camel on her lap while she fingered the scented sandalwood beads.

* * * * *

At Dodd Memorial Hospital, Love is the Best Medicine

When temperatures are rising and pulses are racing, Dodd Memorial Hospital is the place to be. Every doctor, nurse and patient is a heart specialist, and their favorite prescription is a little romance. Next month, finish Lucy Hamilton's Dodd Memorial Hospital Trilogy with HEARTBEATS, IM #245.

Nurse Vanessa Rice thought police sergeant Clay Williams was the most annoying man she knew. Then he showed up at Dodd Memorial with a gunshot wound, and the least she could do was be friends with him—if he'd let her. But Clay was interested in something more, and Vanessa didn't want that kind of commitment. She had a career that was important to her, and there was no room in her life for any man. But Clay was determined to show her that they could have a future together—and that there are times when the patient knows best.

To order the first two books in the Dodd Memorial Hospital Trilogy, UNDER SUSPICION—IM #229, and AFTER MIDNIGHT—IM #237: Send your name, address and zip or postal code, along with a check or money order for $2.75 for each book ordered, plus 75¢ postage and handling, payable to Silhouette Reader Service to:

Silhouette Books In Canada	In U.S.A
P.O. Box 609 Fort Erie, Ontario L2A 5X3	901 Fuhrmann Blvd. P.O. Box 1396 Buffalo, NY 14269-1396

Please specify book title with your order.

IM 245

ATTRACTIVE, SPACE SAVING BOOK RACK

Display your most prized novels on this handsome and sturdy book rack. The hand-rubbed walnut finish will blend into your library decor with quiet elegance, providing a practical organizer for your favorite hard-or soft-covered books.

To order, rush your name, address and zip code, along with a check or money order for $10.70* ($9.95 plus 75¢ postage and handling) payable to *Silhouette Books.*

Silhouette Books
Book Rack Offer
901 Fuhrmann Blvd.
P.O. Box 1396
Buffalo, NY 14269-1396

Offer not available in Canada.

BKR-2A

*New York and Iowa residents add appropriate sales tax.

Silhouette Intimate Moments

COMING NEXT MONTH

#245 HEARTBEATS—Lucy Hamilton

Policeman Clay Williams wanted more than just friendship from Vanessa Rice. But when the drug gang he was after decided to get him by getting her, his campaign to win her heart became a race against time,a battle to prove they had a future together before he lost the chance—forever.

#246 MUSTANG MAN—Lee Magner

To save her father's life, Carolyn Andrews had to find a missing stallion, and only Jonathan Raider could help her. But the search threatened more than their safety. Now that she'd met Jonathan, she knew it would break her heart if they had to say goodbye.

#247 DONOVAN'S PROMISE—Dallas Schulze

Twenty years ago Donovan had promised to take care of Elizabeth forever, but now their marriage was coming to an end. He couldn't let that happen. Somehow he had to prove that his feelings hadn't changed and that the promise he had made once would never be broken.

#248 ANGEL OF MERCY—Heather Graham Pozzessere

DEA agent Brad McKenna had been shot, and he knew that only a miracle could save him. When he regained consciousness, he thought he'd gotten his miracle, for surely that was an angel bending over him. But he soon discovered that Wendy Hawk was a flesh-and-blood woman—and the feelings he had for her were very real.

AVAILABLE THIS MONTH:

#241 THAT MCKENNA WOMAN
Parris Afton Bonds

#242 MORE THAN A MIRACLE
Kathleen Eagle

#243 SUMMER OF THE WOLF
Patricia Gardner Evans

#244 BEYOND FOREVER
Barbara Faith